THE
Scoundrel's Pleasure

THE MACNEIL LEGACY - BOOK TWO

JANE
BONANDER

DIVERSIONBOOKS

Also by Jane Bonander

The MacNeil Legacy
Pleasure of the Rose

Heat of a Savage Moon
Wild Heart
A Taste of Honey
Fires of Innocence
Secrets of a Midnight Moon
Warrior Heart
Dancing on Snowflakes
Forbidden Moon
Winter Heart
The Dragon Tamer

Diversion Books
A Division of Diversion Publishing Corp.
443 Park Avenue South, Suite 1008
New York, New York 10016
www.DiversionBooks.com

For more information, email info@diversionbooks.com

First Diversion Books edition February 2017
Print ISBN: 978-1-68230-345-0
eBook ISBN: 978-1-68230-344-3

To Katie Kotchman

Prologue
The Seduction

ISLAND OF HEDABARR, SCOTLAND—1862

Sometimes, if Isobel listened very carefully, when the island was cloaked in mist so thick it blanketed the earth like a shroud, she could hear the screams. The poor woman still wandered the land, wailing for her lost bairn and cursing her husband, who had taken a shovel to his wife and killed her when his fifteenth daughter was not born a son.

Isobel often thought of that legend, especially on nights like this, when the entire world seemed ghostly. The annual fair, although much anticipated and gay for many, made Isobel's imagination bloom. Probably because of all the oddities the fair brought with it: two-headed chickens, snake people, talking apes. But was there truth to the story of the ghost with fifteen daughters? Did she indeed stalk the land, perhaps in search of her rat of a husband, hoping to do him in as he had done her?

Surely, the incident had happened; Aunt Paula had recounted it to her many times as they sat by the fireplace on bleak evenings, when business at the brothel was slow, and when the storms pelted the house with rain and wind. Isobel hated storms. The girls who worked for Paula sat there too, as fascinated as children by stories of ghosties and little people, goblins and ghouls. In general, Isobel liked the girls who worked for her aunt.

But, Isobel wondered, whatever happened to those fifteen daughters after their mother was killed? Did the vile husband abandon them? She wondered if any of them were still alive and living on the island.

Trying to find answers, Isobel watched her neighbors, looking perhaps for some curious behavior, like the old woman who combed the river's edge for booty, whose constant squirming movements made it look as if she had a ferret in her drawers. Or the woman with the scrunched-in face who cleaned at the inn—she stuttered every time you tried to speak to her. For some, it was embarrassing to listen to her, but Isobel knew the woman couldn't help it, and always waited patiently for an answer. Might she be one of the tragic daughters of a murderer? What about the old whore who still tried to give it away on the streets, or in the back of a bar, lifting her soiled, tattered gown to reveal bony knees, skinny thighs, and no underthings at all. And then there was the woman who had not come out of her house for ten years, or so people said. "She be afraid of crowds," one of Paula's girls had told her. These were things that ignited Isobel's imagination as much, if not more, than the comings and goings of the brothel or the flurry of the annual fair.

Isobel knew what went on in the brothel; she'd lived there most of her fifteen years, except for the times she went off to school on the mainland. The thought of what went on behind those closed doors made her face feel flushed. Many of the girls were not much older than she was. Once she had been walking past one of the rooms they used and heard the bed springs squeaking. Mona, one of Aunt Paula's girls, was urging some fellow on.

"C'mon, luv, that's it, that's it! Oh, ye be so good!"

Isobel had raced down the stairs, her face and neck so hot she thought she might burn the collar of her blouse.

These were thoughts she couldn't shake as she wandered down the paths at the annual fair. The mist had lifted, perhaps shooed away by the wood and peat smoke. Or the noise of the merrymakers, making everything seem normal again. All of her friends had left for the tented freak shows: the goat woman and the fattest man in the world and all the rest of the oddities.

She wasn't interested in any of that. In fact, she was ready to leave. There would be Delilah's clootie dumpling to eat, but only if she got home before everyone else devoured it.

Just as she started to walk away, she saw *them*—one fair and one dark, the dark one like the duke at Castle Sheiling. She stopped and stared. How the lassies on the island had buzzed about the two of them when they first arrived! Since Isobel was at school, she thought little about them until she laid eyes on them. Very, very bonnie, they were.

They were too busy to notice her, of that she was certain. She ducked behind a tent flap to stare without risking them glancing her way. Both of them tall and handsome. The fair one's hair was nearly white and curled close to his scalp and his eyes were so blue they seemed to glitter like sapphires in the lamplight. He had a fine looking, pleasant face; he would be easy to talk to.

The other one…She inhaled a sigh, releasing it slowly. How dangerous he seemed! Reckless, even. He made her body tingle. Aye, she had seen that one before, once when he came to the brothel and Isobel hid behind the door; Aunt Paula had turned him away. He didn't seem upset by her refusal; in fact, Isobel remembered that he had told her aunt in a flirtatious way that he would be back. Indeed, Isobel realized he could have any lassie on the island; he need not go to a brothel to get one.

And one other time she had seen him down at the docks when she returned from school. He had glanced her way, but had not settled his gaze upon her. That was fine with Isobel; she didn't like to be noticed.

Now the two laddies were arguing about what to do next, the fair one anxious to see the performance of *Wallace, Hero of Scotland*, the dark one suggesting a peep show.

"Aw, come on, Gavin, for just once in your boring life give in to your seedy side; you might enjoy it. I hear they have fat girls, ladies with beards, all kinds of great stuff. Even a man with a snout like a pig. And maybe even some naked ladies," he coaxed as he took a swig from a flask. His voice was decidedly harsh compared to the burr of the Scots. She had learned that these were Americans.

7

Americans! Brothers of the duke of the castle, she was told. She had seen the younger sister once; the girl was a beauty, small, delicate, and almost wraithlike, with hair as black as satin, flowing down her back in gentle waves.

The fair one, Gavin, gave his brother a disgusted look. "Why would I want to see bearded ladies? Or a pig man? You do what you want, Duncan, I'm going to see the performance. And you'd better have that flask back in Fletcher's den before he finds it missing."

"What Fletcher doesn't know won't hurt him," Duncan answered, then swore, bringing his hand to his mouth, digging at something.

"What's wrong?"

"Damn nettles," Duncan spat. "They're everywhere on this island."

"You're not even supposed to be here. You're supposed to be mucking out the stables. Why do you constantly challenge Fletcher?"

"Stable mucking is Evan's job. I have better things to do with my time," Duncan said.

Gavin shrugged. "It's your life." With that, he wandered off toward another tent, leaving his brother alone.

Duncan took another swig and turned to leave as well, but his gaze somehow found the very spot where Isobel stood. Well, rot! How likely was that? Her pulse beat hard, high in her throat, and she held her breath. She stood still as a statue; she didn't blink, she didn't breathe, hoping he wouldn't notice her there.

"Are you spying on me?"

Why she jumped she didna' know. Probably because she was embarrassed at being caught. "Nae," she replied. Her fingers went immediately to the scar at her neck, the one left over from the fire so many years before that had killed her parents. She found herself touching it whenever she was nervous.

He strolled toward her, his head bent to one side. As he approached, he said, "I've seen you before somewhere, haven't I?"

She shook her head. "Nae." At least she was grateful for learning English, although often times it was hard to understand him anyway.

He smiled, showing beautiful white teeth and a dimple in one cheek that could hold a lassie's heart. Lord a'mighty, he was a handsome lad. She thought perhaps she could look at him for the rest of her life and never get bored. Just think of having someone so bonnie to touch each and every day. She snuffled softly. What did she know about boys or men? Only that Aunt Paula had warned her to stay clear of them. Not that she ever had reason to; she wasn't exactly the type to draw stares.

"What's your name?" he asked.

Isobel blinked and lowered her gaze. "Isobel."

"Do they call you Izzy?"

There was a smile in his voice and she could smell the whisky on his breath; it wasn't unpleasant. He placed his fingers under her chin and lifted her face toward his. "If you were my girl, I'd call you Izzy." His eyes were dark, his lashes long. His cheekbones were sharp but the dimple in his cheek softened him. She stepped away from him and pulled her shawl up to cover her scar. His hand came over hers. "What are you afraid of?" He moved her hand away and ran his fingers over the bumpy skin beneath her ear.

She shivered at his touch and pushed his hand away, trying to cover the blemish once again. He frowned, displeased with what he saw. Now he would turn away, disgusted.

Instead he said, "Talk to me, pretty girl. Tell me who hurt you."

His soft-spoken voice puzzled her. Why was he being nice? There were many young girls on the island, plenty far bonnier than she. "It…it was a fire, a long time ago. I was but a wee lassie at the time," she managed.

She found Duncan studying her. "And you think that because you have a scar on your neck, you aren't pretty enough; is that why you hide in dark corners and keep trying to cover it up?"

She lowered her head briefly before looking up at him. "I'm not pretty; don't say that I am."

Again he studied her. "Do you know how I knew you were standing in the shadows?"

She shook her head and tried not to stare at him.

"The torchlight from the tent glinted off your hair. It looked like fire."

"My hair is not red," she exclaimed more quickly than she meant to. "It…'tis bad luck to have red hair."

He cocked his head again. "Why?"

"'Tis, that's all." She couldn't tell him that because of the color of her hair, some called her a changeling or a witch. Or that she had fairy blood, which was not a good thing, nae, it was not. And how many times had she been teased by the bullies at school, telling her horrid stories about how her parents really died because of Isobel's red hair?

He broke into her reflections, sounding amused rather than cynical. "And if it's not red, what color would you call it?"

Whenever Isobel whined about her hair, Aunt Paula always reminded her that the long, thick, curly mane was not red, that it was the color of the spice used in broonie, a gingerbread cake. "Ginger," she answered. "It's called ginger."

He chuckled. "Ginger, red, cinnamon—what's the difference?"

She was beginning to think he was simply a great big oaf. "There is a great difference." Her voice was strong now, for this was something she needed to defend.

His gaze was warm; it rattled her. "I don't see how someone as pretty as you could be bad luck."

Twice. Twice he'd called her pretty. Did he see something others did not? Or was she merely wishing it was so?

Just then a gaggle of children ran by, each carrying a stick with a ribbon. They laughed and shrieked and carelessly bumped into Isobel, throwing her off balance and against Duncan. His chest was solid, like the monoliths and the sandstone cairns down at the southeast corner of the island. She tried to picture his body; it would not be the pasty bluish color of so many young Scots. It would be dark, maybe mahogany or cedar. And he surely was as strong as a tree. He took her arm to steady her. His touch was gentle. "Hey! Watch where you're going you little savages!" He laughed when they ignored him. "Are you all right?" When she nodded, he said, "Come, walk with me."

Her emotions in a tangle, she started to say she couldn't, but—

"Come on," he urged, his arm slung around her shoulders. "We won't go far, I promise. In fact, we can go over there." He pointed toward the benches that surrounded a fire. Along with the smell of peat smoke and coal in the air, one could smell toasted nuts, fish and fowl—the smells all mingled to provide a feast for the senses of those who came to the fair because their own kitchens could not provide such delicacies.

Isobel was faintly aware of the people around her. Pipe music wheezed in the distance, the primeval wailing adding a somber note to the festivities. A fiddler played a lively reel. She herself could have been on the moon, for all she really heard was the beating of her own heart and the sound of Duncan's voice. He sat and pulled her down next to him, close. He put his arm around her shoulders once again. She shivered but didn't move away. "All right, tell me all about Isobel."

"Nae," she answered, bravely turning to him. This was not like her. She had little experience speaking to young lads, for her school was all lassies. "You tell me about yourself; 'tis much more interesting, I think." Again, she fell into his beautiful gaze. Again, she compared him to young Scottish men. He took another sip from his flask, stopped a moment, and then offered her some. She almost said no, because she had never had a drink of alcohol before in her life, but she changed her mind. She felt reckless. "Thank ye," she said, hoping she sounded grown up. She bravely took the flask. Before she took a sip, she realized that her mouth would be at the very place his had been. The thought gave her a frisson of pleasure. She took a sip, slowly letting the fire warm her throat—and coughed as it went down. "Ocht." She made a face as tears filled her eyes. "Why do people drink this swill?"

He laughed at her reaction, but it was not unkind. "Because if you take another sip, you'll begin to feel warmth in your belly that matches nothing else." Again, he brought his hand to his mouth, as if it hurt.

"I heard you tell your brother you touched a nettle," she said.

"Yeah, they're everywhere, and they sting like the devil." He shook his hand, as if that would dislodge the pain.

"I can fix it for you."

He gave her a lopsided grin, one that made her giddy. "Will you kiss it and make it better?"

In spite of herself, she had to smile. "Nae." She stood and walked to the far side of one of the show tents, reached down, broke off a leaf, and returned to him. "Give me your hand." He raised it toward her and she took it, feeling the hard palm of a lad accustomed to work. "This is the dock leaf. Wherever the nettle grows, the healing dock leaf grows nearby." She spat on the leaf and rubbed it hard against his palm.

It took only seconds and Duncan looked up at her, amazed. "The sting is gone."

"Aye," she answered. "It's as if nature knows to put a balm next to something as bothersome as a clump of nettles." And what was there to offset a handsome laddie trying with ease to steal a girl's heart?

He took another swig from the flask, then offered it to her again.

Why stop now? "I'll take another sip if ye'll tell me what it's like living in such a fine castle."

He touched her chin, lifting her face once again. "I'll tell you about the castle if you'll let me kiss you."

Before she thought too much she took a swig of whisky, feeling it slide down her throat once again. Only this time it didn't taste nearly so bad. On a whim she took another. She felt all loose and relaxed and found herself saying, "Aye, I would like that." Because she wanted it; this was her adventure! Other girls often spoke of escapades like this, but she had never had one. Before another thought formed in her head, she found his lips on hers, pressing, gently nudging her lips open. She thought she would fall, and grabbed his shoulder so she wouldn't. Oh, how smooth and gentle his lips were on hers! He moved to her cheek, planting sweet kisses everywhere, over her nose, her forehead, her chin. She felt the light stubble from his beard. She wanted in the worst way to reach up and touch it.

He pulled away; she could barely catch her breath. "Oh, Izzy," he said, his voice close to her ear, "if you don't let me kiss you again, I just might keel over and die. But," he added, nuzzling her hair, "not here." She was tingling all over!

She stood, bringing him with her. "Come, I know a spot."

Feeling loose and light headed, she pulled him with her into the woods, leaves and branches crunching underfoot until they could no longer hear the music clearly.

She raced past a cluster of Scots pines and found the little cave that was hidden behind the junipers.

"What's this?" he asked.

"'There's a cave here, behind the brush."

"I like it." He pushed the brush aside to see the opening and poked his head inside. He took her hand and pulled her in with him. Once inside, he took her in his arms and kissed her again. If she hadn't been such a practical girl, she might have thought she swooned. She wrapped her arms around him and returned kiss for kiss—eager, restless, wanting more. His tongue touched her lips and she instinctively opened her mouth, allowing him inside. Their breathing mingled, the whisky fueling her instinct for more.

"Oh, pretty girl," he whispered, "you are so beautiful, can I please, please touch you?"

His voice sounded far away, although he couldn't have been any closer. Her ears were ringing, her body responding to something she had never before experienced. He sounded so needy, how could she refuse?

Her body was on fire; her self-control was gone. "Aye," she said, her voice shaking.

He unbuttoned her bodice; she helped him with trembling fingers. His hand slipped inside, cupping her breast and he moaned with pleasure. When he touched her nipple, she inhaled sharply, feeling a sweet stinging sensation between her legs. "Please let me see your breast; it feels so beautiful, if I can see it I'll know I've gone to heaven."

Isobel let him do whatever he asked of her. Perhaps the whisky had taken the edge off her sanity, but somehow it didn't matter.

"Let me love you," he whispered against her ear. And she did.

• • •

When it was over, she lay there, content, spent. Almost asleep. When she opened her eyes, he was standing above her. "Maybe I'll see you again sometime, okay? And thanks for healing me." He grinned. "In more ways than one."

Isobel nodded as she watched him walk away. She would see him again, she knew it. He wouldn't have told her he wanted to make love to her if he hadn't meant to see her again, would he? A hollowness dug into her belly but she brushed the feeling aside; it was probably just the whisky souring her stomach. She slowly got to her feet, rearranged her disheveled clothing and flinched a little as she walked toward home, all the while telling herself she did not have red hair. She did not. Bad luck would not follow her. It would not. And, she thought with a bite of anger, she never did learn anything about the castle, and by the time she got home, there wouldn't be any clootie dumpling left for her either.

• • •

Duncan sauntered into the room he shared with Gavin, who lay on his bed, reading one of the boring, oversized books he enjoyed so much. The long, large room was split in half, which still gave each of them more room than they'd ever had before. Gavin's side was filled with shelves bursting with books, an enormous globe on a revolving stand, and a neat dresser where he kept his clothing. There was a long table in one corner where he often studied maps, ancient and new. Gavin was smart. Brilliant, really, but according to Duncan, he never had any fun.

Duncan's half of the room, on the other hand, was a typical careless mess. Although his bed was made by one of the young girls his brother had in his employ, the rest of the room was a lesson in disorder, except for the bow and arrows he had brought with him from Texas, displayed on the wall by the window. He had books too, but they were all about horses and hunting. He also had a small stash of trashy dime novels he kept for himself, certain that Gavin wouldn't be interested in them anyway.

"So, what mind-numbing tome is grabbing your attention tonight?"

Gavin lowered the book. "I know you don't really want to know."

Duncan tried to look hurt. "Come on. Tell me."

Gavin shrugged. "It's about the effects of the Industrial Revolution on a small parish in Ayshire by John Galt."

Duncan snorted. "Wherever that is, and whatever that means."

Gavin rolled his eyes. "Who was the 'lucky' girl tonight?"

Duncan heard the sarcasm and disapproval in his brother's voice. He didn't care. "Lizzie, or Izzy or something like that." The first thing he thought of when he saw her was how he'd never had a red-haired girl before. He'd always wanted to see that sultry patch between a girl's thighs to make sure the hair on her head wasn't some kind of crazy dye job. This one, he was sure, had a nice fiery thatch. He could almost imagine his face nestled in the warmth and wetness. Christ! He was getting hard again.

But oh, how he loved sex. He was born to love it. He couldn't imagine living his life without it. In fact, he wondered if he could live at all. He shook his head at the memory of Chet Blackburn, his ranch boss back in Texas, who had told him that one day even he, the horny Duncan MacNeil, wouldn't care a whit about diving between a woman's thighs. Duncan refused to believe he would ever feel that way.

He adjusted his bag of tricks inside his buckskins. Scottish girls were fascinated by everything about him. His color, the length of his hair, his Texas-style clothing and his cowboy boots. Some were even bold enough to be openly curious about his bag of tricks—wondering how they compared with the local laddies'. He played on that interest as often as possible. Tonight he had had to be especially careful, because the red-haired "lassie" was skittish, like a new colt. And she was very sweet. Odd, he'd never really thought about other girls that way, but then, this was his first virgin. He knew this because of all the girls he had ravished, not one had a barrier against his cock. Except this one.

Even so, she had urged him on. He should have spent more time with her. He had wanted to; she was certainly willing. But a roll in the grass wasn't the place to undress a girl. Too many chances of getting caught. How sweet it would have been to take her to the vacant barn off the road toward the castle. To undress her, drink in her luscious body. Even clothed, he could tell she was deliciously curvy. And he loved curvy girls, girls with ample breasts and thighs and hips. And this one would have that special, warm, mysterious place between her thighs covered in dark red fur. How tempting that would be!

He undressed carelessly, tossing his shirt with no concern as to where it landed. The nice thing about being royalty was that there was always someone to pick up after you. He was now His Lordship, Lord MacNeil. He had not ever in a million years thought he would have such a title. But he kind of liked it. He also liked that little maid who scurried in to clean up the room. Unfortunately, Fletcher had warned him that the help was not to be seduced. Didn't really matter; there were girls enough on the island.

Gavin shook his head. "One of these days a girl you've coaxed into the woods is going to come knocking, her belly heaving with your baby. Then what will you do, brother?"

The thought never entered his mind; he was beyond thinking such trivial problems. "She'll have to prove it, won't she? How would she do that?"

"Well gee," Gavin said, giving his chin a dramatic scrape, "maybe when the kid is born he'll be an exact replica of you. Then what?"

Unruffled, Duncan answered, "She'd still have to prove it."

Gavin shook his head and went back to his book. "Fletcher wants to see you before you go to bed."

Duncan snorted. "I'll just bet he does." He continued to undress. The silver flask clattered to the floor.

Gavin glanced up from his book. "Why do you do everything he asks you not to? I heard him tell you not to drink when you're out carousing. It isn't good for the whole damn island to see the duke's brother drunk as a skunk. And you weren't supposed to be out anyway."

"And why does he have to act like such an ass? I mean, he isn't my father; he's just my brother, for God's sake. And just because he's older doesn't mean he can boss me around." He scratched his broad chest then began undoing the fasteners on his britches. "I'm basically an adult and he still treats me like a kid. I didn't even get treated like this by Grandfather."

Duncan could feel Gavin's probing gaze. "Look at you. Kerry finally comes around, and now you're acting like the top turd on the cowshed pile."

Duncan got close, in his brother's face, and stared into his teal blue eyes. "Take a good look, brother, and remember my handsome face and my fine brown ass, because before you know it I'll be out of here." Duncan moved away and pulled his boots off, flinging them toward the wall, where they clattered noisily as they hit the floor.

"Right. And just where would you be goin'?" Gavin seemed to enjoy affecting a Scottish burr, especially when he needled Duncan.

Duncan had decided he would tell no one his plans, but thought better of it. No need to have the entire household in a tizzy over his disappearance. It was only Fletcher he wanted to worry. "Remember Chet Blackburn?"

"Blackburn." Gavin looked over at Duncan. "Wasn't he the rancher you worked for before we came to Scotland?"

"The very one." Duncan flopped onto his bed and put his arms behind his head.

"What about him?"

"He told me before I left that if I ever wanted to come back, he'd hire me on as one of his hands." Duncan watched the shadows from the lamp play across the ceiling. Now and then the flickering glooms looked like the sails of a ship. He was so eager to return to Texas he could almost smell the hot, baked earth.

Gavin gave a quiet laugh. "So you're just going to hop a ship and sail back to Texas?"

"Exactly."

Gavin put his book down and rolled to his side, studying his brother. "You're serious, aren't you?"

Duncan nodded. "I want to go back, Gavin. I didn't want to come in the first place, remember? I didn't fight it because I knew Kerry was counting on me. But she's okay now, and I'm not. I need to get out of here."

Gavin switched to a sitting position on his bed, his bare white feet dangling toward the floor. "I can't simply pretend I don't know this, Duncan. I mean, Fletcher has to be told at some point."

"You can tell him once I'm safely at sea."

Chapter One

ISLAND OF HEDABARR—JUNE 1872

The pungent odor of brine, fish, and kelp wafted up on the damp breeze. Seagulls screeched as they swooped above the brackish water in search of food. The sound was a welcome one, unless they were merely mocking his return. Duncan MacNeil took the smell of the wharf deep into his lungs, holding it there a moment before exhaling. He had missed it.

Fishing boats of many shapes and colors bobbed at their moorings, having already been taken to sea by fishermen in search of salmon, the silver king of the river. Early morning, when the winds were soft and the seas were welcoming, was the best time to fish offshore; Duncan remembered that well. Of all the activities he had experienced on the island, fishing the rivers was one he recalled with pleasure. Some old Scot had once told him that the water's surface was a hypnotic thing, always moving, always changing with the shifting light from the sky. Throughout the journey across the Atlantic, Duncan had become mesmerized by the play of light upon the roiling waters.

He rested his forearms on the ship's railing as it made its way into the port of Sheiling. He pulled in another deep breath, enjoying the brisk, damp air. So different from the air he'd breathed the past ten years. Texas air. Hot. Dry. Bayou air. Hot. Wet.

The sky over Hedabarr was the color of pewter. The fog had lifted; clouds rolled in after a brief interval of weak sunshine. And now he could see the outline of the red sandstone castle far in the distance, and old, nostalgic memories swamped him. Rosalyn's rose garden and the day he and his brothers had trampled it to within an inch of its life. He curbed a smile. How angry she had been! He saw now what his brother had seen in her from the beginning. Beauty, yes, but fire. Placid women excited no man. Of course, he didn't understand that for many years.

He moved suddenly, twisting his shoulder, and it began to ache. The shot from the bluecoat's gun left a permanent scar and it hurt every time he moved the wrong way. The war had left many wounds on Duncan. The worst, perhaps, was the one left by his imprisonment in the bayous of Louisiana. There had been a physical scar, but the one that ached the most was the one left on his heart.

Now he returned to a very different life than those years he'd spent as a ranch owner, the ranch Chet Blackburn's generous gift to Duncan, willed to him before he set off to fight for Texas's right to govern itself. He knew more about cattle and horses than he knew about himself, perhaps because the animals had no mental baggage to drag around. He still knew nothing about being Lord MacNeil. And he had no idea what he was going to do, now that he was here. And had he not missed his family in Scotland, he might never have left America, but stayed to try and find out what happened to the young woman who had helped him escape captivity. But he did miss his family: the people who had always loved him no matter what a jackass he was. He thought about how they must have changed, for certainly he had. Was Fletcher still the man in charge? Had Gavin read every book in the library, then gone on to the mainland where he could find and absorb more? And Kerry. Beauty that she had been when he'd left, he wondered at her beauty now. He had no doubt she would be stunning. A heartbreak waiting to happen to some hapless fellow.

The mates were yelling orders at one another as they lowered the gangplank. Rubbing his aching shoulder, he turned from the sea toward the docks as he heard his name shouted from the pier. His brother Fletcher waved at him; beside him stood the beautiful Rosalyn. He straightened, took one last look at the ocean behind him, and eagerly went ashore.

• • •

Isobel Dunbar had just dropped off some potatoes and turnips to be sold at the market by the docks. Their garden was booming this year; for some reason the rabbits and deer hadn't discovered the feast until late in the season and she had been able to squirrel away many of the root vegetables in the cellar dug in the back of the house long before she came to Hedabarr.

She stopped to watch the latest sailing vessel arrive, listened to the crew shouting orders, and wondered whence this boat had come. It was a grand vessel, larger than most that came into Sheiling's harbor. She tightened the green cashmere shawl around her head and shoulders, covering her ears against the wind. It was a gift from Hamish the Boat, who fished the icy waters of the North Sea and only came ashore once every few months. She smiled as she brushed back a ginger-colored curl that had come loose from her attempt at a practical chignon. Dear, dear Hamish. Perhaps she should give in and accept his marriage proposal. She certainly could do worse, and even though she didn't love him, she knew he cared for her, and his love for her son, Ian, was abundantly clear to anyone who watched the two of them together.

A commotion on the docks drew her gaze as sailing patrons and crew alighted from the broad wooden plank. One such passenger drew her attention, although she wasn't sure why, not immediately. Then she saw the Duke of Sheiling roar a boisterous "Hello!" and drag the other man into a tight bear hug. Her stomach did a somersault and her cheeks were suddenly flushed and hot. Although it had been ten years, she would know the man being embraced anywhere. She had known she always would, should he ever return. And her feelings were not all that pleasant, truth be told.

She took the shortcut home, through a cluster of Scots pines where tiny crossbills were feeding on the seeds. Another rush of memory gusted through her, one more unpleasant than merely seeing Duncan MacNeil returning home. *Lord MacNeil*, she thought with derision. She scanned the pines, knowing exactly where the brush that hid the cave was where he had so skillfully taken her virginity. Never mind that she had given it freely. As she hurried homeward, her mind was filled with visions, memories and feelings she had thought were long dead. Hastily, she pushed open the door to her home, not caring that it banged against the inside wall. Delilah, her business partner and friend, jumped at the noise, which had apparently roused her from a nap.

She frowned at Isobel. "What's the matter?"

Isobel hadn't been running, but her lungs heaved. She dropped her empty cane basket to the floor and unwound her shawl, tossing it onto the coat tree next to the door. Her warm cape followed. She then turned circles in the room, her skirt swishing across the worn, wooden floor that had of late become slanted toward the back door. "He's back."

"Who'd that be? And mind yourself; ye'll be getting dizzy doing that."

Isobel glanced around the room, foolishly expecting to see him hiding there, perhaps behind the wood box next to the fireplace, or the tall, thick curtains that hung from the front window, waiting to see her reaction. Well, that was stupid; he had probably forgotten her the minute he'd ravished her. She sucked in a breath. "Imagine who it is among all the people on this earth I never want to see again."

Delilah's appeared to wrack her brain for something to link Isobel's angst to. Suddenly her expression changed. "Ocht, no."

"Oh, yes," Isobel answered, continuing to march back and forth in front of the fireplace. "He was one of the passengers debarking at the docks."

"How'd you know for sure it was him?"

"The duke embraced him." She neglected to tell her friend that she had instinctively known it was Duncan MacNeil, returned from wherever it was he'd gone to. Back to America, probably, though she had never known for sure. All she knew those many years ago was that he had deflowered her then left her as he'd probably done to a dozen or more lassies on the island. She did wonder how many had been left with his seed firmly planted in their wombs, but oddly, she hadn't seen other signs of it on the island.

Delilah fretted, wringing her hands and pursing her lips. "Well, it doesn't mean naught, Izzy. He isn't a threat to ye as long as Ian is on the mainland—"

"Oh, dear," Isobel interrupted. "I got a letter yesterday from the school saying they were shutting down and sending the students home early because of some mysterious outbreak."

"Even so, why should the big man come 'round here? 'Tisn't a brothel anymore; he'll discover that. And I can't see him caring a whit about our little makeshift school. Nae," Delilah finished, "he shouldna' be a problem."

The burning of the schoolroom attached to the kirk and the disappearance of the schoolmaster had given Isobel a chance to hold things together until everything could be resolved. Reverend Fleming was grateful that she'd stepped in, and although many of the children were waiting for things to get back to normal, a few came to Isobel's little dame school in the interim. There were perhaps no more than a half dozen attending at a time. "Maybe I'm just borrowing trouble." She gave Delilah a self-effacing smile. "I have a habit of doing that, don't I?"

Delilah nodded, then looked over Isobel's head and scowled. "Henry! I asked ye to clean up that corner by the fireplace; it doesna' look any different now than it did before."

Isobel's handyman was a wiry black man whose parents had emigrated from Jamaica before Henry Blossom was born. And Delilah never let him forget that her ancestors had come across the Atlantic from Africa as tradesmen even before the Vikings. Whether it was true or not, no one knew, but it made for interesting conversation. Although, Isobel had learned in school that hundreds of years ago there was an African king in Scotland named King Kenneth Dubh.

Compared to Delilah's "huff and puff or I'll blow your house in" attitude, Henry was as laid back as an exhausted fox hound. He raised a huge hand to fend off her peppering of words. "I'll get to it after I fix the leak in the roof," he announced, and languidly made his way through the kitchen and out the back door. The door never banged shut when Henry left a room; not so with Delilah. The slamming of a door was to Delilah like an exclamation mark.

Most likely, he would gather some materials that he would need, and then eye a cozy spot under a tree, the work forgotten as he napped. But she hadn't the heart to let him go; where would he end up? Along with everything else—the condition of the building, the leaky roof and the warped floor—she had to worry about Henry. He was sweet and old and arthritic. Someone had to care for him.

Now Duncan MacNeil was back, and every secret she'd been harboring for the past ten years was being threatened. Isobel was happy she had never let herself get too close to the duke's wife, even though she had been kind and generous with supplies for the children after the school's accident. And in the beginning, she had often lingered, as if wanting to stay and help, but Isobel always told her she had plenty of that, and surely the Duchess of Sheiling had more important matters to attend to. There was always the chance that Ian might be home and accidentally be seen by Her Grace, and she might wonder...Isobel was a bit sad she wouldn't ever know her better, for she seemed like a lovely woman, one Isobel could easily have something in common with—outside of *that*.

But sweet as the duchess was, Isobel couldn't help remembering the one and only time she had been anywhere near that castle. It had not been pleasant.

Chapter Two

ISLAND OF HEDABARR—OCTOBER 1862

Isobel stepped out of the bathtub and took the towel her aunt offered her. Paula eyed her up and down, her face pinched into a frown and her hands on her hips. "Ye be pregnant."

Isobel's heart leaped into her throat as she shook her head, her aunt's words falling on her like icy water. "Nae, I...I'm not." How could she be? She had valiantly blocked out that one night of her life, hoping it would be erased from ever happening.

Paula pulled in a sigh. "Isobel Crawford, I wasn't some fool born yesterday. I be knowin' a pregnant belly when I see one, and I'm lookin' at one right this minute. And your chest be twice the size of normal." At Isobel's gasp, Paula replied, "Don't get starchy on me, sweet girl. Now is not the time."

Isobel brought the towel in front of her, over her breasts and stomach, as if she could protect them from her aunt's tirade. Her teeth began to chatter, either from the cold or from fear. "But how can that have happened?"

Paula studied her, her expression cynical. "How, indeed. Unless ye're going to have only the second virgin birth in the history of the world, someone got ye pregnant."

Isobel flushed and turned away. The embarrassment came flooding over her. She swallowed several times to keep her dinner down. "But...but I still bled, Aunt Paula. Truly, I did."

Paula drew in another deep breath, releasing it quickly. "I guess there aren't any hard and fast rules about that, my dear." She frowned again. "Ye haven't been sick?"

Isobel shook her head. If anything, she'd been ravenous. "I

feel fine." She bit her quivering lip and looked eagerly at her aunt. "Maybe it's not real."

Paula still stood before her, arms now crossed across her ample chest, an angry V between her eyes. "Who be the father?"

Isobel had the sudden urge to sob, to wail and scream and cry. "I'm serious as sauce, Isobel, who be the father?"

"It was only one time," she whispered.

"One time with who?"

Isobel shook her head, the dreadful reality hitting her, filling her chest with panic. "I can't tell ye."

Aunt Paula swore. "By God, girl, ye will tell me or I'll take a switch to your backside, pregnant or not. Understand?"

Isobel bit down on her lower lip again. It didn't help. She dissolved into tears and collapsed into the chair by the fireplace, drawing her knees up to her chin and burying her face.

Paula was at her side immediately, a dressing gown over her arm to clothe her niece. "Ocht, my dear, this is terrible," she insisted, wrapping Isobel in the soft, flannel gown. "Was it rape? Lord, child, why didn't ye tell me? Something could have been—"

"Nae," Isobel said. "He...he didn't...do that. I...I thought he loved me." She burst into tears again.

Paula drew her into her arms and rocked her. "He told ye that, did he? My poor, innocent lass. I guess I've kept ye too ignorant in the ways of the world. This is my fault as well as yours." She sat up and brought Isobel's face between her palms. "Please, dear. Tell me."

For all of her aunt's sputtering, Isobel knew her to be a kind soul. And she'd kept her dark secret for five long months. She wanted to let it out, get rid of it. So she told her aunt everything.

"That scoundrel of a half breed. I know exactly who ye mean. Both Delilah and I have had to turn him away from here time after time. Maybe if I'd let him in, this wouldn't have happened. Well," she said resolutely, "we're going to make a little visit to that castle, Isobel. They might own the blasted island, but that doesn't give them the right to use young lassies and then leave them as if they were nothing."

Now, ten years later, Isobel could still remember the rebuff they encountered on the steps of that grand, red structure. How would she have proved that the shining young sire of the manor wooed her and lured her and coaxed her into believing he'd instantly fallen in love with her? Aunt Paula had been so upset she'd threatened to sue them. She was told that she hadn't been the first person to try to extort money from the duke; scams had abounded when he first arrived to take control of the castle.

Isobel recalled the doddering old servant they'd dealt with. He was bent and skinny and had only a rim of white hair just above his ears. He did tell them to come back after the family returned from holiday, but Isobel was sure they wouldn't, and he wasn't very convincing anyway. They returned to the brothel with nothing, not even Isobel's fragile self-esteem. And four months later, Isobel had her beautiful son; she was glad no one at the castle knew of his existence, because then they couldn't come and try to take him away from her.

There had been that ordeal about conjuring up a reason for her condition. If nothing else, Paula had been a very creative woman. The story was that while in school on the mainland, Isobel had met a dashing young soldier named Robert "Rabbie" Dunbar. Robert or Rabbie after Scotland's favorite son, Robert Burns, and Dunbar after an obscure Scottish poet from the sixteenth century, one that Isobel had studied in school. The two married hastily when Isobel discovered she was pregnant, lying about her age, for she was not yet sixteen at the time. And shortly after that, the story went, poor Isobel learned that her new young husband was killed in a freak accident while practicing with his mount.

And now, Ian's real father was back. Could she keep him from learning that he had a son? She must. After all, she had been one of many that he had seduced, she was certain. There was no way he would ever remember her. Without thinking, she raised her hand to the scar below her ear.

• • •

A cannery. Fletcher wanted to build a cannery, and he offered Duncan the job of finding a site for it, recruiting the men and overseeing the building of it. Duncan took the opportunity happily.

He rode Miley, a gray gelding with a white face, which he had picked out at Fletcher's stable. It reminded him of his favorite horse, Lucky Boy, back on the ranch in Texas. Just before he entered the village, he stopped and took a sharp look at the buildings and how they were built, each attached to the next by adjoining walls. That wouldn't do for his purpose.

As he rode into town, he noticed the sign above the pub was different. No longer the Potted Haugh, it was now called Danny's by the Glass. The exterior was freshly painted and there were pots of flowers beside the door. Just then, the owner stepped out into the street with a broom and began sweeping away debris.

Duncan dismounted, tossed the reins over a post, and called out, "Danny McKay isn't it?"

McKay stopped sweeping and leaned on his broom. "Aye, 'tis. And I've been hearin' you'd be back soon enough. Word gets around fast."

Duncan came forward and the men shook hands. "The place looks fine, indeed."

With a harsh chuckle, McKay said, "Aye, that good-for-nothing MacNab drove the business into the ground, he did. 'Tisn't nice to speak ill of the dead, but that nasty bastard got what he deserved, being thrown from the horse he was trying to steal."

"My brother's horse."

"Aye," McKay replied.

Duncan looked up and down the street. "I don't suppose any of these buildings are empty."

McKay tilted his head. "What're you thinking?"

"Can we talk inside? I've got a bit of a thirst."

"Aye, my treat," McKay said, and ushered Duncan into the pub. A long polished oak bar stood along one wall, behind it a mirror and dozens of bottles of scotch from McKay's distillery. "Tessa," he called to a pretty young woman who was tending the bar. "Two pints to the back table, if ye please."

Once settled, McKay asked, "Now, what's on your mind?"

Duncan told him of the plans for a cannery. "We'd like property close to the water, of course. I thought you might know if there's any land available."

McKay pulled out a pipe and, without lighting it, stuck it between his teeth. "A cannery, you say?" He shook his head. "None of the row house buildings would work, but…"

Sensing interest, Duncan said, "But?"

The bartender, Tessa, set two big pints of ale in front of them; she gave Duncan a warm smile and left.

McKay noticed. "Tessa used to work for the madam. Nice girl, even so."

Duncan merely nodded.

"Now mind ye, I don't know if the place is for sale or if the owner would sell if offered a good price."

"What building is it?"

"Ye do remember the old brothel, then?" It seemed a rhetorical question.

"How could I forget? I was tossed out of there more times than I could count."

"'Tisn't a brothel anymore; the old madam died some years ago. I don't know exactly what it's being used for now, but it's close to the water, it's a free-standing building, and you just might find it to your liking. The building itself is in poor shape. Even so, the owner may not want to sell."

Duncan finished his pint and stood. "Fine ale, McKay. Thanks for the information, too." He rode to the brothel and sat astride as he studied it. It looked to be in pretty bad shape. The roof slanted and the place needed a good paint job. But, it was in perfect proximity to the water. Duncan could almost envision the new building now.

A black woman came out with a rug and shook it; Duncan recognized her as the one who had often turned him away. She glanced at him, nodded, then tucked the rug under her arm and hurried inside.

Duncan didn't dismount, but stayed astride and continued to study the building.

• • •

Delilah came in and slammed the door. "Don't look now, Izzy, but himself is out there, sittin' on a horse, studyin' the place."

Isobel's heart bumped against her ribs. She crossed to the window and carefully pulled the curtain aside. And there he was, bold as brass, staring at her building. Closer now than he was at the docks, she realized he had matured into quite a fine-looking man. "What in the devil is he doing?"

With an indelicate snort, Delilah said, "Maybe he's reliving all the times I escorted him out of the building. I should have booted him in the arse."

Isobel dropped the curtain. "What will I do if he comes to the door? What in the name of heaven could he want from me?" There was no way he could have discovered her secret; at this point Delilah and Hamish were the only ones who knew.

Delilah continued to stare out the other window. "Want me to go out and shoo him away? I could use the broom."

"That would only make him more curious." She pulled in a breath as she watched him turn his mount. "He's leaving. Thank God."

She sank into an overstuffed chair by the fireplace. Ian was coming home from school early, and his biological father had turned up, practically on her doorstep. She felt her carefully woven life of lies begin to unravel.

• • •

Duncan joined Fletcher in his study and accepted the snifter of brandy. "I rode into the village to have a look around. McKay has done a nice job with the pub."

"And MacNab's widow is living out her life without being used as a punching bag," Fletcher answered.

"McKay mentioned that one of the few free-standing buildings in the village is the brothel, which I understand is closed. Have you any idea what it's being used for now?"

Fletcher shook his head. "Not really. Whoever owns it now rents out rooms. Our rag man stays there on occasion when he passes through. And it's close to the water."

"Perfect location."

"What are your thoughts?" Fletcher asked.

"You say they rent rooms? If that's the case, maybe I should rent a room for a while, just to get an inside look before I make a decision. I realize the condition of the building is moot, for we'd tear it down anyway. The woman who used to kick me out of the brothel recognized me as I was studying the place. We don't know if the owner is willing to sell, either."

"We can always sweeten the deal; if the location is perfect, money isn't an object." Fletcher refilled his snifter and raised the bottle in Duncan's direction, but he waved him away.

"How do you want to do this?"

"Geddes is still your solicitor?"

"Of course; he and Fenella are doing well. That was a match no one but my wife anticipated."

Duncan put his empty snifter on the table beside him. "I'd like to get in there, but the owner deserves some kind of warning. I was thinking Geddes could send him a letter in advance, make him an offer, or at least propose an offer. What do you think?"

Nodding, Fletcher said, "I'll have Geddes get right on it."

. . .

Less than a week after Isobel's life took a turn for the worse, rather like a boil that needed lancing, she received a letter from the local law office. Curious, she opened it and scanned the contents. The words that jumped out at her were "meeting," "Thursday next," "condition of property," and "lucrative offer." After reading it thoroughly, she understood the entire meaning and fear thrummed through her veins. Someone wanted her building and its close proximity to the water. She dropped into a chair and brought shaky fingers to her mouth. Hadn't she thought that this day might come? Hadn't she been waiting for it? Well, here it was, and still she wasn't ready to consider such an offer. She had never even toyed with the idea of selling.

Determined, she stood and stuffed the letter into her apron pocket. She had two days before the meeting. There was nothing she could do in two days but fret and stew and worry, which she undoubtedly would do. She was good at that. But she would keep the news to herself. No need to stress Delilah, Henry, or Lily, her new young teacher. Whatever happened would be common knowledge sooner or later. Isobel would deal with it then. In the background, she heard Delilah nattering at poor Henry. It was time to intervene. Again.

• • •

Fletcher leaned back in his chair and studied Duncan. "Forgot to mention when you first arrived that you looked like hell."

Duncan returned his brother's gaze, noting the lines that bracketed his mouth were deeper and the hair at his temples was salted with gray. Small wrinkles fanned out from his eyes. Duncan wasn't surprised, but he was taken aback a bit. What had he expected? That time on the island would stand still for him? He quickly scanned the den, the bookshelves, the cribbage board that sat on a nearby table. No matter how many times he and Gavin had played, Gavin beat the pants off him. And this was where he could always find his brother, his nose in a book so dry Duncan was surprised dust hadn't dropped into his brother's lap as he read.

"Three months on a ship will do that to a person," he responded. They had met with some foul weather that had taken them far off course. "If I remember right, you didn't ever develop your sea legs, or anything else on board a ship. At least I kept my food down."

Fletcher threw his head back and laughed. "Touché. The first thing I saw after I was carted upstairs was the face of that huge beast of a dog. And then Rosalyn burned my buckskins."

Duncan had heard the story many times before, but after ten years, it was like hearing it anew. "Rosalyn is as beautiful as ever."

Fletcher's features softened. "She is, isn't she?"

Duncan dared to broach the matter of children. "Not that it's my business, but I'm surprised there aren't more little MacNeils running about the place."

When he left the island the twins, Rory and Rabbie, were babies. They would be rambunctious ten-year-olds now.

Fletcher cocked an eyebrow at his brother. "So far, they have been enough of a handful, but we continue to try, just the same."

Duncan, anxious to see his nephews, asked, "Where are those rascals? I probably wouldn't recognize them if they came up and tackled me."

"It does seem quiet around here without them; they're currently on a field trip to Skye. They'll be home soon."

"Do you still have sheep?"

"We've got them over near Ben Rothsay. It won't be long before we do some shearing." He raised a black eyebrow at his brother. "You do remember how to shear sheep, don't you?"

Duncan clasped his hands together and cracked his knuckles. "I can still beat you by a dozen."

Fletcher cracked his knuckles as well. "In your dreams, little brother. In your dreams."

They sat in comfortable silence. The grandfather clock in the hallway outside the library door gave notice that it was seven o'clock. Although he had been back in Scotland for over a week, Duncan felt exhaustion seep into his bones.

There was a gentle knock on the library door, and when Fletcher called, "Enter," the housekeeper, a pleasant-looking woman of perhaps forty, rail thin and ruddy, stepped in. "Yes, Mrs. Miers?"

"I'm sorry to interrupt, Your Grace, but there be auld Barnaby roamin' about without his breeks again."

So, Duncan thought, the ancient valet still appeared to prefer a breeze on his bony behind.

"Take him back to his quarters, if you will, and pour him a whisky. Hopefully he'll sleep until morning. Oh, and Mrs. Miers? Lord Duncan should have hot water for a bath. Can you see that it's done? Perhaps Evan and one of the girls can give you a hand with the buckets. Please don't try to do it by yourself."

After she left, Duncan said, "It's going to take a mighty long time for me to get used to that title."

"Hell," Fletcher answered, "I'm still not accustomed to being Your Grace and Duke of Sheiling, and it's been over ten years."

Fletcher brushed dog hair off his trousers. "So, you'll meet with the brothel owner tomorrow. I wish I could join you, but there's an important meeting of the crofters I don't want to miss."

"I'll be anxious to see who owns the property now. You know, that was the first time I realized all black people didn't talk like they did back home. That big woman manning the door sounded every bit as Scots as Geddes, albeit she peppered her speech with more colorful words."

Fletcher took another sip of brandy. "With its closeness to the river, it's the perfect place to build a cannery, and the island is screaming for some new opportunities. We've got the distillery, where they're refining a beauty of a scotch whisky, but other than that there aren't many prospects for work. The crofters are doing better now that I won't accept payment from them; even so, some of them are looking to leave if they can't get wages." He studied Duncan again. "Times are changing, brother."

"I'll get it done, trust me. Since we last talked about it, have you learned what the building is being used for?"

Fletcher was thoughtful. "Sometime last year, the schoolmaster disappeared after the schoolroom burned. It's right next to the church, but fortunately the fire was put out before it got that far. According to Rosalyn, there is a woman running a small dame school at the old brothel now, for those who want to be in school until the building is ready, but I'm not aware of who she is or where she lives. She may stay there for all I know. I'll leave it to you to find out."

"You mean you're going to toss a bunch of kids out onto the streets to fend for themselves just so you can open a business?"

"It isn't like that," Fletcher said in his defense. "Rosalyn has been to the brothel on a few occasions since the fire and smoke damage to the school. The school should be ready to use again by the time we make arrangements to buy the property." He shook his head and raked his fingers through his hair. "This may be a small island, Duncan, but there's so much to be responsible for. As soon as Reverend Fleming returns from the mainland, I'll have to get in touch with him and see how things are progressing with the school. The main thing is we want that piece of property."

"We should be prepared for a negative response. Is there any place we could suggest the inhabitants of the old brothel move to, if indeed they live on the premises?"

"I'd be willing to cede them any number of pieces of land. Perhaps offering them free land to build on would be a good incentive." Fletcher rubbed his chin thoughtfully. "If that's not an immediate option, I believe there's a vacant croft cottage near the village that would suffice until more permanent arrangements could be made."

"Well," Duncan said, "it's all worth a try."

Chapter Three

Isobel returned from the meeting shaken. Yellow the Cat, their mouser, raised her head, then snuggled back into a ball in the sunshine, apparently content that nothing was being asked of her. When Delilah met Isobel at the door, Isobel knew there was no hope of keeping the problems to herself. Delilah offered to make her "a wee cuppa." While she waited for the tea, Isobel picked up the handmade booklet lying on the rosewood side table, one Ian had made for her at school. Until now, she hadn't gone through it entirely, for she was constantly interrupted by one thing or another.

In it were pictures he had drawn of her, Delilah, Henry, Hamish, and Lily. They were caricatures, really, although Isobel didn't think Ian knew the name for what he'd drawn. For instance, her caricature's most outstanding feature was her hair. Red as flames. And there was a bright red circle on each cheek. She put the back of her hand against her cheek and felt the warmth. She knew they would be rosy. Of course Delilah was enormous and black and she was depicted knitting something that was so long, it went off the page. Henry was also black, but he had a wide smile on his face, and carried a huge hammer, which amused Isobel, because as many times as Henry picked up a hammer, he got distracted and forgot what he was going to use it for.

There was nothing funny about her new teacher, Lily; she had been drawn with skill and care. She was blonde and lovely, just as she was in real life. Of course he couldn't put her idiosyncrasies to paper, like her affinity for cleanliness and her odd habits about food and laundry. Ah, but Hamish. He was drawn big and brawny with lots and lots of red hair—like hers—and his mouth was open with a bubble over his head laughing. *Ho ho ho!* it said, as he stood beside a well-drawn seafaring craft. Puzzling, however, was that beside the figure of Hamish Ian had written *Hamish the Boat, PD.* PD? Down in the corner she saw in parentheses *(pretend dad).*

She turned to the final page and gasped, bringing her hand to her mouth. She had never gotten this far before. On the page was an oblong box with the letters *RD* printed across it. At the bottom were the words *(real dad—Robert Dunbar).* She sagged against the back of the chair and closed her eyes. As far as Isobel was concerned, Ian's father was dead to her and would continue to be so. Suddenly all of the inner rage she'd experienced at the meeting softened. She could not lose control. One tiny slip and her life and Ian's would be ruined.

Delilah returned with their tea and a plate of scones. "So, how did it go?"

"Someone wants to buy the property."

"What for?"

"Apparently it's the perfect location for a new cannery." Isobel pushed a tendril of hair from her forehead, recalling the oh-so-very logical plan the solicitor had laid out before her. And himself, acting like typical royalty, merely sat there, smug as any monarch could be at the idea of turning so many lives upside down. "I can understand the need for jobs, I really can. But…" She felt deflated. "I can't sell this place!" She gave Delilah a frantic look. "What would we do? Where would we go?" She took a sip of tea, noting that her hand shook.

Delilah nodded and flicked a crumb from the corner of her mouth. "Ye mean they didn't offer a solution?"

Isobel straightened. "Of course they did. Something about an old crofter's cottage on the edge of the village until permanent arrangements could be made."

Delilah was thoughtful. "At least they came up with something. Not hardly goin' to be a positive response if they put us out on the street."

Isobel threw her a hard glance. "They also said the duke would give us property to build on."

Delilah brightened. "Now that sounds fair."

"I know I have many bills to pay. It doesn't make things any easier. After all the years we've been here, how can I simply hand the building over to someone who will knock it down? All of our memories will be lost forever."

"Memories are things we take with us, darlin'. The house is just a place to hang our clothes."

"But we have the children to think of. Until I hear otherwise, I'm responsible for their education. I can't be forced to do something I don't want to do. So many changes coming. With Reverend Fleming retiring, there will be another new situation to deal with." She took a sip of tea. "He's been such a big part of our lives; replacing him will be very hard."

"Have you heard if they've hired someone?"

"I haven't, but Birgit told me there's a young missionary in America whose family is rooted in one of the other islands. He's one of the candidates, I believe."

Delilah barked a laugh. "We're being inundated by Americans. I suppose it's the duke who wants to build."

Isobel toyed with her teacup, studying the dainty pink and green flowers that circled the rim, then gave Delilah a grim smile. "Yes, it is."

"I guess it makes some kind of sense for him to want to extend his hold on the land, as if he doesn't already own enough," she groused. "He was at the meeting?"

"That's the other thing. No, he wasn't. He sent someone there in his stead."

Delilah took another scone and placed it on her saucer. "That advocate with a broom handle up his arse?"

Isobel laughed. "Yes, Mr. Gordon was there, but someone from the family was there as well. Guess who?"

Delilah put her cup down on the tray a tad harder than was necessary. The sound pinged loudly in the room. "Ye don't say." She studied Isobel closely. "Did he recognize ye?"

"Nae. I don't think so." He hadn't given her too much notice;

she was grateful for that, even though ten years had passed, and she had recognized Duncan MacNeil at a distance in an instant. She was just another one of his flings. Why should he remember her at all? "It's better that he doesn't. I don't want to give him any reason to suspect…you know."

"I guess ye be right," Delilah agreed. Suddenly she stood; the chair scooting out behind her, sliding along the warping floor. "But it ain't right that himself can come waltzing back into your life without so much as a how do."

"Don't worry," Isobel promised. "I've already decided that there is no way on this earth that I will sell to him or to anyone else. I don't have to, and I won't. I don't care how many jobs a cannery will create for the villagers and crofters. They can find suitable land somewhere else." And she meant it.

• • •

Duncan watched the restless wind push the waves against the rocks. A cold rain battered the windows, all of which reminded Duncan he wasn't in Texas anymore. He moved toward the fireplace, settled into the comfortable armchair beside the fire and accepted a snifter of brandy from his brother. He hadn't gone over the details of the meeting yet; dinnertime was not the time for business. "You haven't told me what Gavin is up to."

Fletcher poured himself a similar snifter and relaxed into the chair opposite. "Well, you know he went off to Glasgow and then Edinburgh," he said. "He finished studying the history of the world, decided that wasn't challenging enough, and so went into the priesthood."

Duncan nearly choked on his drink. "Priesthood? Why not just the seminary? What man would choose to be celibate if he didn't have to be?"

Fletcher gently swirled his brandy. "I guess he thought of that afterwards, because he studied for a year, then decided it wasn't for him."

"I'd have killed myself."

"I've sent Gavin off to the Borders. I learned a few years ago that we have an estate there, and it needed managing. He went happily."

"Sounds like it would suit him," Duncan mused.

They sat quietly, enjoying each other's company and the good brandy. The fire spit and crackled up the chimney, sending warmth into the room.

"Do you remember the Fleming twins?" Fletcher asked.

Duncan tipped his head back, glancing toward the ceiling. "Can't remember their names, though."

"Birdie and Robbie," Fletcher reminded him. "That's what we called them anyway."

"Ah, yes. Which one was the pretty one?"

Fletcher gave him a chiding look. "I thought they were both rather attractive."

"Well, I remember that Gavin was head over heels for the pretty one, the redhead, and she sure knew how to make herself available when he was around."

"That was Birdie; she didn't have much between the ears. Robbie, on the other hand, is currently studying in Edinburgh."

"That's what happens when you're not the pretty one. A woman can't be pretty and intelligent."

"I beg to differ," Fletcher said with a laugh.

"You got lucky. Rosalyn is the most perfect package: beauty and brains." He turned and gave his brother a wry smile. "And then there's Kerry, who is also beautiful and bright. She seems content; is she?"

Fletcher let out a rush of air. "There's an underlying current of restlessness there. She keeps it pretty well hidden."

"I met Evan in the barn; he's become quite a help around here."

"I've given him complete responsibility for the horses and all the outbuildings. He's also been working with Geddes to learn the legal ins and outs of our businesses here on the island. He and Kerry are very close." He waved his arm toward Duncan. "Not physically, not like that, but they've had a bond since the day she arrived and it's only gotten stronger." Fletcher made a sound in his throat. "Actually, he's a better brother to her than I am."

"You don't think she'd leave, do you?" Duncan asked, curious.

"And go where, and do what?"

A flash of the ranch and its need for future competent management raced through Duncan's head.

Fletcher studied him. "Did it ever bother you that you spent most of your time on this island chasing the lassies?"

"And trying to avoid any work you asked me to do? No," he admitted. "Certainly not while I lived here. When I left, I felt like I'd escaped from prison." He gave his brother an apologetic glance. "For my behavior to you, I've felt guilty for years, especially when I realized how much work and responsibility it took to run the ranch."

"Well, I have to admit I'm surprised we didn't see proof of your legacy all over the island," Fletcher said with a grim smile.

Duncan shuddered and took a sip of brandy. In his pensive moments he had often wondered that himself. "The thought horrifies me."

"So, tell me about the meeting. Did it go well?"

"I guess that depends on which side you're on," Duncan answered.

Fletcher frowned. "What happened?"

"You did tell me the place is now some kind of temporary school."

"Yes, but not for long. As soon as the repairs are made and the roof is replaced on the schoolroom, it can open again. Of course, we still haven't hired a new schoolmaster and the tutor we had for you, Gavin, and Kerry—"

"And the Fleming twins," Duncan reminded him.

"So you remember that much. You left before you really settled in. Anyway, your tutor stayed on to teach our boys, but he wasn't interested in taking on the job at the school. And," he added, "the brothel building won't pass inspection."

"Well, the place is a safety hazard and a firetrap. I could tell that from the outside. I have to get inside to really check out the rest of it."

"How will you do that? I'm assuming the owner doesn't feel he has to accommodate you."

"She," Duncan corrected, recalling the fiery redhead who had sat across the table from him. "The current owner is the niece of the late brothel owner. She's also the temporary teacher for the children who chose to stay in school. And you did tell me that they have rooms to let for travelers passing through."

"So?"

"So, she can't discriminate in who she rents to, can she? After all, I'm not some troublesome rag man, although she'll probably treat me like one." It had taken him until he returned to the castle to realize that there was something familiar about the woman. It was the way she fidgeted with a scar on her neck. That triggered something in his memory, and as he mulled it over, he remembered the night at the fair. Oddly enough, she had been his last conquest on the island. The virgin. She'd become quite a luscious-looking woman, rounded in all the places he liked his women round.

At first, he'd thought her animosity at the meeting was because of the circumstances. Now he wondered if she recalled that night as well and the memory didn't appear to give her any pleasure at all. And why should it?

In any case, he was about to find out.

. . .

Isobel stood in front of Delilah, nearly incapable of speech. "You did *what*?"

"I rented Lord Duncan a room," Delilah repeated with an easy calm. "He paid for a month up front and I couldna' see any reason to turn him down."

"He has a castle a few miles from here. Why would he even want to stay in one of our rooms? They're plain and serviceable; that's all. I think even a monk would find them lacking."

Delilah stood her ground. "The money is more than we could count on for three months. And what's the harm?"

Again, Isobel was nearly speechless. "Have you forgotten Ian?"

"Well, course not, but who's to say the man would even recognize himself in the lad?"

Isobel fidgeted with her apron strings, tying and untying the ends. "It's still a worry. In a few days, Hamish is coming by and we're going to fetch Ian at the docks."

"We'll figure out something," Delilah promised.

Isobel found it difficult to catch her breath; she was warm and felt a headache starting at the base of her skull. She rubbed the area with her fingers. "I don't want Duncan MacNeil here, Delilah. I don't want him anywhere near me or my family or my business." She picked up a leaflet from the table beside her and fanned herself.

Delilah studied her, concerned. "Ye be all right, Izzy?"

Isobel nodded, continuing to try to cool off. "I'm letting my emotions get the better of me. This entire situation gives me a headache, that's all."

"Well, I can't return the money; I've spent some of it to pay the butcher for the last two orders of mutton we received."

Isobel closed her eyes briefly and rested her head against the back of the chair. "That came due already?"

"'Fraid so, and as long as the money was there, I thought it best to pay him. After all, we don't need much meat, but we need some, and we don't have our own sheep to slaughter."

"I could probably take in some more dressmaking." Although the thought of it made her feel exhausted before she'd gotten the words out.

Delilah slapped her palms on the arms of the chair. "Nae. Your hands haven't healed since the last precious gown ye sewed for that fancy lady who was visiting her brother the alchemist."

It was true; Isobel's skin was delicate and her hands cracked and bled when she worked with them too long. That was one of the reasons she had worn gloves when she sewed that last gown, otherwise the skin on her fingers would have snagged the fabric and ruined it.

"Has His Lordship moved in already?" She tried to curb her

sarcasm, but wasn't successful. At Delilah's nod, Isobel said, "You know what I'd like to do? Go up, take his precious belongings, and toss them into the river."

Isobel pulled herself out of her chair and headed for the empty makeshift classroom where Lily, who was humming a tune Isobel had come to recognize, was preparing an art class for the children. Although her speech was often a mixture of Gaelic, English, and Creole, Lily strove to make her English stronger.

She worked hard to teach some English, so there were alphabet letters printed on heavy paper on the walls. Most of the children still spoke the ancient Gaelic tongue at home, as did their parents. The number of daily students varied. There were a few of the crofter's children, but the sheep shearing season would be coming up soon, and the children were always eager to help.

The teacher looked up and smiled. "I'm hoping I can get this restless bunch interested in something other than catching frogs at the river."

Isobel still found it almost amusing when Lily spoke, for although she certainly looked like a Scot, she didn't sound like the rest of them. She examined the large sheets of paper. "Where did we get those?"

"They were brought over by one of the girls who works at the castle. Apparently the duchess found them somewhere on the mainland and thought of us."

Once again, Isobel realized how fortunate it was that she had never become close to the duchess; it would only add to her guilty burden if the whole family suddenly descended on them now that His Lordship was staying here.

The moment she laid eyes on Duncan MacNeil, she saw evidence of her son in every feature. Ian was lighter, but he promised to become as handsome a young man as his father. But, she vowed, he would never, ever become the scoundrel his father had been—or perhaps still was.

Chapter Four

Duncan studied the street below. There was little fortification in his rented room to keep out the outside sounds and winds, and as a wagonload of peat clattered over the cobbles, he could also hear the *clip clop* of the big horse's hooves. Ragged-looking children ran and shouted in the street, some trying to taunt the horse, who, much to their dismay, didn't respond.

The sight of the animal poked at a sore in his mind, and he was back in battle.

LOUISIANA—JULY 1864

Duncan fought to catch his breath. Sweat dripped into his eyes as he peered over the breastwork and realized that whatever small skirmish they had started was now at an end. Bluecoats lay all around them, some face up, their eyes sightless against the burning heat of the sun. Brain matter where it shouldn't be. He swallowed hard, attempting to get past the nausea that rose in his throat.

And the battery horses…torn by shot and shell, suffering for man's sake, not their own. They were the sacrificial lambs of the army, on both sides. It sickened Duncan.

A shout from the street brought him back, and he saw that many of the buildings in Sheiling were handsome—tall, three story row house structures, colorful and neatly kept, fronted with timber, finished with stone or slate. The only building needing repair, it seemed, was the one he was standing in. Also, it was the only building that stood alone, without other structures attached. It backed up against the waterway, making the property perfect for a cannery. Duncan had glanced at the roof of the brothel and noted the snags and cracks in the corners where the eaves met the siding. And inside, on the third floor where the rental rooms were, the ceiling was spotted with circular stains where the rains had broken through.

He wondered how long it had been since any serious repairs had been done to the building. Even though he hadn't been in the structure more than an hour, he already knew the place was a firetrap. It was with that truth that he would try to convince the owner to sell.

The owner. Isobel Dunbar. A widow with hair so bright it could glow in the dark. No doubt she had a temper to match. Although she had been stoic all through the meeting, he'd seen a glimmer of anger in her eyes, especially when she looked at him. Was it because she remembered who he was, or was it just because of the nature of the meeting? At any rate, how does one approach such a dilemma? *Hello, there. Remember me? I took your virginity ten years ago.* Or maybe: *You look vaguely familiar. Have we me before?* He combed his fingers through his hair and shook his head. Either way, it was going to be awkward. For him, anyway. It was possible she had forgotten him the minute he'd left her. Although he had to admit it wasn't probable, since there had been no other half-breeds stalking the girls on the island all those years ago.

Hoping to put the incident out of his mind, at least for now, he sat at the small desk in the corner of the room and wrote a list of things he wanted to show her, to make her understand that selling the property would be in her best interest.

· · ·

Duncan met Isobel on the stairs. She looked deliciously heated; her cheeks were rosy and her hair had come loose around her face, framing it with curly tendrils. Her bosom was full and round beneath her clothing. He cleared his throat. "I would appreciate speaking to you about something," he began.

She narrowed her eyes. "Tell me." Her voice was tight. "Why is it you want a room here when you have a castle mere miles away?"

Her straightforwardness didn't surprise him. "First of all, it isn't my castle. Secondly, I wanted to check out the building. There are things I'd like to show you that may surprise and dismay you."

She gave him a cool, unwelcoming smile. "Really. You don't think I know my building better than anyone? Don't you think I'm aware that some things are falling down around me? That doesn't mean I'm in any way willing to sell this property to you."

"Please indulge me." He motioned for her to go ahead of him.

With a twist of her mouth, she lifted her skirt, whipped past him, and went upstairs.

First he showed her all the water spots on the third floor ceilings. "You're lucky it isn't worse," he noted. "After another storm, you may find the ceiling on top of my bed."

Her eyes glittered as she replied, "With you in it, if I'm lucky."

He enjoyed her plucky attitude. It was refreshing. "Yes, well, don't kill the messenger."

"So I should plan the demise of the duke, then, is that it? Surely this isn't the only property close to the river that would meet your needs."

"There may be others, but to be frank, this building is on land that is perfect for what we plan to use it for."

She studied him for a long while. "And you think you can bribe me into selling you my property just because you've offered a nice little bonus?"

Duncan shrugged, keeping his demeanor professional. "I didn't think it would hurt."

"Well, what if I took your bonus and hired someone to make the repairs?"

His gaze lingered on her. "You wouldn't do that."

"Why not?"

"Because you're an honest woman. If you weren't, you'd have found some shady way to get the building in better shape by now."

Surprise flashed in her eyes; she planted her fists on her hips, her color high. "I am not interested in selling at any price."

"I'm hoping you change your mind once I've shown you the other problems."

She opened her mouth to say something, but obviously thought better of it, and followed him downstairs. He stopped in the great room, picked up a toy ball that was in a chair by the fireplace, and put it on the floor. It rolled right across the room and into the kitchen, stopping at the back entrance. "I'm sure I don't have to explain that if a floor slants like this, it's likely that the boards beneath it are rotting away. Water damage and mildew, no doubt. Could even be an infestation of some sort."

He continued over to the windows above the kitchen dry sink, poking at the frame. It broke off and fell into his hand. "These keep out very little from the outside. In the winter, I imagine things get quite chilly in here."

"We make do." She appeared resolute. Stubborn, even.

Apparently she needed further convincing. "What if I told you the building is a firetrap, and you're risking the lives of every person who lives in it?"

Her eyes widened in shock. "What do you mean, firetrap?"

"Exactly that. The chimneys are full of peat soot; I'm surprised the place hasn't caught fire already."

"The lums can be cleaned out," she countered. "And I've been meaning to do just that."

He watched as she ran nervous fingers over the scar on her neck. "The brickwork on the outside around the chimney is broken. What if a piece were suddenly to fall into the street and hit someone? One of the children, perhaps?"

"I hardly think that's likely," she said. "If you don't mind, I would like to have someone else come in and give me another opinion. I'm suspicious of yours."

"Certainly. I think that's a fine idea," he answered. "Just remember, I've only scraped the surface of what's wrong with this structure."

• • •

Isobel paced back and forth in the kitchen, wearing a path in front of the fireplace. "He is out for blood, that's for certain."

Lily, who had finished in the schoolroom, sat at the long, plank table with her cup of tea. It had startled Isobel at first when Lily refused to use any cup, dish or cutlery that wasn't her own. She had brought all of her own dishware with her, explaining that that was the way she'd been raised. "Are ye sure he's like that?"

"I hadn't planned on mentioning this to you, because until now it wasn't necessary. But for you to understand my position, you also must know some of my more sordid history."

Lily bit her lip to stifle a smile. "Ye? Sordid? That's hard for me to believe, Isobel."

Isobel took a seat across from the teacher and folded her hands on the table. "Well, it certainly isn't a fairy tale, but I'll start with 'Once upon a time, ten long years ago…'"

She finished by showing Lily the booklet Ian had drawn that depicted his natural father in a coffin. Lily simply sat there and stared at her. "Ye mean His Lordship, Duncan MacNeil of the clan MacNeil, brother to the famous duke, is Ian's father?" She brought her hand to her chest. "The other story was all just made up?"

Not feeling too proud of herself, Isobel simply nodded. "Yes, and now it could all come crashing down around my head."

"And they wouldn't listen to your aunt at the castle?"

"There was some old valet or butler there at the time, and I suppose we could have returned when the duke and his family were there, but truthfully, we both decided it wasn't worth the abuse. And by that time, Paula was determined that we would raise the bairn together. She was just as afraid as I was that they might try to take him from me."

"Do you really think they would have done that?"

"Why not?" Isobel replied. "I've read that it's done all the time. And no doubt Ian would have had much more than he has now. He's always wanted a horse, you know, and certainly if he'd been raised by the duke and duchess, he would have had one by now." She felt tears well up and blinked them back. "If I would have had to give him up, I don't think I could have stayed here, close enough to watch him grow and not know of my existence, yet how could I have left?"

She sniffed and wiped at her nose with her handkerchief. "I guess I'm lucky I was able to send Ian off island to school. The mystery of his birth would have been solved by anyone who looked at him closely had he been here."

Fifi, Lily's little dog, came running into the kitchen and leapt onto Lily's lap. Lily scratched the pup's ears. "What have you been up to, scalawag?" She glanced at Isobel and grimaced. "She's wet. I guess the river is just too much of a lure for her."

"Delilah is going to have her for dinner when she sees the muddy paw prints all over the kitchen floor."

"Ocht, she's all bluster."

"It didn't take you long to figure her out."

Just then, Delilah stepped into the room with a basket of vegetables. "Aha! That mutt has been fishing in the river again. Wouldn't be so bad if she'd catch something big enough for us to eat," she grumbled. She dropped the basket onto the table, put her fists on her hips, and focused her attention on Isobel.

"Well? What did His Lordship have to say for himself?"

Isobel pulled in a deep breath. "He says the place is a firetrap and I'm endangering everyone who lives here."

"Course he'd say that. Didn't he have anything specific to say?"

Isobel rubbed her hands over her face. "The roof is bad and the outside is falling apart, the floors are damp and moldy and they slant towards the back door, the windows aren't sealed, the lums are full of peat soot and need cleaning or we'll all burn to death...need I go on?"

Delilah harrumphed. "We know all that, except that he thinks it's a firetrap. Do ye suppose he said that just to scare ye into selling?"

Isobel reached over and picked up an apple off the side board, rubbed it on her apron, then took a knife from the cutlery drawer and began slicing it into chunks for baking.

"I don't think he's trying to scare me, but I've already contacted

Ferris the Peat and he's going to come over tomorrow and give me an honest consultation. I have to hear from someone I know and trust."

Lily turned from the sink, a potato in her hand. "That is something I've found so colorful about living here."

"What's that?" Isobel asked.

"I'm sure Ferris has another name; why do you call him Ferris the Peat?"

"Because," Delilah stepped in, "he cuts and stacks our peat when 'tis dried so we can use it in the lums."

"Ah," Lily answered, digging furiously at an eye on the potato. "That's why Hamish is the Boat. I understand now. But, what if Ferris finds the same things wrong with the place?"

Isobel stopped cutting up the apple; the knife slid from her fingers. "Then I don't know what I'll do."

Delilah joined Lily at the sink and began scrubbing a squash. "Let's think about something pleasant. Like Ian's return the day after tomorrow."

"That's both pleasant and frightening," Isobel answered around a small bite of apple, hoping the meticulous Lily didn't notice.

• • •

The next day, Duncan made another cursory tour of the building, and his conclusions hadn't changed. If anything, he was even more concerned about the safety of the occupants. He discovered some of the boards on the back porch were rotting, others loose with nails popping out of them. He stood at the ledge where the washbasin sat next to a pump, presumably for children to wash up after playing by the river, and glanced through the window into the kitchen.

Isobel sat with her back to him, discussing something with an older fellow Duncan assumed to be her "other opinion." She was upset; he could see that, and he could also hear bits and pieces of their conversation, although he could only understand Isobel.

"What am I going to do, Ferris?" Isobel's voice was high.

Ah. Ferris the Peat. Now older, he had a thick head of white hair. He put a large, work-worn hand on Isobel's arm. He said something to her in a soft voice.

"Sell? Really? You too?" Her voice rose higher and she stood, nearly toppling the long bench at the table.

Duncan didn't hear the older man's answer, but clearly it wasn't what Isobel wanted to hear, for she hurried from the room, her hand over her mouth.

Duncan actually felt some guilt over what he'd brought about. But there wasn't any other solution. He opened the door and stepped into the kitchen. The older man looked at him and a broad smile wreathed his face. "Is that ye, young Duncan?"

Duncan crossed the room and they shook hands. "It's me." He glanced at the door that Isobel ran through. "She's pretty upset."

"Aye, she's been livin' in a bit of a fantasy here, since her aunt died. Too much money going out and not enough comin' in to pay for the upkeep."

"So you and I agree on the condition of the building?"

"That I do. But ye will tread lightly, won't ye?"

"I'll do what I can, I promise you that."

"Have ye thought of where they'd go once the deal is done?"

"A couple of suggestions. We would offer them property on which to build, of course, but in the meantime there's a vacant crofter's cottage outside of town on the Meade Road."

Ferris nodded. "Aye, I know the place. Been empty for a few years, a family of rodents has probably taken up residence."

"That can all be rectified," Duncan replied.

"I can give ye a hand wi' that, young Duncan. Isobel is a young woman who has always been close to me heart."

Chapter Five

The following morning, Duncan prepared to ride to the castle but stopped at the wharf to see if there was any mail. As he approached a quaint tea shop, he noticed Isobel, a big man, and a young boy ahead of him. The man had his beefy arm around the boy's shoulders and the boy leaned into him as they walked. Duncan, feeling like a voyeur, entered the shop a few moments behind them and pretended to study some imported hand-blown glass. Isobel was so engrossed in her company that she didn't even look his way.

The man had the look of a fisherman. His face was ruddy and wind burned. He was big, brawny, with wild red hair and a big laugh. Curious, thought Duncan. The three looked like a family. She was a widow; what was her relationship to the big fisherman? And was the young lad hers? Isobel was enjoying the company of both of them, and Duncan noticed a glow in her face that he hadn't seen since he'd arrived. For some odd reason, that bothered him. He left before they could notice him, but he was determined to find out for sure who her two companions were.

When he reached the castle, he found Fletcher in the stables with Evan and Kerry. They greeted him warmly, then each saddled a mount and were gone. Two large hounds followed them, loping easily beside the horses. A couple of collies paced in the yard, attempting to herd some chickens.

"Kerry has become a beautiful young woman," Duncan noticed.

Fletcher eased Ahote's saddle off and slung it over the railing. Duncan noticed the round silver concha that secured the saddle strings was shiny as a new coin. He also noticed that Ahote was getting gray around the muzzle. Fletcher took up a brush and began grooming his mount. "I agree." He continued his labor of love, brushing his steed methodically.

"I don't imagine there's much chance of her marrying an islander," Duncan mused.

Fletcher gave him a wry look. "Sometimes I wonder if she'll ever marry. It would be a shame if she didn't. But she's been in Rosalyn's loving clutches so long she refuses to even consider marriage until she's fallen madly in love."

"And where is she to find this perfect man?"

Fletcher shook his head. "Every eligible Scot on this island leaves as soon as he can. But even if one were here and wooed her, I…well, I don't mean to sound arrogant, but Kerry is so damned brilliant, I don't think he'd have a chance. I don't know what she's looking for, but I can safely say she probably won't find him here. And no amount of posing and posturing would interest her; in fact, she'd see right through any attempt at flattery."

Duncan pondered that bit of news. He filed it away along with his other notations about the ranch in Texas.

"So, what have you discovered in the village?"

"The place is definitely a firetrap. She even brought in her own consultant who apparently agreed with my findings."

"That must not have gone over well," Fletcher mused.

"It certainly did not. Is there any reason to believe she can get by without selling?"

Fletcher shook his head. "I went over the history of the property with Geddes, and she has a loan out, plus she owes most of the merchants in town for one thing or another, trying to pay them by giving them produce they've grown. And with a new schoolmaster coming, she won't be needed in that capacity."

"Has she been told about this change?"

Fletcher frowned and stopped his chore. "I believe so. She and Reverend Fleming are in contact."

Duncan rubbed his temples. "She's a stubborn woman, I'll give her that. Even after all that we offered, she's still standing firm."

Fletcher fixed his gaze on his brother. "Is there something else I should know?"

"No, no," Duncan said hastily. "But I did check with Ferris the Peat, who was the person she went to for another opinion."

"Ah, Ferris. Fine fellow."

"Yes. He agrees with me and of course is concerned about everyone in the house. He's aware of the accommodations we've offered. Even said he'd help spruce up the place. No one has lived in the cottage for a number of years, so there may be critters."

Fletcher briefly stopped brushing. "Just who all lives in the old brothel now?"

"Well, the owner of the building, Isobel Dunbar, her business partner, Delilah something or other, who used to refuse me entry to the brothel all those years ago, Henry the handyman, which I believe is an overstatement, for if he were truly handy, the place wouldn't be in the shape it is, and a young woman schoolteacher with a yappy little dog."

Fletcher ran strong fingers through his hair. "As for the building, how can she want to stay there when we've practically offered her the moon?"

"Like I've said, she's stubborn. She really can get her ire up."

"Truthfully, I've never seen her at all. Is she elderly?"

"If she had been, maybe she'd have been easier to deal with. Actually, she's a young, healthy, beautiful redhead who has decided you and I are devils. She won't be easy to convince of anything."

Fletcher studied his brother with interest. "Beautiful, you say? Can't you do what you did best years ago? Flatter her, letting your charm ooze from your pores like honey?"

Oh, if he could tell Fletcher that he'd already done that—ten years before. "I'm afraid my days of charming are over." The idea that she had a new beau still rattled him. But why shouldn't she have someone? It wasn't like they'd had any kind of relationship; he'd spent more tender moments with his horses.

Fletcher thumped him on the back. "Tough luck for both of

us, I guess. But if the place is a firetrap, and she cares for the people who live with her, she'll decide to sell."

"There you two are." Rosalyn stepped into the stable. Beneath her scarf her hair was that glorious shade of summer wheat, and even though she'd borne children, her figure was perfect. His brother was a lucky man.

She strode up to Fletcher, her arms folded across her chest. She didn't look happy. "So you asked me about the old brothel because you want to tear it down?"

Fletcher looked a little guilty. "I was afraid you'd try to talk us out of it."

"Well, of course I would," she answered. "At least until the new schoolroom is ready. Why are you in such a hurry for this project of yours to get started?"

"Rosalyn," Fletcher began, "the young men on this island are leaving in droves because there's no work. The sooner I have a cannery open and running, the sooner some of them will stay, because there will be work."

She frowned and looked away. "I just wish you'd wait until everything else has come together. She's doing a good job. I may not know this firsthand exactly, but from what the reverend says, the young woman is educated and capable."

"Rosalyn, the place is a firetrap. Duncan has gone over every inch of it and tells me it's so. She may well be educated, but she is not a qualified schoolteacher, nor is the young girl she has working with her. Sooner or later this was going to happen. And we have offered her accommodations."

She looked a bit perturbed. "You could have told me. I still don't understand why you're in such a hurry."

Duncan was curious. "Do you know the owner, Rosalyn?"

"I've been over there a few times with supplies and I've offered to help her on many occasions, but she's determined to do everything on her own. I'm truly sorry she feels that way because I think we could be friends."

"Do you know anything about her circumstances?"

"Does she have children?" Duncan probed. "I saw her in the village with a big red-haired man and a boy."

Rosalyn shook her head. "I know she was widowed at a very young age, so I suppose the boy could be hers. She's a very private person, keeps everything close to her chest. Since her aunt died, she's become almost reclusive. I could ask the twins if they know anything about the boy, but I doubt it because if that is her son, he doesn't go to school on the island. She must send him to the mainland."

"With a school right here, why would someone go to that much trouble?" Duncan asked.

Rosalyn lifted one delicate shoulder. "I heard somewhere that she went to school off island as well. Perhaps that's why."

Fletcher went to her and put his arm around her waist. She leaned against him and they looked at each other, their gazes warm. "Do you forgive me for not including you in my plan for the building?" Fletcher touched his nose to hers.

"I can forgive you anything. But don't keep me in the dark again, all right? We used to do everything together." She kissed his chin.

Duncan cleared his throat. "Before you two ask me to leave you alone, I'd better get back to the task at hand."

They were still arm in arm when Fletcher left them. Duncan was a bit jealous, but he was also profoundly happy that his brother had found peace and pleasure in his life, for he surely had not.

• • •

LOUISIANA—AUGUST 1864

They trudged along, the soles of their feet blistered from holes in their boots. To Duncan, each stone in the road was like a shard of glass, cutting his flesh, causing it to bleed. They were no longer interested in or able to march in unison.

Duncan cast his gaze on the spectators who had come to watch them shuffle through town. Three young women, all dressed in fine clothing and pretty hats, put their heads together as the soldiers passed and started to giggle. One even pinched her nose, implying that the lot of them stank.

Of course they did. They hadn't bathed in weeks; they'd had no opportunity to do so. Their ragged uniforms not only smelled, but were also damp from the rain that had fallen unceasingly as they huddled in their trenches—no tents available. And no food to eat, for there was no way to make a fire.

Some of the men had eaten plants from a field, but shortly after they were throwing up on the road, their faces green under their dirty whiskers.

Yes, they were a stinky, damp, dirty, moldy, motley lot. So much for a fellow in uniform impressing the ladies.

•   •   •

Seated in the kitchen while Delilah prepared a special dinner for Ian and Hamish, Isobel's heart was light. Her darling boy was home and her dear friend was staying for dinner. Ian's cheeks were rosy and his skin was clear; he was such a handsome lad. He was honest and open and hung on Hamish's every word. She noticed that his hair had changed a bit since he'd last been home; it was still kinky curly, but had some auburn highlights that hadn't been there before. Did he look like his father? All those years while Ian was growing up she could still conjure up an image of that boy.

Yes, she thought, as she studied her son, there was definitely a likeness, but fortunately Ian had much lighter coloring and hair. She didn't think the similarity would be evident to just anyone. She was grateful she had never resented Ian for the way he came into the world, but she could, however, resent the reckless boy for the way he planted the seed.

And dear, dear Hamish. She was using him, she knew, only because he had such closeness with Ian and the lad really did need a male figure in his life. Delilah said something and Hamish laughed his big, brash laugh, making everyone in the room laugh too, if only because the sound was so infectious.

Later, at Ian's insistence, the three of them went down to the river and Ian and Hamish skipped stones on the water. Isobel turned her back on the water and stared at her house. The only place she'd ever lived except for her short life in school on the mainland. A lump formed in her throat and she fought tears. His Lordship was not only a threat to her personal existence; he was also a threat to everything she held dear. She wished he had never returned to turn her life upside down.

. . .

Determined to have his curiosity satisfied, Duncan returned to the brothel and found Delilah in the kitchen mixing up something that had the potential to taste delicious. He noticed the small bowls of currants and raisins.

She nodded toward the table. "Don't be steppin' on Yellow."

Puzzled, Duncan looked around. "Yellow?"

"Aye, Yellow the Cat. She's yellow and she's a cat and she's under the table. Don't be steppin' on her."

Duncan glanced down and saw the big tabby curled up near Delilah's feet. She opened one eye and looked at him, made a small, threatening sound in her throat, then went back to sleep. The damn place was full of females.

"Clootie dumpling," he said, inhaling deeply. The sweet, tasty round bread made from suet and dried fruits had been one of his favorites. He couldn't stop a chuckle as he recalled the awful army grub he'd been grateful to have, when it was available.

"What's funny?" She sounded offended. He poured himself a cup of coffee and slid onto the bench at the table. "Just remembering how happy I was to eat bacon and biscuits three times a day when I was in the army—if I was lucky to eat at all."

She gave him a curious look. "Ye be an army man?"

"Fifth Regiment out of Texas," he answered.

"Do any fightin'?"

"Yes."

She gave him a good once over but said nothing more.

"Tell me something, Delilah."

"I could tell ye a lot of things." She formed the dough into a ball.

Her Scottish burr still surprised him. "I saw Mrs. Dunbar in town this morning with a big, red-haired man and a little boy. Do they both belong to her?"

He noticed the snick of fear that came into her eyes. It was gone, immediately replaced by suspicion.

"'Tisn't a secret. She has a son. His da, Rabbie Dunbar, died before the lad was born and she raised him all by herself. She's a very fine mother."

Her words came out sounding defensive. "I have no doubt about that, I was just curious. And I'm sorry about her husband. Who's the big fellow?"

Delilah cleared her throat and covered the bread with a cloth. "That'd be Hamish the Boat. He fishes in the North Sea, comes home every few months." She paused and added, "He's her fiancé."

Duncan sipped his coffee. "Hamish…the Boat?"

"Aye," she answered, a frown of her own appearing on her forehead. "He be a fisherman. He has a boat. Hamish the Boat."

Yellow the Cat and Hamish the Boat. These were little idiosyncrasies that he hadn't thought about for ten years. "So she's engaged." An odd feeling of loss washed over him, surprising him so much he felt off balance. "Well, he seems like a fine fellow," Duncan managed.

"Oh, he's more than fine. He's a dandy father figure for Ian."

"Ian?"

"Ian be Isobel's son. He adores Hamish. When Hamish comes home from the sea, they're almost always together, those two."

Duncan had other questions but thought he'd heard enough for the time being. More than enough, actually. He swore to himself. Was he jealous? No, not jealous of those involved, but perhaps jealous of their situation. A family unit. Something that had never been possible for him. If he was a religious man, he might think he was being punished for his past behavior. He didn't believe in a vengeful God, even though he'd had a few reasons to wonder if it was so.

• • •

Later that evening, as Isobel was taking inventory of her stock in the pantry, Duncan entered the kitchen and poured himself coffee, settling himself at the table. She knew he could see her from where he sat.

"I do remember you, you know."

Isobel held her breath. She turned, giving him a tight smile. "Amazing that you could remember one young lassie out of so many."

He seemed unaffected by her sarcasm. "You were the girl who wasn't a red head. You said it was ginger. Isn't that right?"

She was stunned that he would remember her at all, much less the comment about her hair. She lifted a nervous hand to the collar of her dress and attempted to hide her scar.

"So you're still trying to cover up your mark of distinction. I would have thought you'd outgrown that, Izzy."

She couldn't hide her anger. "Don't call me that."

"Don't call you Izzy? Why not?"

"It isn't appropriate, you being a lord and all. I'd think you'd have a bit more propriety."

He sighed and ran his finger around the rim of the coffee cup. "Propriety isn't one of the things I've ever been good at."

She shot him a quick look. "I'll attest to that…My Lord." Those two words would never come out of her mouth eagerly or with any amount of respect.

"I'm sorry about my past behavior. It was despicable."

His candor surprised her. "Well," she said, hoping to lighten the dreadful mood, "no harm done." She turned toward her duties so he couldn't see her face. She must not let him think his appearance in her life meant any more to her than it did to him.

"You have a son."

Be careful. She took a deep breath as the image of Ian laughing with Hamish floated before her. "Yes," she answered, continuing to fiddle with the cans stacked on the shelf. "He's the light of my life, but then, what mother would say otherwise?"

"I understand his father died before he was born."

She held her breath again, expelling it softly. Her heart didn't seem to want to stop drubbing against her ribcage. "How did you know that?"

"Delilah informed me—not that it was any of my business; I was merely curious. And your fiancé, Hamish the Boat? I saw him in the village the other day; he seems like a fine fellow."

Fiancé? Ah, dear Delilah. "Hamish is a fine man." She saw no reason to contradict him.

Duncan changed his position on the bench at the table. "I saw your boy and your fiancé playing catch outside earlier this morning. They seem to be very close."

He sounded wistful. Almost vulnerable. She studied him briefly, noting that age had crept up on him slowly, because he still had a youthful quality about him, even though his face had become more handsome. If that was possible.

"You don't have a family?"

He looked away, toward the window. "No. Other than my brothers and my sister, and a cousin, I have no one. Not that I'm aware of anyway."

Oh, wouldn't he be surprised! Although he sounded wistful, she had no problem vowing never to let him know he had a son. She almost pitied him, which made her angry, with him and with herself. She didn't want to feel anything toward him at all, much less pity. She glanced at his cup. "We have ale in the cooler. You can help yourself any time." She pretended to finish counting supplies and shut the pantry door. "It's not as if you haven't paid for the privilege." She turned to him, her hands on her hips. "The huge amount of money you gave Delilah was a bribe; I have no doubt of that."

He shrugged. "Whatever I can do to sweeten the deal."

Now she was annoyed. "Just what makes you think I'm going to give in?"

"The safety of your loved ones," he answered.

She didn't respond at first, but already she knew it was going to be hard to hate him. "Why are you doing this for us?"

"Because we aren't devils and we aren't demons. We want your land, but we don't want to put you out into the street. We want to make sure everyone is happy in the end."

For some reason she didn't want to appear too eager. Then he smiled that smile she had never completely forgotten, and she fell headlong into the dimple in his cheek.

He stood, took his cup and put it on the counter beside the pump. "Good night Izzy."

• • •

He left her, feeling proud of himself. She was weakening. So was he. He wasn't immune to her at all. She'd been a sweet, lovely girl ten years ago and she was a luscious woman now, and filled with confidence. And she had that spirit that he'd seen only briefly when they had first met. Duncan only hoped he could make good on his promise to her.

• • •

Delilah met Isobel in a room that had once been where the women gathered to be selected by the johns. No trace of that was left—not the red velvet couches, the wallpaper with the naked women on it or the bar in the corner where the men could buy a drink to fortify themselves before joining the girls.

"Ye've been talking to His Lordship." Delilah was direct. "Maybe ye should just tell him the truth. Why dig yourself a deeper hole than the one you're in?"

Isobel gave her a scolding look. "I will do no such thing, and you won't either. Do you hear me? He's already seen Ian and has no clue that he's the boy's father. Let's just hope it stays that way."

Delilah sighed and looked a bit hurt. "I always do what's best for ye, Izzy, and I'm not sure your decision is the best one."

Hamish ambled into the room smoking his pipe. "What're ye lassies gabbling about?"

"She wants to keep Ian's parentage a secret from 'ye know who.'"

"I certainly do, and Hamish, I want you to promise me you'll do the same." Isobel put her hand on his arm; he covered hers with his paw.

"Ye know I'll do whatever ye want, if I can, Izzy, but when a man doesn't know about the family he has abandoned, he is innocent, unlike the man who knowingly deserts a family. That da doesn't deserve any respect, y'see. Me own da left us when I was eight, and I've never stopped hating what that did to my mam."

"I know how it hurt all of you, Hamish, but—"

"I won't tell him, Izzy, but if he should ask, I dinna know if I can lie. The man doesn't even know he left ye with a bairn. He may have been a wild rascal, but ye don't know what he'd have done if he'd found out."

"I have a pretty good idea he and his noble family would have found a way to take Ian from me, that's what I know."

Hamish furrowed his brow and sucked hard on his meerschaum, smoke snaking out around it. "A man who leaves knowing what he's done is different from one who leaves ignorant of it, y'see." He raised both hands in defeat. "I'll try to keep the secret, if that's what ye wish, Izzy, but…We could make this easy if ye'd only marry me. I'd adopt Ian in a heartbeat and no one could take him away from ye."

Never before had Hamish's offer sounded more inviting. "But, how do we know he wouldn't find a way to prove he's the father? I think the natural father would have more influence than either of us. And remember, he has money and power."

"Aye, there is that. But," he continued, a twinkle in his eye, "ye could run away with me and he'd never find ye." Yes, if there was a way to disappear with Ian, her whole life would be perfect. Well, almost perfect. Hamish still deserved a woman who loved him with all her heart.

"I see how the breed looks at ye, Izzy," Hamish continued. "He likes what he sees, and who wouldn't? You're the bonniest woman on the island in my opinion."

"Nonsense," Isobel said, yet she'd felt Duncan MacNeil's eyes on her as well. Or maybe it was because of what she still felt for the father of her son. She was foolish to think of him at all, especially when she had a perfectly wonderful man who cared for both her and her son, a man who would sweep all of her problems away. And yet…

Isobel hugged him. "Thank you. But I simply can't change my story at this point. It's too late. My whole life has been a fabrication; how will it look if I spring this on everyone now? But thank you, you two, for helping me dig a deeper hole." She wished His Lordship hadn't called her Izzy. Now, whenever she heard it she would think of him and how his voice uttered the name so smoothly it would have melted butter on an ice floe.

Lily stepped into the room and noted the embrace. "Am I interrupting?"

Isobel pulled away from Hamish. "Of course not, Lily. I was just getting their promises that neither would spill the beans about Ian's birth. I hope I have your discretion as well."

Lily had Fifi in her arms. "Since I don't know who my natural parents are, I can't really understand why either Ian or His Lordship wouldn't like to know one another, but I'll abide by your decision, Isobel."

Isobel knew very little of Lily's history, other than that she'd been abandoned and brought up by gypsies somewhere in the south of Scotland. It was certainly an unusual upbringing for any child, for travelers never stayed in one place long enough to put down roots. Therefore, education wasn't a priority for their children. But Lily was very well read and an excellent teacher; her rapport with the children spoke to that. Although, Isobel recalled, the young woman had some very strange quirks.

Isobel didn't believe she, herself, was in any way an unhygienic person, but Lily's proclivity for washing her upper body and lower body clothing separately puzzled Isobel. When she asked, Lily explained that the lower body was unclean. Wash water used for those garments should not be mixed with water used for blouses, camisoles and such. At first Isobel thought she was kidding, but now, with all of Lily's other oddities, she realized the girl was absolutely serious.

Hamish laughed, bringing Isobel out of her reverie back to the problem at hand. She could not allow Duncan MacNeil to learn he had a son. He hadn't appeared suspicious at all. She hoped to keep it that way.

• • •

Duncan had arranged to meet Archie, Fergie the Burn's son, at Danny's by the Glass to see if he was really interested in work at the new cannery.

When he'd last seen Archie he was a lad of twelve or thirteen. Now the man was tall and wide shouldered like his father, but had a full head of dark hair. His father's scalp was tanned like leather from years of working in the sun.

The two men, Duncan and Archie, sat in a quiet corner, pints in front of them. A new father, Archie was anxious to make a decent living and had mentioned to his own da that if something didn't come up soon, he'd take his young family and go to the mainland.

He leaned his meaty forearms on the table and held Duncan's gaze. "If I understand ye right, there'll be work a' plenty when this gets goin'. I want in."

Duncan appreciated his candor. "Tell me what you do, Archie. I mean, are you a carpenter? Can you manage people? What are your skills?"

"Aye, I can handle a hammer and saw well. Me da made sure of that. I built a shed behind me place out near the river; tight as a drum it is. Come by and see it fer yerself."

"I may do that." Although Duncan believed the man, he always liked to see for himself how a man worked. Early in his ranching years, he had hired men who boasted of their talents only to discover they weren't worth a tinker's damn.

"Me brother, Reuben, is also good with his hands. He's just

turned eighteen, but he's a hard worker," Archie said. "Clive is only eleven, but he'd be a good and proper runner."

"I'll need a number of good carpenters, Archie." He thought a moment and then came to a conclusion. "Tell you what. You know these fellows on the island; I don't. Can I leave you in charge of getting a crew together? If you can, try to find men—or boys even sixteen years old—who can do a variety of jobs. There will be plenty of work to go around, and I guarantee the pay will be good. And we can use Clive to run errands, something the older boys probably wouldn't like to do."

"So, what kind of work needs to be done, then?"

Duncan took a deep drink of ale. "I need men who can make stone cladding, masons, joiners, framers, roofers, glaziers, and a good bunch of laborers. I do intend to see if Ferris the Peat wants to oversee the roofing, since he's done such a good job on his own."

Nodding, Archie said, "I can think of a few fellows. Some of them will know others. I'll get the job done for ye, count on that."

"How much time will you need?"

Archie scratched his square chin. "If ye can give me two weeks, I'd appreciate it."

"Two weeks it is," Duncan answered.

They stood and shook hands. Duncan felt good about this. Things were beginning to happen. Now he only hoped it would be this easy to convince Isobel Dunbar to sell him the property.

Chapter Six

Later that week, as Duncan returned to Sheiling from Fletcher's, he noticed a wagon ahead of him and a man appearing to study his horse's leg. As he got closer he realized it was the big fisherman, Hamish. Hamish the Boat. *Hamish the Fiancé,* Duncan thought grimly.

He reined his mount alongside. "Got a problem?"

The fisherman squinted up at Duncan. "Aye, the mare threw a shoe. I've been a fisherman all me life and can do most anything on a boat, but never did learn how to shoe a horse, y'see."

"You're in luck," Duncan answered, cracking his knuckles. "Horse shoeing is one of my specialties." He dismounted and introduced himself. They shook hands and Duncan, who was not a small man by any means, felt as if his hand had been swallowed by the big man's paw. "Aye," said Hamish, "ye're the one hopin' to buy Izzy's place, that right?"

Duncan squatted by the horse's flank, grasped the animal's back leg, and studied the hoof. "That's the plan. There are obstacles, of course."

The fisherman laughed his big laugh. "Aye, Izzy isn't an easy one to persuade, no matter what the topic."

Duncan pulled out his knife and cleaned out around the animal's cuticle. "You managed to convince her to marry you."

Hamish laughed again. "Don't I wish! Can't tell ye how many times I've asked and the lass has turned me down every time. Just asked her again last night and she still refused y'see. What made ye think we were engaged?"

"I guess I misheard some information."

"Aye, that ye did."

Duncan felt the man studying him. He glanced up, meeting Hamish's gaze. "Tell me something about the boy, Ian. I've noticed how good you two are together."

Hamish was quiet for so long, Duncan thought he wasn't going to say anything. On a deep, rumbling sigh, Hamish replied, "That's a long, complicated story, mate, one I sorta promised I wouldn't tell. Sure ye want to hear it?"

Duncan stroked the mare's flank. "Why not? Until the other day, I didn't even know she had a son."

Hamish cleared his throat, took out a pipe and smacked it a few times against the wagon, dislodging tobacco. "The lad is schooled off island. Comes home pretty often, but stays close to his mam. And to me, when I'm here."

So Rosalyn had been right about that. Duncan continued to work on the mare's hoof. "Sounds like you're protecting him from something."

Hamish let out a whoosh of air, seeming to have come to some conclusion. "I'm going to break a promise and tell ye a little story, mate."

Duncan looked up, noting the fisherman stood with his feet wide apart and his beefy arms over his chest. "Sure. Go ahead."

"There once was a sweet, naïve young thing," the fisherman began, "who had been kept from the cruelties of the world, making her perhaps too gullible and trusting. She lived in a place that might have made other lassies promiscuous. But not this lass. She fell in love with a rascal of a fellow who swept her off her feet, took what was hers, planted a seed, and left her without a backward glance."

Duncan chuckled at the set up and brushed off the mare's hoof, letting the animal put her foot on the ground. "Except for the seed planting, it sounds a lot like me."

Hamish studied him a while, and then said, "'Tis."

At first, Duncan didn't understand. "What? Wait. I thought her husband was killed before the boy was born."

"Aye, that's the story all right," Hamish answered.

"Well, which is it?" Duncan's heart was banging against his ribs.

"'Tis the story made up before Ian was born. The lad had to be told something, and the truth was not what any lad would want to hear. And people around here loved Isobel; whatever story she and her aunt concocted was good enough for them. They may believe her story or they may not. 'Tis been nine years since the lad came into this world. Ye were gone," he said with emphasis. "She was safe to tell her own story, y'see."

Duncan's ears rang. "How does she know it's mine?" The minute the words were out, he could have kicked himself.

Hamish gave him a scornful look. "I told you that Izzy was never a loose lassie, sir. And if ye look carefully at the boy, ye might see some things that are familiar."

Isobel. The virgin. The mother of his child? How could he not have noticed? Duncan was thunderstruck. He staggered, leaned against the wagon, and rubbed his hands over his face.

"I promised Izzy I wouldn't say anything to ye, but being a man whose da ran off and left his family of his own free will, I didn't think it was fair for ye not to know what ye left behind when ye sailed away, y'see."

Duncan shook his head in disbelief. "And I thought she was aloof because I'm trying to buy the building she's so attached to."

"Aye, that too. Ye got the double whammy."

Duncan didn't know whether to laugh or cry; either way, his eyes welled up. Hamish clamped a paw on Duncan's shoulder, dragging him from his musing. "Well mate, what are ye going to do with this information?"

Duncan was still processing the news. "The boy thinks I'm dead?"

"Well, not ye, personally, but the image of the man who supposedly wed his mam."

Duncan heard the contempt in the fisherman's voice. "I was an arrogant son of a bitch when I lived here ten years ago. I've regretted my behavior countless times since then." His thoughts turned to the castle.

"Why wasn't my family notified? Surely they wouldn't have let her carry the burden all by herself."

"'Twas no burden to Izzy, mate. And you'd best talk to her about those details; I've done enough damage." He turned to leave, then added, "Izzy's biggest fear is someone from your family learning his parentage, and Ian being taken away from her. Now ye're here; she has the same fears, y'see. Money is a powerful weapon; ye have it, she does not. At any rate, she'll probably take a broom to me arse when she learns what I've done because I sorta gave her me word I wouldn't tell ye."

Hamish bent to check the mare's hoof. "She'll be all right until I get her to the smithy?"

Duncan nodded absently and wasn't even aware when Hamish and his wagon began lumbering on toward Sheiling.

• • •

Isobel and Lily folded laundry in the small room off Isobel's bedroom. It had once been Paula's suite, so there was a nice tub, filled with bubbly water just waiting for Isobel. There was also a rather large mirror over the dry sink. A square table was tucked into a corner, making it the perfect place to fold and stack clothing and bedding.

"These dish towels look like they're ready for the rag man's pickup," Isobel announced, frowning at the condition of the cloths. "And look at these drawers! The ties are so tangled it'll take me a week to untangle them."

Lily picked up the drawers. "I don't know how ye can wash everything in the same water."

"I've been doing it for years, my dear, and nothing has happened to me yet."

Lily picked up the pile of underthings. "As I was growing up, we were constantly on the move, rarely staying in one place for long. My parents were field workers; when the work was done, we left. The roads were dusty and dirty, and by the end of a single day, we were all filthy. So we washed. Often. We bathed upriver from where the underwear was washed."

"Why?" asked Isobel, remembering her first glimpse of Lily.

"Because it covered the dirty part of our bodies," she answered, as if that would make perfect sense to Isobel. Then she gave Isobel a mystified look. "I suppose 'tis different when you stay in one place all the time, ye don't get as dirty, but still, I will never be able to wash all of my clothing in the same tub." She nodded at the clothing she had picked up. "Here, let me take them downstairs. I have some work to do in the great room. I can get these untangled and folded and put away."

Relieved, Isobel stretched her back and yawned. She had been up since four in the morning, fussing and stewing about things over which she had no control. And she'd been in the garden today and felt grimy. Earlier she'd asked Henry to bring up some hot water so she could bathe; she hoped she didn't fall asleep in the tub.

After tossing her clothes onto a chair by the door and pinning her hair high on top of her head, Isobel stepped into the tub and audibly sighed as she sank into the now lukewarm, sudsy water. She must have drifted off, because she was awakened by the sound of her name being shouted in the hallway. Before she had a chance to react, Duncan MacNeil, the lord from hell, barged into her private bath. And stood there. And stared. She sank deeper into the water, hoping to salvage some of her dignity. "Get out of here, ye big ass!" Heat raced through her; she flushed red all over.

• • •

Duncan was rooted to the floor; his feet wouldn't listen to his brain telling them to move. Isobel was exquisite. Heat from the water had curled her tendrils even tighter around her face, and her cheeks, neck, and chest, were pink and glowing.

"Get out!"

Finally he shook himself. "Well, now that I have you defenseless,

I want some answers." He continued to gaze at her chest, now and then seeing a perky pink nipple pop through the suds.

"Didn't you hear me? You shouldn't be in here, by all that's holy," she huffed, her arms crossed over her chest, hiding anything he might wish to see. "Please leave…Your Lordship."

He ignored her. "When in the hell were you going to tell me we have a son?"

She gasped, seeming prepared to sit up but remembering where she was. Her chest heaved. "*We* don't have a son," she said, her voice rigid. "*I* have a son."

He smirked at her. "It takes two, I believe."

"Ocht, yes. I forgot your part; seduction and deflower; sweet talk and retreat. The perfect romance." Her voice was filled with scorn.

Duncan cringed. "I admit to being a jackass, all right? I admit I was a wild kid who had no boundaries. I took what I wanted when I wanted it. I admit what I did to you was wrong, but if I had known—"

"Ye would have stayed to make an honest woman of me?" she interrupted, her face a mask of mock anticipation.

Duncan had the decency to look away. "No. I don't know. At the very least I would have seen that you were properly taken care of."

"I was taken care of by my aunt, good and proper, who had birthed babies before I was even born. I was in good hands, thank you very much." She sank lower into the water, a scowl on her face.

He couldn't stop the questions that slammed against his brain. "Even if you'd needed money, my family—"

"No," she interrupted again. "Don't talk to me about your family. We had already been there. Aunt Paula insisted we face the duke and tell him what happened."

Duncan couldn't imagine anyone turning her away. "But it doesn't make any sense. Did you speak with Rosalyn? My brother?"

Isobel shook her head. "An old man, perhaps a valet or butler. I don't know. All I know is that we were told the family was on holiday and we weren't the first to try to extract money from them, and he promptly slammed the door in our faces."

"But later…" He didn't even know how to finish.

"Later, when I thought there might be some resemblance to you, I was afraid your family would take him away from me. After all, he was born and lived in a brothel, for God's sake. The landed gentry on this island could have had him removed from my care. They could have taken him to live at the castle and he would have eventually forgotten me." She pressed her lips together as though to keep them from trembling. "And if that happened, I couldn't bear to look at him and not even have him recognize me." She glanced away, innocently offering Duncan a view of her lovely profile. Her nose was pert and her lips generous. She had a smooth neck, despite the scar, and her shoulders were feminine.

"My family isn't like that," he murmured, suddenly aware of her vulnerability.

She swiftly turned her gaze back to his, her eyes glistening with tears. "But how was I to know? My first experience with them was not exactly a positive one." She began to shiver.

Duncan swore. He reached for a large towel and motioned her out of the tub.

Her teeth chattered; she hugged her chest. "Ye must think I'm crazy."

"Isobel," he scolded softly, "please get out of the tub before you catch a chill."

Resignation showed on her face. "The least you can do is close your eyes."

He did as he was told and felt her step into the towel, then he wrapped it around her and brought her close to his chest. Surprisingly, she didn't resist.

"Isobel, Isobel," he crooned, enjoying the feeling of her body against his. "So the late Mr. Dunbar doesn't exist."

"Nae," she answered. "It always seemed like a reasonable story; only now does it sound ridiculous."

"I'm glad there was never a husband, Izzy, real or not." He glanced into the mirror in front of them and looked at her. "You have freckles across your nose. I hadn't noticed them before."

"Aye, it was dark, or don't ye remember?"

"Oh, I remember. I offered you a swig from my flask and you tried bravely to act as if you drank the stuff every day." He chuckled against her hair, drew in a breath and smelled jasmine. "You sputtered and coughed, but took another sip just to prove you weren't some innocent virgin, wandering around in the woods alone."

"Aye," she said, giving him a small grin in the mirror. "But that's what I was."

He ran his fingers over her bare arm, noting with delight that his touch created gooseflesh on her skin. "I discovered that, didn't I?"

"Aye." Her voice was almost a whisper. In the mirror, he could see that she'd closed her eyes and that the pulse beat hard against the hollow of her neck.

"We are quite a pair, aren't we?" His gaze lingered on her face, pink and healthy, her neck, glowing from the bath, her body, naked under the towel. Desire rose inside him. He nuzzled her ear, her soft curls tickling his nose, and without a thought blew gently into her ear.

She suddenly pulled away and grabbed the towel, wrapping it tightly around her. "You still have a way of ruining the mood. Now you can leave, like you did the last time."

He deserved that. "We haven't resolved the issue, Isobel. Our son thinks his father is dead. I'm very much alive and I'm not going anywhere."

She snugged the towel even tighter and gave him an angry glare. "And how do I know that? I don't even know you. You could try to sweet talk me into sharing the news with my son, and then, fast as you please, leave again and never return. Or worse, take him with you. Do you realize what that would do to all of us?"

Duncan rubbed the back of his neck. "I'll admit my track record isn't good, Isobel, but I'm not a cad. I have a son, and I want to get to know him. I would like to be a part of his life."

She frowned and studied him. "Who told ye about the boy?"

"I met Hamish on the road; his horse had thrown a shoe."

"Well, a pox on Hamish! A lot of good it did to tell him to keep his mouth shut."

Duncan couldn't stop looking at this Isobel, this partially clothed woman he had deflowered ten years before. She was angry and she was beautiful and once, just once, she had been his. "I'll be grateful to him for the rest of my life," he said quietly.

Isobel studied him. "I'm probably a wee bit insane, but I'll give ye a chance. You'll have to give me a little time. I can't just blurt it out."

"I want to be there when you tell him," Duncan insisted.

She muttered something and then said, "I should have let Hamish adopt Ian years ago."

Anger flared in Duncan's gut. "That is not going to happen. Ever. I don't care if you marry the gorilla. No one is going to be that boy's father but me."

Isobel tilted her head and looked at him, her eyes narrow. "You wouldn't care if I married Hamish? Because he's asked me every time he visits and now with your royal approval, I suppose I might as well say yes."

The thought stung Duncan. He had blurted out the words without thinking. No, he didn't want her to marry anyone and take Ian away. That left one solution, but he couldn't quite form the words. "I would imagine that if you haven't agreed to wed him yet, you won't. Just...don't make any hasty decisions." With that, and against his better judgment, he stormed from the room.

● ● ●

Isobel sagged into a nearby chair. Blight on Hamish! She should have known he couldn't keep quiet about such a thing when it had bothered him so as a bairn. But did she really believe he wouldn't? Did she, somehow, hope he would tell Duncan about Ian?

Lily poked her head around the door. "Are you all right? I just saw His Lordship stomp out of here. I swear there was smoke coming out of his ears."

Isobel grabbed her robe, slipped into it and tied the sash around her waist. "Hamish told him he is Ian's da."

Lily gasped. "And after he vowed he wouldn't. What happened?"

Isobel sat at her vanity and tried to comb out her hair, noting with some disgust that her hands shook. She tossed the comb on the table. "Truth to tell, I don't exactly know. By the saints, he's already taken possession of Ian and the lad still doesn't know Lord MacNeil is his da."

"It's a tangled web, that's for certain."

Isobel studied her fair-haired teacher. "Don't you ever wonder about your life before you were found?"

Lily spoke pensively. "I have, of course. But what good does it do? I was raised by a kind, if unusual family, they cared for me the best they knew how, they fed me and clothed me. Travelers are stern parents, Isobel, although to look at them one wouldn't think so."

"Stern? Did they beat you?" Isobel always wondered about the Travelers' family life, for she had seen many wagons of them come through Sheiling from time to time. The children seemed wild and the men dangerous and the women dark and mysterious.

"Oh, no," Lily responded. "They didn't punish that way. But they expected their children to do what they were told. Except for me," she said with a soft smile. "I was the ugly duckling they plucked from the river. They let me do as I pleased, and oddly, I had this desire to learn and read and my questions were so annoying, sometimes I think they rued they day they saved me." Her smile remained soft. "I think they were as grateful to be rid of me as I was to go on my own way."

"You came here from Ayr, didn't you?"

"Aye, not so far away, but when you're alone without means of transportation, it might as well be the moon." The water had drained and Lily wiped down the tub. "After I left my family, I found the position with the elderly rector and his wife, who reveled in teaching me things and answering all my questions."

"They did a wonderful job. But you called yourself an ugly duckling earlier. You're hardly that."

Lily dipped her head. "Perhaps not, but I was the odd one, to be sure. My brother and his friends were dark, their eyes so brown they were nearly black. They preened and pranced around, trying to impress all the girls, even me." She stopped wiping down the tub for a moment and her eyes misted over. "Except Stefan."

"Stefan?"

"Stefan was a throwaway child, like I was. I mean, his mum had been taken against her will by some lofty gentry person, and she refused to raise the boy. So, my mum and papa took him in, just like they did me."

Isobel tilted her head and studied Lily. "You care for him."

Flustered, Lily quickly finished wiping the tub and folded the towel over the edge. "Nae, it wasn't like that. Actually, they all frightened me more than anything. My sister, Kizzy, began to fill out into a woman overnight it seemed. She was…very curvy. She wore low-cut blouses to show off her, you know, cleavage. And mind you, it was abundant." Lily refolded the damp towel and replaced it again. "We weren't close. Kizzy and her friends were eager to grow up, eager to catch some boy's eye. They dressed very provocatively, always hoping that the boys would notice them. They thought they were ready to marry the first boy they were attracted to. And they were encouraged by their parents.

"But they knew nothing of marriage. They weren't even allowed to kiss a boy until he asked her to marry him." She looked off into the distance. "There was something exotic about my family, and to an outsider I imagine they seemed dangerous, just because of the way they looked." She tucked a stray strand of hair behind her ear. "Before I left, Kizzy was sweet on some fellow. I wonder if she's married by now. Even though I was raised in the same household, my brain wouldn't surrender to their ways of thinking."

"Was Stefan expected to do the same?"

Lily shook her head, her gaze focused once again on something far away. "Nae, Stefan could do anything he pleased," she answered, her voice soft.

"Do you miss them?"

Lily's expression became thoughtful. "It's strange. I never really felt loved. Oh, I was well cared for, but my mum was a bit distant with me as I grew up, like she didn't know what to do with me. I think we were all content when I decided to leave."

Just then Fifi bounded into the room, tail wagging, tongue hanging over the side of her teeth. She ran to Lily, who picked her up off the floor. "Have you been in trouble again? Has Delilah chased you from the kitchen? You're lucky she doesn't have a cage built for you so she can put you away when you're a naughty pup."

"How long have you had Fifi?" Isobel asked.

Lily nuzzled the pup's furry neck. "I found her when I was living with the rector. I guess I rescued her just like I was rescued, but I couldn't bear to lose her; she's become such a treasure to me. I hope Delilah doesn't truly mind Fifi's antics."

"Delilah is a pussy cat in truth and we both know it." There was clomping on the stairs, and moments later Delilah stormed into the room.

"There's that rapscallion! Do ye know what she did? Do ye?" Delilah's fists were on her ample hips and her bounteous bosom moved as she spoke. Her dark eyes blazed.

Lily flinched. "Oh, dear." She clutched the pup to her and it peered over her shoulder at the Amazon, apparently thankful to be in a safe spot.

"She dug up them newly planted rose bushes we worked so hard on just this morning," she said. She shook her finger at the dog. "If ye weren't so bloody scrawny, I'd cook ye up for supper."

Delilah threw both women glances that were warmer than her words. "I guess I can put a wire fence around the flowers." With that, she stomped off, but not before Fifi yipped at her.

• • •

Duncan's ride to the castle was swift. He left his mount at the stable and ran into the building, shoving the door open so hard it banged against the wall, startling Rosalyn, who was placing fresh flowers in a vase on a table by the stairway.

"Duncan? What's—"

"Where's Fletcher?" he interrupted, immediately sorry for being so brusque.

"He's in the library with Geddes." Her answer was cautious as she studied him. "What's wrong?"

He strode to the library door and yanked it open. "Come in here and find out."

The two men inside glanced up, appearing surprised at the interruption. "Duncan?" Fletcher's face was guarded. Geddes reacted more slowly, carefully placing some papers back into a file.

Duncan was so upset he hardly knew how to begin. "I have a son." He nearly choked on the words, not from despair but from disbelief.

Behind him, Rosalyn gasped and before him, both men stood in unison.

"Tell me what's happened," Fletcher ordered. "You can't be sure—"

"Damn it, Fletcher, I'm not a kid any longer. Don't tell me what I can or cannot be sure of."

Fletcher appeared at odds. "Well, then, let's hear it."

Rosalyn entered behind Duncan and closed the door. She took a seat by the fireplace, her face creased with worry, her hands clasped in her lap.

Duncan paced and began his story. When he had finished, everyone was silent.

Rosalyn spoke first. "We were never notified of such an event," she recalled, her voice quavering. "I suppose it was Barnaby who took the message…" Her voice trailed off, because even back then Barnaby was a bit addled. "But why didn't they stop back when they could speak with someone from the family?"

"They were told that they weren't the first to try to blackmail the family by some means or other. Knowing Isobel as I do now, I imagine both she and her aunt wouldn't be humiliated twice."

"But they wouldn't have been," Rosalyn urged.

"How would they know that?"

"What do we do now?" Fletcher asked.

"*We* do nothing," Duncan answered. "I need to sort this all out myself. Isobel is a very proud woman. If she senses any push from this house, she's liable to ship the boy off with the fisherman, just to keep him out of my clutches. She's already threatened to let the giant adopt him."

Rosalyn's hands flew to her mouth. "She wouldn't, would she? I mean, I've met her several times and she's a fine young woman. Hardworking, honest…" She glanced at the men. "Now that I think about it, she never let me get too close to her…"

"Now you know why." Duncan stood before her, arms crossed over his chest.

"There could be a legal way to handle this," Geddes spoke.

Duncan reared up. "Don't you think that's just what she's afraid of? That's why she did nothing after the initial attempt. She knows we have the power and the money to do whatever we want to. Hell, it wouldn't take much to convince a judge to let us have the boy; after all, he was raised in a brothel."

Rosalyn sagged against the back of the chair. "Oh, dear."

Fletcher came around the desk. "So let me understand this," he began, his hands clasped together behind his back as he strolled the room. "Once the boy was born, she was reluctant to let us know about it for fear that we'd take him away from her. She concocted a story about a husband and father to the boy, who has believed, all these years, that his father is dead. Now she's threatening to let some big red-haired goon adopt him and whisk him away to sea just to keep him away from you?"

"I know it sounds bad, but I truly believe they are empty threats. She's so damned mad at me on so many levels; she's bound to say anything to get my dander up."

"Have you seen the boy? What's his name?"

Ian's face, smiling, handsome and happy, floated before him. "His name is Ian."

"Ian. I like that. Does he look like you?" Rosalyn's voice became soft and wistful.

"If he had, I might have noticed the likeness earlier, but I didn't even when I saw him up close. Now, though, although his hair is a riot of reddish brown curls, I can see myself in his eyes and his mouth, maybe the cut of his cheekbones. And damned if he doesn't have the same dimple in his cheek."

"He doesn't know about you?" Geddes asked.

"No. He still believes his father died in an accident with his horse."

Rosalyn let out another gasp. "Well, he has to be told. How will the poor laddie feel about being lied to all these years?"

"Isobel has that same concern," Duncan answered. "I told her I had to be with her with she told him the truth."

After a quiet moment, Fletcher said, "I guess we shouldn't be surprised you left a part of yourself behind. After all, I think you bedded most of the lassies on the island."

Duncan winced. "You don't have to remind me what a selfish bastard I was back then. I've often wondered if I was being punished for it."

The three of them studied him.

Rosalyn stood, went to Duncan, and put her arm around his waist. "The God I love doesn't punish people by taking away their happiness even if they've caused someone else pain in the past."

At that moment Duncan knew that any involvement he had with his son in the future would also involve this family. He also knew he had to tread lightly, softly, and feared that even then his son might not want to believe the truth.

Chapter Seven

The following morning, Rosalyn went out into her rose garden, a place where she always felt at peace and could work through her thoughts. She was pruning a small bush that would yield gorgeous pink buds and eventually flower one day, when a shadow passed over her. She glanced up.

"Good morning, Fen, good morning, Ruby."

Her friend and sister-in-law, Fenella Gordon, dressed in her trousers and a casual shirt, squatted down beside her. Ruby, the 'sicky' lamb Fen's caretaker Reggie had adopted when its mother died, munched on nearby grass. Oddly, it had attached itself to Fen, although it stayed with Reggie in his rooms off the clinic.

"I hear there's a storm abrewin'." She exaggerated her own burr.

Rosalyn sat back on her haunches. "Of monumental proportions." She watched the lamb graze. "Don't you think it's a bit odd to have a lamb for a pet?"

Fen shrugged. "Perhaps, but it's really Reggie's responsibility. I can't help it that it follows me everywhere." At the sound of Fen's voice, Ruby looked up and bleated.

"You realize she'll probably outlive you. Remember Harris the Road had one that lived to be nearly thirty years old?"

"Reggie and I will leave her in the care of your boys," Fen promised.

"They'd love it. What does Geddes think of her?"

Fen tilted her head to one side. "He doesn't care as long as she doesn't end up tearing the clinic apart."

"But she's a lamb, Fen. She isn't a dog. She can't be trained."

"You'd be surprised. Watch this. Ruby?" The lamb looked at

her. "Ruby, sit." The lamb nosed around in the grass, then plopped down, still looking at Fen. "Ruby? Come." The lamb stood and made its way to Fen, nudging her pants pocket. Fen pulled out a treat and tossed it in the air. Ruby caught it and ate it. "Good girl," Fen cooed.

Rosalyn was impressed. "I guess I could be trained too if I knew there was a treat at the end."

"Ocht, you've been trained, don't think you haven't." The innuendo hung in the air between them.

Rosalyn touched her fingers to her chin and gave her a wicked grin. "Hmmm. You might be right." They laughed together. "And how about you, Fen?"

Before Fen and Geddes fell in love, they were as different as two people could be. Fen, always dressed in trousers and blousy shirts, her curly hair cropped close to her head, brooked no nonsense from anyone. As a nurse in the Crimea, she had seen every hideous thing that man could do to man.

Geddes, on the other hand, was quiet, straight laced, meticulous in his habits, and a bit of a chauvinist when it came to women. He and Rosalyn had many arguments about Fen in the beginning.

"I'm not sure who trained who, but I won't deny my life has never been so good," she admitted. She was quiet a moment, then added, "One of my patients told me they have hired a new minister to replace Vicar Fleming."

Rosalyn looked up. "Who?"

"That I don't know. But," she added cryptically, "I do know he comes from America."

"Really? How very interesting. One has to wonder why a parson from America would want to have a little kirk on a small island off Scotland."

"Oh, Roz, everyone knows this is paradise." Fen's voice was filled with sarcasm.

Rosalyn raised her eyebrows. "Back to the brewing storm." Fen had learned the whole story from Geddes when he returned home the night before.

"Ah yes: the school and the prodigal son. As for the school, I don't get called there too often; they usually call Doc Mac."

Rosalyn had been relieved when they finally got another doctor, for Fen had worked herself nearly ill during the time they didn't have one. "Well, this whole thing is such a shock. Imagine. There's a laddie on this very island whose father is my brother-in-law and I've never seen hide or hair of him. Fen, he's my nephew."

"I imagine the young woman had good reason to think she must keep things secret."

Rosalyn studied her roses, absently plucking off dried leaves. "But you and I both know she has nothing to worry about. Nor would she ever have had."

"So dear old Barnaby sealed their fate." Fen let out a mild chuckle. "Who would have thought he could cause such a ruckus."

"Barnaby is a loyal servant. No matter what he may have thought personally, if he even did think about it, he has always protected the family. Oh, I know he's a dotty old soul, and he's certainly not going to get better—in fact, his memory worsens every day—but perhaps we are at fault. We should never have left him in charge."

"Wasn't there anyone else here at all?"

Rosalyn took her handkerchief from her apron pocket and dabbed at her face. "Oh, let me think." Suddenly she remembered. "It was Geddes."

Fen straightened. "My Geddes?"

"Yes, yes, but Barnaby was instructed to contact Geddes if there was any trouble, and obviously he must have forgotten the incident the moment he closed the door on them. And I know Geddes came by nearly every day to check things out and make sure everything was running smoothly."

Fen appeared deep in thought. "Can you imagine what might have happened if Geddes had been alerted to them?"

"What would he have done, do you think?"

"Knowing Geddes, he would have gotten to the bottom of the situation. And he would have reported back to the duke, a thorough investigation would have been made, and when the bairn was born, we'd all have studied him closely to see if there was a resemblance. Frightening the young mother into wishing she'd never said anything at all."

Rosalyn tucked her handkerchief into her pocket. "Yes, I suppose. But you're not taking into consideration the mindset of the young woman. From what I understand, she's strong willed, leery of the lot of us, and very proud. Since she'd been turned away once, she may not have been interested in what either Fletcher or Geddes had to tell her. I dare say I wouldn't have been too keen on it after having the grand door shut in my face once."

Fen stood and brushed off her trousers. "It's water under the bridge now, that's for certain. But," she added, a sly smile on her lips, "I'd like to be a fly on the wall as this situation continues."

Rosalyn gave Fen a sad smile. "Poor Duncan. 'Tis one thing to learn you have a nine-year-old son, and another to learn the mother of your child is threatening to let another fellow adopt him."

"Do you think she would do that? Out of spite?"

"I honestly don't think so. I've met her a few times, tried to be more helpful to her as she copes with the school situation, and although she isn't forthcoming with me, I don't think she's vindictive."

"Do you suppose she's using the threat to rope Duncan into marry her?"

Rosalyn was appalled at the thought. "Nae, she isn't like that. I don't know what their relationship was, but knowing Duncan, when he was seventeen all he thought about was himself. Fletcher nearly tore his hair out worrying over whether or not we'd see his likeness in some of the young ones on the island. Surprisingly, we never did. Apparently Isobel and her aunt were very careful to keep the bairn hidden until they could send him off to school on the mainland."

"Duncan always was a charmer." Fen helped Rosalyn to her feet. "He seems to have settled down quite a lot. The trip to America must have been good for him."

"It gave him a world of responsibility that he never acknowledged before. And apparently he did a grand job managing the ranch."

"Did he ever tell you much about his life in Texas?"

"We would hear from him periodically, mainly to update the state of the ranch, the cattle, the wheat, the horses. Only now and then would he allude to a private life." Rosalyn placed the trowel into the bucket beside her, brushed off her apron, and gazed up at the castle windows, noting with a bit of weariness that they needed washing. She couldn't let Mattie do them all by herself, and she didn't trust the maids to do a good job. "I have the feeling a great deal happened to him that we may never know about."

She turned her gaze on Fen. "Anyway, about Isobel. I think you should make her a little visit. Make up an excuse if you have to, like inquiring about the children and asking if they need anything. See what you think about the mother of Duncan's child."

Fen nodded absently. "Maybe I'll do just that." With that, Fen walked off, Ruby stepping lightly by her side.

• • •

The afternoon weather spelled gloom, the clouds resembling dirty laundry tumbling from the heavens. Isobel shivered and moved closer to the fire, wishing she dared use more coal with the peat. But coal was expensive. Peat was everywhere. Moments earlier she had heard the children leave the classroom, no doubt anxious to get out into the fresh air. Children didn't seem to care whether the sun was shining or not; they simply wanted to be outside. Had she been like that? She couldn't remember not having chores or lessons. To run and play had been for other children, not her. She could remember pressing her face to the window and watching children roll hoops past the brothel, longing to join them, only to hear Paula's voice calling her from somewhere, asking her if she'd finished her chores or her lessons.

Ian was off somewhere with Hamish, who had promised to be the lad's close guardian until Isobel and Duncan could talk with him. She had just finished darning one of her threadbare petticoats when Lily rushed into the room carrying Fifi.

"I think there's something wrong with her," she announced.

"What happened?"

"She just keeps scratching her ear, like she's trying to dig deeper into it. She's even drawn blood. I looked inside her ear, but all I could see was the redness she'd already made with her nails."

Fifi whined and tried to squirm loose as Lily held her. "What can we do?"

Isobel understood Lily's concern. After all, Fifi was all that she had. "Have you talked with Delilah?"

Lily looked embarrassed. "I haven't. I'm afraid she might tell me it's high time to get rid of my pup."

"Do you really think she'd say that?"

"I don't know. Most of the time I can tell she's more bluster than anything, but with Fifi, I'm sure she's serious."

"Who's serious about what?" Delilah's girth filled the doorway.

Lily cuddled the dog closer to her chest. "Oh, it's nothing, Fifi's ear is red, and that's all."

"She need a doctor?"

Both Lily and Isobel laughed. "Be serious, Delilah."

"I'm serious as sauce. We don't have the doctor, but in the parlor is that nurse, Mrs. Gordon. She's here to see ye, Izzy." She threw a glance at Lily. "Maybe she can take a look at the mutt."

. . .

Fen studied the room. It was clean and comfortable, if quite bare. Once, years ago, she had been here when it was a brothel to treat one of the girls who, unfortunately, had developed a bad case of pneumonia. Fen could not save her.

She heard footsteps approaching and two women, one holding a small dog, stepped into the room.

The one she knew to be the owner stepped forward. "Mrs. Gordon? This is a nice surprise. What can I do for you?"

Fen studied her. The woman had a rare kind of beauty. "Well—" Fen wasn't even sure what to call her.

"Isobel," she prompted with a warm smile.

"Isobel. I had thought to come here to make sure all of the children were fine and that none of them needed my attention. And if you do need anything like that, I'd be happy to help. But, the real reason I'm here is that it appears that on the return of one Duncan MacNeil, a storm of enormous proportions is about to erupt." She tried to make her words lighter than the picture they evoked.

Something flashed in Isobel's eyes, and she brought her hand, which Fen noticed was red and work worn, to her chest. She tossed a quick glance at the other woman. "Oh, pardon my manners. Mrs. Gordon, may I present Lily Varga? She's helping me with the children."

The woman was actually little more than a girl. Another beauty. Hair the color of dark honey, eyes a purplish-blue, like the bluebells of Scotland. Her skin was fair; she had been in the sun, for her nose was a little sunburned. She smiled at the girl, and then looked at the dog. "Is something wrong with your pup's ear?"

Lily gasped. "Yes. How did you know?"

Fen reached out to the dog. It sniffed her fingers. "I don't have any formal training with animals, but I've treated a few in my time. This little fellow is moving his head around as if trying to rid himself of something."

"It's Fifi. She's a girl."

Fen studied the pup. "Fifi. Do you mind if I look at her ear?"

"No. Not at all."

Fen gently pulled the floppy ear away from the pup's head and glanced inside, noting the redness. "How long has she been like this?"

"Since yesterday. She was out romping in the woods with some of the children. Ever since she returned, she's been digging at her ear."

Fen always carried a few supplies with her. From her back pocket she drew out a small pair of tweezers. Before going to the pup's ear, she scratched her chin and crooned her name, hoping to settle the pup down before she went in. "You will hold onto her good and tight, won't you?"

"Of course." Lily then bent down and nuzzled the pup's other ear, talking in soft soothing tones.

Fen went into the affected ear with the tweezers and almost immediately found what she was looking for. She plucked it out and showed it to Lily. "She had a briar embedded in there. She'll be fine, but I suggest you take a cloth and wash her ear out with warm water. I have some salve in my bag in the buggy; I'll get you some before I leave. Pups with long, floppy ears often have ear trouble. This could very easily happen again."

A very grateful Lily hustled away with her dog firmly in her arms.

"How very kind of you," Isobel said.

Fen felt motherly warmth for the girl. The emotion surprised her. She'd never really been the maternal sort, except for Ruby. "I do things like that without thinking," Fen admitted. "Now, where were we?"

Isobel released a long sigh. "You mentioned something about a storm and Lord Duncan MacNeil."

Fen spread her hands in a defensive manner. "I'm not here to stick my nose into anyone's business. All I want to say is that you have nothing to fear from the MacNeils. They are fine, generous people. Rosalyn has admitted to me many times that she wished she could do more to help you with the school, but you've seemed reluctant." She gave Isobel a side long glance. "Maybe now we all know why."

Isobel's cheeks reddened further. "Yes. I will admit I've been wary of them ever since the day my aunt and I were so abruptly dismissed at the castle door."

"No one is sorrier than Rosalyn that happened," Fen stated. "If you had returned when they were home—"

"No. Under no circumstances would I have returned. I hadn't wanted to go there in the first place but Aunt Paula insisted, and I was only fifteen; she was my guardian. And then, when Ian was born…" She released a soft sigh. "He became my world. I had to protect him, don't you see?"

"So, now what?" Fen persisted.

Isobel rubbed her hands over her face and took slow steps toward the window. "I don't know. I honestly don't know."

Digging further, Fen said, "Duncan is afraid you will let that big fisherman adopt the lad."

Isobel's laugh was short and harsh. "Don't think it hasn't been tempting."

"After all these years, why didn't you go through with it?" Fen could tell something was fighting inside Isobel, something fierce.

Isobel's gaze went from the window to the floor. "I don't know that either."

Fen wondered about that. She walked toward the door. "This isn't a threat, please don't take it that way, but we're all very fond of Duncan. He's finally come home and we want him to stay."

With that she opened the door, stepped outside, and went to her carriage to retrieve the salve. She returned and handed it to Isobel. "And please, send for me if you ever need to. I'm close by and I'd like to help." She had come to do what she'd planned to do, but there was something else niggling at her now. She couldn't put her finger on it, but it was there, just the same.

. . .

Isobel slumped onto the settee by the fireplace. By the holy, now what was she supposed to think? That woman may not have thought she was a threat, but Isobel deemed all of them a danger to the quiet life she'd been living for the past ten years. Things were getting so messy.

Lily came in without the dog. "Are you all right?"

Isobel waved the salve at her and Lily took it, slipping it into her apron pocket. "I fear that soon I'll be inundated by every member of that family."

Lily sat down beside her and took her hand.

Isobel looked down at both hers and Lily's, hers red and sore and Lily's dainty and white. "And that's another thing. Look at my hands. I'm a worker. I barely make a living. My hands are red and sore because I do my share of scrubbing and cleaning—" She sucked in a breath, hoping it wouldn't become a sob. "And besides that, how can I compete? Once Ian discovers the truth, he'll be enthralled. What lad wouldn't be?"

"But you're his mother," Lily encouraged. "He will always love you."

Isobel drew out a handkerchief and dabbed at her eyes. "Oh, he may always love me, but will he want to stay here when he could be living like the royal lad he is?"

"Whatever happens, I imagine you can work something out."

Isobel twisted the linen until it looked like a tassel. "And what if after he learns the truth, he's resentful because I've kept him ignorant about it?"

"Oh, Isobel," Lily soothed, patting her hand, "you're only inviting trouble thinking that way."

"I'm not inviting it, but by the holy, it's going to come calling anyway."

• • •

Rain spattered the castle windows. The sky was the color of slate. Crashing waves pushed against the rocky shore below. Duncan looked out, studying the rugged landscape, remembering the many times he and his brothers had raced their mounts along the beaches, into the wind. He'd had a good life here. Had he wasted ten years by leaving?

He turned away and watched the fire spit and snap as it roared up into the chimney. No. He couldn't think that way. He may never have matured if he had stayed. He would never have taken over the ranch, discovering that he had a very good head for business.

And he wouldn't have joined the Confederacy to fight for the rights of Texans to govern themselves. That year, those horrifying memories, would be with him always.

LOUISIANA—SEPTEMBER, 1864

A short siege left them in a tiny town on the edge of a swamp. A man in a ragged black coat and top hat stood on a box, spouting rhetoric.

"We've got to stop the despot, Lincoln! We want to govern ourselves, not be under his deceitful thumb! We've suffered enormously these past years; it's time to put a stop to it!"

Duncan had heard others complain about the northerners, invading and polluting their land. He had always believed in self-government; he was a Texan after all. But entering the fray when he did, so late in the game, he wondered if deposing Lincoln was just an empty threat, something to keep men from believing that perhaps for them the war was over. If it was, it would be a bitter pill to swallow for all of them.

A log snapped loudly in the fireplace, bringing Duncan out of his reverie. The question of Isobel and Ian clogged his thoughts. He didn't see any reasonable solution. Not one that would placate both him and Isobel. When the boy learned the truth, would he want meet the rest of his family, or would he refuse to have anything to do with the lot of them?

But when the boy discovered what the twins took for granted, he could easily change his mind. A pony of his own. A whole new world to explore. What kid wouldn't? If he and Isobel split their time with him, would he be content to return to the brothel after he'd stayed here?

Another thought struck him. What if the lad wanted nothing to do with him, refusing to believe he was his true father? What if the boy resented him for not returning for him, even though Duncan hadn't known the boy existed?

He dug the pads of his thumbs into his eyes. Everything had to be in order before Ian was told anything. He and Isobel would have to hammer out the details so there would be no question that couldn't be answered.

Chapter Eight

Fen glanced up when Geddes came through the cottage door. She still found him incredibly handsome. He was still blond, tall, broad shouldered, and when he looked at her, something flipped in her stomach. Every time. Even after ten years.

He dropped his leather briefcase on the chair by the door, gave Ruby a scratch, then crossed the room and bent and kissed Fen. "Why is Ruby still here? Where's Reggie?"

"I sent him out for a few supplies. He'll take her back to the clinic when he returns, I promise."

"Ah. What have you been up to today? Any patients?"

"Just one. Fifi."

He arched a tawny eyebrow. "Ah, a French mademoiselle, *oui?*"

She stood and went into his arms. "Speak to me in French, my dear, and you'll find yourself being dragged off to bed."

He pulled her tight and answered, sounding wistful, "Too bad *oui* is the only word I remember." He leaned away and looked down at her. "So was she French?"

"Hardly. A floppy-eared mongrel that had a briar in her ear."

"Since when have you started treating animals? Other than that one," he nodded toward the lamb.

"It isn't the first time, but today it was just by chance." She wondered how much she should divulge about her trip to Sheiling. "I went to visit the school."

"What you mean, is that you went to have a good look at the mother of Duncan's lad."

"Of course I'd met her before. I thought it unusual that she rarely summoned me when there was a medical problem, but now I guess I can see why she wouldn't."

"And you saw the dog there?"

Fen nodded, still resting her head against her husband's chest. "The little makeshift school has a new young teacher. Her name is Lily Varga, and she was the one with the pup." She pulled away and looked up into Geddes's face. "Something is eating at me." She shook her head. "I can't put my finger on it, but the girl reminds me of someone."

"She looks like someone you know?"

Fen shook her head. "No, it's not that she looks familiar. And she speaks like no Scot I've ever heard, but still, there's something about her. I know it sounds weak, and maybe I'm just imagining it, but something makes me want to really like her and I don't even know her." She stepped out from the circle of Geddes's arms and went to the kitchen to begin supper. Geddes followed her.

"I suppose I could go over and see what you're worrying about. I am the advocate in the case of the cannery, and it should be perfectly innocent if I stop by to conduct a tour of my own. In the meantime, perhaps I can get a chance to speak with this young lady and see if anything joggles my memory."

"You're a love," Fen said, and kissed him on the mouth. The kiss ignited a flame in her belly. "Supper can wait," he said, drawing her with him toward the bedroom. "Ruby? Stay."

Ruby stayed.

• • •

Two days later, after Duncan had spent time at the castle with his family, he rode toward Sheiling, and the sunshine seemed a good omen. He had convinced Isobel to meet with him to decide just how they would tell Ian the truth about his father. She hadn't been terribly approachable, but the idea that she would see him at all was a small victory. Now he had to watch himself. Behave himself. Be a man she couldn't refuse.

As he passed the wharf, he glanced at the boats moored there, noting how well kept they were, as was most of the town. There wasn't much to Sheiling beyond the water, maybe three or four blocks of residences and shops and the pub, and today the water was blue and light bounced off it like brilliant raindrops.

The brothel loomed in the near distance. Blue peat smoke snaked from the chimney. He had learned on his first visit to the island that peat was plentiful, but it smoldered and didn't truly burn like coal, therefore wasn't terribly warming. Was everyone who lived in that eyesore freezing at night? He glanced up at the window of the room he had rented. He hadn't spent much time there so far.

He dismounted, tossed the reins to a waiting boy, and went up to the front door. He was nervous. It was an odd feeling for him. Rarely was he under the kind of scrutiny he would be under today and from this day on.

Isobel had seen Ian and Hamish off once again, this time for a trip to the wharf where Hamish's fishing boat was moored. Of course, this time it was planned. She checked herself in the mirror by the door. Her gown, an emerald green with sprigs of white flowers, was homemade, and the cameo at her neck had belonged to her mother; it was not expensive. She had tried to tame her hair but gave up and merely smoothed her chignon into place. What did it matter what she looked like? Duncan had seen her before. Heat rose into her cheeks. All of her. Now they were supposed to "hammer out a deal" (his words) for Ian's care. Isobel's stomach was in knots and earlier she'd almost lost her breakfast.

There was a knock on the door. She thought it odd that he would knock; he had a room on the third floor and could come and go as he pleased. She opened the door and thought, *He looks almost contrite.* She opened the door wider and stepped back so he could enter.

Duncan nodded. "Good morning, Isobel."

She merely nodded, unsure of her voice, then took his western-style hat and his leather jacket and hung them on the coat tree near the door.

"So," he started. "Where do you want to do this?"

Curt. Business-like. She appreciated that. She cleared her throat. "We can use the small room off the kitchen. No one should bother us there."

She led him to the room, which held a small table and two chairs plus a sofa and a table with an oil lamp on it. A single window looked out onto the back garden. "I'm sorry I don't have anything grander for you to sit on," she said. "I'm sure you're accustomed to quite a bit more luxury than this."

"Isobel, Isobel, don't be that way. I've lived comfortably in cabins and lean-tos. I've slept outside in all kinds of weather. I've slept in a hole I dug myself that filled with water, using two fence planks for a bed to keep from getting soaked. If you're trying to make me feel guilty about being a MacNeil, you're not succeeding." He pulled out a chair and offered it to her. She sat and let him push her closer to the table. He was being such a gentleman; she almost let down her guard.

He sat across from her and neither spoke. She reflexively touched her scar.

"Don't."

She blinked and looked at him. "What?"

"Every time you're nervous, you press your fingers to your scar."

Indignant, she asked, "Is there something so terribly wrong with that?"

"I don't want you to feel nervous when you're with me," he said softly.

She hadn't been bothered by her scar for years. Not until he came back into her life. "I admit you make me nervous, but only because I don't know what to expect from you."

He leaned back in the chair, still handsome, still a bit roguish, and still the only man she had ever been with. How he would laugh at that! She might as well still be a virgin.

"I've been thinking a great deal about our situation," he began. *Do tell,* she thought. *Who hasn't?* "And what's your grand conclusion?" She frowned, unable to curb her wayward, sarcastic tongue.

He smiled easily, his dimple sucking her in, apparently not injured by her jab. "You'll have to marry me."

She sat there, stunned, unwilling to believe what he'd just said. "What?"

"We will get married."

"But…but…but why?"

He leaned across the table and took her hand. Once again, she cringed at the state of her skin, foolishly wishing she was soft and delicate. Surely he could tell she was not gentry material.

"I'm the boy's father. You're his mother."

"Ian," she said softly, her heart on her sleeve when she spoke of him.

"What?"

She cleared her throat. "If you are going to speak of the lad, use his name. He has one, you know."

His smile crinkled the skin at the corners of his big, brown eyes, and Isobel thought she might swoon.

"I know his name. Ian. It's a good, strong name, Isobel."

How could he sit there so calmly? He'd just asked her to marry him. Marry *him*. He must have been insane. How could he propose such a thing?

"What's going through that pretty head of yours, Izzy?"

She expelled a huge sigh. "Don't call me that."

"What, Izzy?"

"That. And don't call me pretty. I never have been, you know."

"Why, because you have red hair and it's supposed to be bad luck?"

"My hair is not red," she said firmly. It still puzzled her that he would remember their conversation all those years ago.

"Ah, yes. Ginger, isn't it?" He leaned back in the chair and crossed his arms over his chest. "I can still remember our little argument—"

"We didn't argue," she interrupted. "You tried to call it cinnamon and under my breath I called you a big oaf."

He looked at her, eyebrows raised. "A big oaf? Really?"

"Aye, but that was before…"

He leaned forward. "Before what?"

"'Tisn't important."

"Oh, but it must be, or you wouldn't mention it. That was before what, Izzy, before I kissed you?"

She was mortified. She gave him a slight nod, refusing to acknowledge the incident further.

"You seem to think I wouldn't remember anything about you, Isobel. If you were to ask, I could recall for you much of what we did that night."

She was overheating; she wanted to escape. Lord, why didn't he just shut up?

"I told you I think we should get married. What's your answer, Isobel?"

"You can't expect me to give you an answer so quickly," she cautioned, trying to keep from panicking. "I personally think you must be crazy to suggest such a thing."

"Why is it so crazy? Ian is our son. We are his parents." He cocked his head at her. "I've already lost nine years. I want to be a normal part of my son's life, not some peripheral figure who sees him only occasionally. I wouldn't like that, Isobel, not at all."

She pressed her lips together. "You could take him away from me, couldn't you?"

He raised his eyebrows, thinking. "That's one solution, but I don't want to do that."

"Is there no other way we can agree on?"

"Is marriage to me so terribly unbearable, Isobel?"

How could she answer that? "It just never occurred to me that you would…I mean, why would you want to marry me?" What answer did she want from him?

"Marriage would legitimize Ian. Isn't that something you want?"

"Of course." It had always pained her that Ian was a bastard. That's why she had concocted the story about his father's death all those years ago.

"Then what's stopping you?" he asked.

She looked at him, confusion on her face. "You're a MacNeil." As if that explained everything.

"So I am. So is Ian. You could be, too."

She bristled. "It isn't my dream in life to become a MacNeil."

He actually laughed at that. "Our dreams change, Isobel. I know mine have."

She felt befuddled. Married to Duncan MacNeil? Had she ever thought of such a thing? Oh, maybe ten years ago when she was a foolish, stupid girl, pining for a lad long gone from the island. But not now. *Really?* Really. She had more belief in Nessie, the Loch Ness monster.

"So? What are you thinking, Isobel?"

"What arrangements would have to be made?"

"Do you mean will we be married in name only, just to make Ian legitimate?"

She felt herself relax. "Aye, that would do."

"Oh, no. That won't do," he said, his voice smooth as cream.

Her heart rate suddenly doubled. "No? Then what are you saying?"

"I will not force myself on you, Isobel, but we will live together as a couple who are raising a son."

"Where?" If he dared tell her they would live at that damned castle, she would upend the table on him.

"Well, that's the rub, I guess. Your building will be demolished, and the church will see to it that a new schoolmaster will be installed. They have also promised to do some work on the current schoolroom off the church." His gaze rattled her. "You've done a remarkable job here, without any instruction. I should think you'd be relieved to have it come to an end."

"I'm responsible for three other people, as you know."

He studied her. "It's not a problem that can't be solved. Mrs. Beard, who runs the tea house, has rooms to let."

"She certainly doesn't have room for all of us," Isobel protested.

His expression was patient. "You, Isobel, will be living with me and Ian, somewhere else. I don't know just where yet."

Oh, of course. If they were to wed. "I must know that all three of them have a place before I even think of a wedding," she threatened. Suddenly she felt like she was being swallowed up by the landed gentry. They were coming at her from all sides, pulling her away from everything she was and had ever been.

"Then you will marry me?" His face lit up; she still wasn't sure if he was teasing or not.

She held up her hands to fend him off. "I don't know. You seem to have taken care of everything. Did you think me so docile that I'd swoon at your proposal because it would save me from ruin?"

"Isobel, you're anything but docile." His eyes twinkled with humor. "I've thrown everything at you too quickly, I can see that. But please, think about my offer. Where we live together as a family is not important to me. The castle isn't my home, Isobel, I've told you that before. It's Fletcher's. We can build a place of our own. Just don't say no before you think about it."

He rose from the table. "I'd tell you to take your time, but I'm eager to become a father to my son." With that, he left her there, sitting alone at the table, staring into space. She quickly followed him, stopping him at the door.

"I see no reason to pretend this won't happen," she said.

"So your answer is yes?"

With some reluctance, she replied, "Aye."

He lifted her hands to his lips and kissed them; she still cringed, knowing they were red and rough. She watched him leave, wondering if she'd just made the biggest mistake in her life.

Delilah poked her head into the room. "I thought I saw Himself riding off. He sure don't make much use of that room he rented, does he?"

Without preamble, Isobel said, "He asked me to marry him and I said yes. I could see no other choice."

Delilah's mouth hung open. Suddenly she dipped into a clumsy curtsey. "Nae, My Lady, ye have no other choice." Delilah's antic sent Isobel into a fit of giggles. She could hardly imagine becoming a titled lady. How far-fetched was that?

. . .

Duncan rode to the castle slowly, taking the long route that went around the cairns. So. He would be married. He had never believed that would happen, not to him. At one time, when he was fighting in the war, he thought he might die, half believing it, half hoping it wouldn't be so.

Ponchatoula, Louisiana—November, 1864

The Confederate sharpshooters stayed motionless among the thickets of young pines, up in the cypress trees, along the slick, damp, spongy grass of the bayous, waiting for their signal. The ring of dense cypress surrounding sluggish Lake Tickfaw shut out any breeze. Katydids, frogs, and crickets harmonized in the humid air, stopping abruptly when the enemy approached, tromping through the tangle of briar and brackish water like a herd of water buffalo, shouting orders. A bugle sounded the signal for double quick, and the enemy picked up their pace.

No stealth there, Duncan thought with a shake of his head, as he brought his Sharps rifle to his shoulder. Up high in a cypress tree, he waited for the signal. When he heard it he took aim and paused. Another signal, the Rebel cry, and he caught sight of a Yankee coming toward him. He took the shot, downing the enemy with one bullet. A cacophony of shots followed, and the enemy scattered.

Suddenly he felt a stinging pain in his shoulder, and then another, and the last thing he remembered was falling out of the tree onto the swampy ground.

It had been close; too close. But everything that had happened after that was etched into his mind; something he would never forget. And someone he could not save.

Chapter Nine

Geddes left his buggy and tossed a lad a coin to keep an eye on it. He glanced at the roof of the old brothel building, noting the places where it needed repair. Duncan had said there were water spots in every room on the third floor, which could be dangerous if they got a heavy storm.

There was a young woman in the garden, weeding. She wore a big, wide-brimmed hat tied under her chin, and garden gloves.

"Can I help you?" she asked.

"Miss Varga?" At her nod, he continued. "I'm Geddes Gordon, solicitor to the MacNeils."

Lily Varga smiled at him; it was a stunning smile. She was quite a lovely girl. "Of course. Did you want to see Isobel?"

"No," he admitted. "I actually came to see you. You see, I've learned that you are helping with the children until another schoolmaster arrives, and I discovered I have many supplies that could possibly be useful to you." He told her what he had, and she appeared extremely interested. He was glad he had a legitimate reason to be here.

"Would you like some tea, Mr. Gordon?"

Although he was in a bit of a hurry, he said that would be lovely, and he watched as she called to a young lass who was playing nearby and instructed her to get them tea and biscuits.

A moment later Delilah brought them out and plopped them on the garden table that sat between the two of them. She didn't leave directly, standing and observing them both silently, but someone called her name from inside, and she reluctantly trudged off.

"How's your pup's ear?"

Lily reached down and stroked her dog. "She's much better, thanks to your wife."

"Varga. That's an unusual Scottish name."

She laughed, showing him bright, even teeth. "I'm quite sure it isn't Scottish. You see, I was raised by Travelers whose ancestors came over from Romany a generation ago."

His curiosity was piqued. "How did that come about—if I may ask?"

"Naturally I don't know what led up to my rescue, but apparently the family was traveling from Ayr and stopped by a river to have their meal. My mum claims she heard a mewling, like a small animal, down by the water. When she investigated, she found me, bawling, almost naked, and lying among the lily fronds. That's why they called me Lily. She often told others that if I'd have been a boy, she would have called me Moses."

"Amazing." Geddes bit into a buttery biscuit. "How old were you?"

She raised her eyes and thought a moment. "I'm not quite sure, but perhaps two or three."

An eerie sensation crept up the back of Geddes's skull. "That's quite an unusual story. Were you ever curious about how you got to that place?"

"Oh, yes. From time to time I wondered, but even after I left the family and settled with an elderly couple in Ayr, I discovered it was almost impossible to learn anything."

"And this doesn't bother you?"

The girl toyed with the strings on her apron, tying a bow, then untying it. "Sometimes, I suppose. As I grew up I did wonder what the circumstances were, why someone would simply leave me there." She gave him a shy look. "I don't usually admit that to anyone; I'm surprised I said it to you. I try to make people think it doesn't bother me, but that wouldn't be true at all. But," she added with a sigh, "there's nothing I can do about it. At least I'm alive, and whatever happened to put me in that place at that time can be of no use to me now." She leaned back against the chair and took off her hat;

a tumble of honey-colored curls fell to her shoulders. She laid her hat on the ground near the table. "There are worse things than not knowing where you came from."

Indeed, thought Geddes. He stood. "It's been delightful taking tea with you, Miss Varga. I'll have one of the boys collect the materials from my buggy and bring them into the building."

She stood as he left, and he heard her say, "Fifi, stay."

Isobel came out just as the advocate was leaving. "He wasn't here to see me?"

Lily shook her head. "He just had some supplies he thought the school might find useful, so he dropped them by."

"We're being inundated by that family and all who are associated with them," Isobel murmured.

"Oh, I don't think there was anything sinister about his visit, Isobel," Lily said firmly.

Isobel couldn't think of a reason either, but even so she felt crowded, recalling Duncan's recent visit. "I guess you haven't heard my news."

Lily put her gardening supplies away in the shed and returned to where Isobel stood. "News?"

"His Lordship, Duncan MacNeil, has asked me to marry him." She had been surprised at Delilah's reaction, but Lily's stunned her.

"Oh, Isobel! That's wonderful news! I'm so happy for you." She pulled Isobel into a warm embrace.

"Easy, now, it wasn't as if he'd fallen in love with me. It's just for the sake of Ian."

"Naturally, but Izzy, he could have done any number of things to gain fatherhood. This is so beautiful."

"He merely wants to be part of a family."

Lily pulled away. "Of course he does. You are perfect for him. You know each other, well—intimately, if I may say so." She added, blushing, "And you're quite pretty and he's handsome gentry. It's like a fairy tale."

"Like Cinderella?"

Lily nodded with enthusiasm. "Exactly."

"So I'm the scullery maid, relegated to the cellar to clean and scrub and haul away the fireplaces ashes. And who, then, are my ugly stepsisters?"

Lily giggled. "Oh, you know what I mean. You'll end up like Cinderella with her prince and if you should try to leave, he'd come searching for you until he finds you."

"Like he simply can't live without me?"

Lily inhaled deeply then released a sigh. "Yes."

Isobel patted Lily's cheek as she prepared to return to the building. "I hope you always have such happy fantasies, Lily." For a child who was abandoned at the river's edge, Lily had more joy in her heart than Isobel would have thought possible.

She left Lily as the girl picked up a ball and began to play fetch with her dog. Fantasies had no place in Isobel's life; she had to focus on the reality of telling her son that his father was not only alive, but close enough to touch.

• • •

The next afternoon, Isobel and Duncan sat down with a curious Ian.

Isobel gave her son a warm smile and squeezed his hand. Lord, she didn't even know how to begin. He glanced at her, then at Duncan, whose gaze was direct and sincere.

"Ian, I have something to tell you and I'm not sure exactly how…"

Ian looked at Duncan. "We read about Indians in America at school. You are an Indian, aren't you?"

Duncan nodded. "My mother was a pure-blooded Comanche and my father was a Scot. He was raised right here on the island."

"Why did he go to America?" the boy asked.

"I guess he wanted an adventure," Duncan answered, and Isobel was glad he hadn't said anything about growing up at the castle. Not yet.

"Did he ever come back?"

"No, I'm afraid not. He loved Texas. You know where Texas is, don't you?"

Ian nodded eagerly. "It's very big and it's hot, and there are a lot of Indians living there. Spanish people, too."

"You sound like you enjoy your history lessons," Duncan said.

The boy shrugged. "They're okay."

"What's your favorite subject, Ian?"

"Holiday."

Both Isobel and Duncan laughed. She was grateful that Duncan had drawn Ian into conversation before she dropped the bomb.

Suddenly Ian asked, "Why are you here on Hedabarr?"

"Well, some of my family still lives here. I lived here as well, a number of years ago, and then I returned to America. But I missed your island, Ian. I missed my family and I missed your island."

"How long have you been gone?" Ian asked.

"Ian," Isobel interrupted, "you're asking him too many questions."

"Nonsense," Duncan said. He was quiet for a moment and then said, "Years ago, your mother removed a nettle from my hand. Did she ever tell you that?"

Isobel gasped. What was he doing!

"You knew my mam?" Ian's hazel eyes grew large. He swung his gaze to her. "Why didn't you ever tell me you knew an Indian?"

Isobel's gaze bore into Duncan's. How was she supposed to answer that? "It was a long time ago, Ian—"

"Ian," Duncan interrupted, "do you believe in miracles?"

The boy shrugged again. "I guess."

"Do you believe in forgiveness?"

"Sure," Ian answered. "We learn about that in religious studies."

Isobel didn't know where he was going with this, but she held her tongue.

"How do you feel about people who lie?"

Isobel's stomach dropped.

"Lying isn't right, is it mam? I know that lying is wrong."

Isobel squeezed his hand again.

Duncan leaned forward, his brown, toned forearms on his thighs. Once again, Isobel thought she could look at him forever and never get tired of it. "What if someone you loved very much lied to you to protect you? Could you forgive that person?"

Ian frowned. "Protect me from what?"

"Something that could hurt you as you grew older; something that society often looks upon as a sin."

"Isn't telling a lie a sin too?"

"You know," Duncan began, "I believe that sin comes in all shades of black and gray. Some sins, like murder, are the worst. Some, like telling your teacher your dog ate your homework when in fact you didn't do it all, is a lie, yes, but not so very bad."

Isobel realized he had completely taken over the conversation and she found that she was strangely relieved. But the worst was yet to come.

Ian processed every word Duncan said. "Who lied to me?"

• • •

Fletcher stepped into Fenella's clinic. Both she and Geddes were cleaning up after the patients she had tended for the day.

"I got your message," Fletcher said. "What's this about?"

Fen pulled out a chair by the table. "You might as well sit, this might take a while."

Fletcher noticed that both Fen and Geddes glanced at each other, appearing to share some sort of secret that wasn't necessarily good news. "What's happened? Has something happened to the cannery deal? Has Duncan—"

"No, no," Fen interrupted. "This has nothing to do with Duncan or the cannery."

"Well then, what?"

Geddes cleared his throat. "We may be way off here, but we believe it's worth relating to you. If you are as curious as we are, we'll leave it up to you to take it from here."

Fletcher sat back and waited. When Geddes was finished with

his story, he felt both fear and anticipation. "She was found by the river? By Travelers?" He found that a bit unsettling no matter whose child it was.

"Yes," Fen answered.

"But, why would you think it's anyone we know?"

"There are many coincidences, Fletcher. She was abandoned, she was two or three years of age, which would make her the same age as Fiona, if Fiona had lived. Her eye and hair coloring are different from Rosalyn's, but her mannerisms I found eerily similar," Fen added.

"And she calls herself Lily Varga?"

Geddes nodded. "That's not all. She has a dog. Fen found a briar in the pup's ear when she was over there the other day."

Fletcher shrugged it off. "So?"

"The pup's name is Fifi," Fen explained.

Something clicked loud and long in Fletcher's brain. "Like Fiona's doll?"

They both nodded.

"Are you sure?"

"I'm quite sure," Fen answered.

Fletcher stood and paced the room. "We can't just present this information to Rosalyn without knowing for sure. We can't let her get her hopes up; it would destroy her. She's agonized over Fiona's death for years. She loves our boys, of course she dotes on them and adores them, but I know for a fact that she still mourns the death of her daughter."

"But Fiona's body was never found," Fen reminded him.

He suddenly turned toward them. "I have to see this girl for myself before we do anything further."

They all agreed that it was the best way to proceed.

• • •

The shock of Duncan and Isobel's news sent Ian scrambling from the room.

Isobel couldn't hold back her tears. She pressed her handkerchief against her eyes. "Poor laddie, what can he be thinking of me? His own mother, lying to him like that when time after time I've told him it isn't right to lie to anyone. About anything." She stood. "I should go after him."

Duncan took her hand. "Let him process it all. There's plenty of time for you to—"

"To what?" she interrupted. "Prostrate myself before him and beg his forgiveness? I've dreaded this moment since the day I saw you walk down the gangway into your brother's waiting arms."

"So you recognized me?"

She sniffed. "A woman never forgets the first boy who woos her."

"I'm sorry I hurt you, but truthfully, now that I'm here and I know I have a son, I can't say I'm sorry it happened."

She wasn't sorry either, for if not for that night, she wouldn't have her wonderful son. Who, at this moment, probably hated her. She pulled her hand from Duncan's. "I must go after him."

Glancing out the window as she hurried from the room, she saw Hamish and Ian in the garden. As eager as she was to console her son, she also wanted to hear what he and Hamish talked about. She stopped near the back door next to an open window.

"Now, now, laddie," Hamish soothed. "'Tis not such bad news, is it?"

"Why didn't she tell me the truth?" Ian asked.

"Ye'll have to ask her, my boy."

With such an opening, Isobel stepped outside. "Yes, Ian, you'll have to ask me."

He turned toward her and she was relieved she didn't see tears. Just questions.

"Mam?"

Isobel led him to the garden chairs and they both took a seat. Hamish stood nearby. "Oh, my darling boy," she began. "All those years ago it seemed just an innocent story to smooth over all the questions that people might have had of me. Questions about the father of my baby, who, unfortunately, had sailed for America before he even knew about you."

"Mister Duncan."

"Actually, I believe his title is His Lordship. And I had no reason to believe he would return. It isn't easy to admit, but we didn't know one another well, I'm afraid. And making up a story about a man who died bravely seemed an innocent thing to me at the time."

Ian was quiet for a long while. Suddenly he turned to her and asked, "Does that mean I'm an Indian too?"

"Partly, yes."

His eyes got big. "Wait 'til the kids at school learn about this."

"That's all you have to say about it?" She nearly laughed.

"It's something no one else I know can say," he replied.

"That's true enough."

"Where does Mister Duncan live?"

Isobel wondered when, or if, he'd ever call the man Da. "I'll let him tell you about that," she answered. "He's still in the great room. Why don't you ask him?"

She watched Ian dash inside. "He's taking this better than I expected."

"Aye, Izzy, he's a happy lad. He was lied to, aye, but to learn his da is an Indian, why that's about as good as living in a fairy tale, y'see."

There it was again: fairy tale. "Lily is bound and determined to compare this entire story as a fairy tale; I'd have thought ye were beyond such dreams, Hamish."

"Nae, everyone loves a fairy tale."

She studied her big friend, noting the weather-worn face, the bright blue eyes, the wild red hair. His expression was wistful and Isobel felt a stab of guilt. How different all of their lives would have been if Duncan MacNeil had never returned.

Chapter Ten

Duncan was just leaving the great room when Ian nearly skidded to a stop in front of him. "Yes, Ian?"

"Mam told me to ask you where you lived on the island."

"She did, did she? Where is she now?"

"She's in the garden with Hamish," he answered.

"I tell you what. You go and ask her if it's all right for me to take you there." He watched Ian race back outside. When he returned, Isobel was with him.

"You want to take him there?" Her question was cautious.

"Is there a better way to explain it all to him?" Duncan asked. He could see the anguish she was trying to hide. "Do you want to ride along?"

She quickly shook her head. "No. No, no. I'll have my baptism by fire soon enough."

He felt a jolt of sympathy for her situation. Suddenly being thrust into his family, their lives, their inquisitiveness about her and Ian; certainly it was terrifying for her. "I'm sorry you feel that way." He gave her a lopsided smile. "We're really not such a bad bunch."

She appeared reluctant to return the smile, but it appeared anyway. "I'm sure you're not, but after all these years…I've been here, in this ramshackle building, and they've been up there," she said, glancing toward the window.

"They will love you, Isobel." He almost said "as I do," but stopped himself. Where in the hell had that thought come from?

She waved off the comment. "Off with you two or you won't be back before dark."

"Isobel," Duncan said, "think about a day for the wedding.

Do whatever makes you feel comfortable. We can do it alone, or with family. Naturally I'd prefer to have my family there, and I know Delilah, Henry, and Lily would be very put out if they weren't invited."

Isobel watched them go off on Duncan's mount, Ian tucked comfortably in front of his da. *His da.* She would have to get used to that. And she had to plan a wedding. She was to marry His Lordship Duncan MacNeil! Unbelievable. Her emotions were in tatters. What would she wear? She had sewn beautiful gowns for many women in the community, but had never had one herself. And she didn't have time to sew one now, nor did she have the means to purchase the material. All of these preparations suddenly made her want to curl up into a ball and go into hibernation. And she had butterflies, just as if this were something she had looked forward to all of her life. But these butterflies were different; they weren't ones of excited anticipation; they were of fear of the unknown, maybe even dread.

Lily called to her from the classroom. "Could you come here a moment, please?" She was holding a letter and her expression appeared quizzical.

"What is it?"

She handed Isobel the letter and she read it. When she'd finished she glanced up at Lily. "So, the elderly couple you helped and lived with left you something in their will. That's wonderful, Lily!"

"But that means I have to travel to Ayr to meet with the solicitor. How can I leave the children for that long?"

Isobel returned the letter. "Oh, Lily, I can manage for a while, believe me. I did it before you came along, and although you're much better at it, I can fill in while you're gone."

"Will I miss the wedding?" Lily asked.

"Hmmm. I don't even know when it's going to be yet. Don't worry about that—we'll all be here when you return and we'll be so excited to hear what the solicitor had to say."

"What about Fifi? I can't take her with me."

"Fifi will be just fine with me. I'll watch her carefully and keep her out of Delilah's hair."

Lily glanced at the floor. "You know, she always sleeps with me, Isobel."

"She can sleep with Ian. He'd probably be delighted to have a bedmate."

Lily hugged her. "You are such a dear."

Someone rapped lightly on the schoolroom door. "Excuse me, ladies."

They turned to find the duke standing in the doorway.

The MacNeil gave her a short bow.

Isobel supplied a small curtsy. "Your Grace." Of course, she had seen him before, but not this close. He was every bit as handsome as his brother. Older, of course, showing some flecks of gray in his thick, black hair, but very distinguished.

"Please, call me Fletcher," he asked. "And I should have come before. I've been very narrow sighted about this entire cannery project, not taking into consideration anyone else's feelings but my own. For that I apologize. Sometimes I get so wrapped up in a project I don't see warning signs around me."

Isobel was pleased. "I must say I felt as though I was losing control of everything. But truthfully, if we can make all of us happy, you included, I won't cause any more trouble." What good would it do? This man standing before her was going to be her brother-in-law. He had a lawyer on his side. He had money and power and… holy saints, they were going to be related. Suddenly she felt faint and steadied herself by grabbing the back of a chair.

"I've been meaning to meet Miss Varga as well. I hear she's been a very big help to you while we look for another schoolmaster." He turned to Lily, whose eyes were like saucers. "Do you have training as a teacher, Miss Varga?"

Lily, who was surprised at being addressed by the duke, shook her head. "I have no formal training, Your Grace," she answered, a slight quaver in her voice.

"Be that as it may, perhaps there will be a place for you in the school anyway."

Lily appeared too startled to respond, but she smiled and nodded.

He looked at Isobel, his expression grim. "May I speak with you on another matter?"

"Certainly," she said with caution. "We can go into the small salon off the great room. This way," she said.

The duke bade farewell to Lily and followed Isobel from the classroom into the room she used as a study. She offered him a chair, and they both sat.

He bit his lower lip and studied the worn carpet. "I'm not quite sure why I feel I must confide my suspicions to you, but I'm compelled to."

Isobel was instantly alert. "Suspicions?"

The duke appeared troubled. "Many years ago, before Rosalyn and I were married, indeed before she came to live at Castle Sheiling, she endured a hideous marriage. She had no notion that it was bad until after they had a daughter, whom they named Fiona. Soon after Fiona's birth, Rosalyn discovered her husband's ugly proclivities and left him.

"To make a long story short, after Rosalyn left her husband, he kidnapped Fiona. There was a search, of course, but the only body that was recovered was his. He had drowned. There was no sign of Fiona; everyone assumed she had drowned as well."

"How terrible." Isobel felt a sting behind her eyes.

"Yes," he said. "She still carries a wound in her heart from the loss."

"Why are you telling me all of this?" She wondered if it was because they would all soon be related, but it was a strange introduction to the family.

He inhaled deeply, releasing the air in a rush. "After hearing Miss Varga's story from both Geddes and Fenella, I thought I should look in on the young woman myself. You see, Rosalyn's daughter, Fiona, had a little doll she kept with her always." He paused, as if waiting for Isobel to gather it all in. Then he added, "She named it Fifi."

Isobel gasped, finally understanding. "You're saying that…you think it's possible that Lily is your wife's daughter?"

"I know it sounds irrational, but the moment Fen met Lily and heard her story, she was overwhelmed with a feeling that she already knew the young woman. Geddes, too, said he got chills up the back of his neck when he spoke with her."

"Considering how she was found, I guess it's certainly possible. What are you going to do now?"

The duke scrunched his forehead into a frown. "I have to think of a way to introduce all of this to Rosalyn. Even though we might be enthusiastic about the possibility of reuniting mother and daughter, we have to be absolutely certain before we do so. Otherwise it would send Rosalyn spiraling, I'm afraid."

"Indeed it would," Isobel agreed. "Just before you came into the room, Lily showed me a letter she has received from a solicitor in Ayr. The elderly family she lived with has apparently left her something in their will, so she'll be gone for a bit. I don't know if this is good news or bad for you."

"It actually gives me good reason to put off approaching Rosalyn about this."

"I'll be sure to let you know when she returns," Isobel promised.

"That would be fine. Thank you." He stood. "I'm glad we could talk. And perhaps one day in the next few weeks we can all sit down and work out a satisfactory deal for the cannery."

She didn't want to give him any reason to regret taking her into his confidence. "I'm sure we can come to an arrangement we all can live with."

She walked him to the door and watched as he pulled himself easily into the saddle of a beautiful mount.

Delilah came up behind her. "What did he want? Was it about the wedding?"

Isobel shook her head. "Just to say that in a few weeks we can sign the paperwork for the sale of the building."

Delilah studied his retreating form. "He never did visit the brothel, you know."

Isobel raised her eyebrows. "I didn't know that. It's nice to hear there are a few men who take their marriage vows seriously."

"'Course your future husband tried many times, but I never let him in. Never."

"That's probably why he scoured the island looking for willing lassies. We all might have been better off if you'd let him in."

"Then we would never have had Ian, would we?"

. . .

Duncan and Ian had arrived on castle grounds. The boy sat straight as a board, trying to take everything in. "This is really all yours?"

"Well, not mine exactly. It belongs to my brother, Fletcher. He's the lord of the manor, so to speak."

"Gee. I've seen it from a distance, you know, but…It's really a castle." His voice was filled with awe. He turned and pointed to one of the out buildings. "Is that the stable? Do you have a lot of horses?"

"Yes, that's the stable, and yes, we have horses." They trotted to the stable and Duncan helped Ian slide off the mount. After he dismounted, he threw the reins to Evan.

"Evan, may I present to you my son, Ian? Evan, as it turns out, is your uncle."

Evan reached out and shook the boy's hand. "Nice to meet you, Ian." A huge, scruffy dog with bushy gray eyebrows meandered over to them and stuck his nose into Ian's face.

"This is Bear," Evan said.

Ian reached out and stroked the dog's chin. "Well, hello, Bear."

Duncan was proud that his son wasn't afraid of the beast. "Let's go up to the house."

But before they got there, Rosalyn came running outside, her skirts flying out behind her.

"Oh, oh, this must be Ian." She stopped in front of them, her face wreathed in smiles. She appeared to want to hug the boy, but restrained herself. "Come inside. Rabbie and Rory have just finished with their French lessons and are ever so eager to meet their new cousin!"

Ian stared up at Duncan. "I have cousins?"

Duncan nodded and placed his hand on Ian's shoulder. "And much, much more." He watched Ian and Rosalyn walk swiftly to the castle.

Duncan strolled to the stable, stepped inside, and found the old hound, Bear, sprawled on a blanket. He raised his enormous head as Duncan sat down on a stool beside him. Duncan scratched the hound's scruffy ears. Evan came out from the back room.

"I have to apologize to you," Duncan began. "I treated you like the hired help when I lived here before, and there's no excuse for my behavior."

Evan reached down and stroked his dog's back. "I was the hired help. No harm done."

"What have you been doing these past ten years, besides keeping my brother in line?" Duncan teased.

"Actually, Geddes has been teaching me the ins and outs of law. Not that I ever want to be a lawyer, but both Fletcher and I agreed that it would be good to have the knowledge under my belt." He saddled his mount. "I imagine we'll be seeing a lot of each other," he said as he urged the mount out of the stable. "I'll be looking forward to it."

He looked up as Kerry stepped in, leading her mare. "Duncan! What a nice surprise. You've been terribly busy." She brought the horse to her stall, made sure the mare had water and oats, then began grooming her. "What are you doing out here all by yourself?"

Kerry was petite and lovely, although she wasn't a fragile woman. Her long, thick, dark hair was pulled back and held in place with a length of leather, and she wore a pair of wide-legged trousers that were hemmed just below the knee. Her white blouse was open at the neck and the sleeves were rolled up above her elbows.

"Ian is inside getting acquainted with his cousins."

"Oh, how wonderful. Duncan, can you really believe you have a son after all these years?"

"It's nothing short of a miracle," he answered. He watched her work for a while, recalling Fletcher's words about Kerry and the island. "Are you happy here, Kerry?"

She turned and gave him a strange look. "Why wouldn't I be?"

"Have you ever thought of returning to Texas?"

She stopped brushing her mount and studied him. "Why do you ask that?"

"Because you didn't want to leave in the first place."

"Oh, but that was ten years ago. I've adjusted to Scotland, although I admit there are things about Texas I will always miss." She began her grooming again. "How about you? Are you here to stay, or will you return to Texas?"

"No, I'm here to stay." And he was. There was no going back now, nor did he have any desire to.

"You left the ranch in good hands, did you?"

"I did, but it's temporary. I hate to leave it at that indefinitely. I'm thinking of hiring someone to take over the entire operation."

She finished her chores and pulled up a stool beside him. "Someone from Texas?"

"Not necessarily." His mind was going fast. He looked at the young woman who had been such a troublesome child when she arrived at Castle Sheiling ten years before. They had all changed for the better. "How about you?"

Kerry studied him. "Why me?"

"I've given this some thought, Kerry. If you've learned anything from Fletcher and Evan, you've learned the business of managing animals. You're smarter than anyone I know, kid, and you always have been. You're even more brilliant than Gavin, but don't ever tell him I said that."

Kerry looked into the distance and didn't speak for a long moment. "Back to Texas. I just don't know…"

Duncan put his hand on her knee. "Think about it. Take your time. I don't mean to pressure you." He stood. "In the meantime, there's an old brothel to buy and tear down, and, oh, by the way, I'm getting married."

Once again he had her momentarily speechless. "Duncan! Really? You're going to marry Isobel?" She stood up so fast the stool tumbled over, startling Bear, who stood and shook himself violently. Kerry threw herself at Duncan and hugged him hard. "Oh, I'm so glad you're home."

Chapter Eleven

Isobel stood at the railing as the vessel carrying Lily to Ayr made its way toward open water. Truth be told, Lily didn't appear to want to leave, despite the surprise of an inheritance. "I have everything I want right here," she insisted. And Isobel thought she might have more here on Hedabarr than she ever imagined if things played out.

She raised her hand in farewell, once again noticing their redness. She had not felt inferior to anyone for many, many years, not since her school days when other girls took for granted things that Isobel either would never have or had worked hard to get.

She hated feeling like she didn't measure up to the MacNeils. She was a woman who had always worked with her hands. It was good, honest work and she'd never been ashamed of it.

Now, however, after she returned to the house, she took inventory of herself. Her hands were chafed and her knuckles were red. She glanced into the mirror and touched her face; her cheeks were red and a bit chapped. Her hair, wild and curly, could never be tamed into something presentable. And the color—when compared to the women in the family into which she would marry—was not soft and blonde, like Lady Rosalyn's, nor was it long, dark, and thick like the lovely Kerry's. For years she'd tried to pretend she wasn't a red-haired woman. But truth be told, although it might not be as red as Hamish's, it was definitely red.

And Isobel was not what one would call willowy. As she'd grown into a woman, she had cursed her ample bosom and womanly hips. She was told to be grateful for her tiny waist, but all it did, she found, was emphasize her other attributes.

And come her wedding night, she would not expect her future

husband to join her in their "marriage bed," for he'd already made it clear that she didn't have to worry about that. But what did he really mean? He had said they would live together as husband and wife, but that he wouldn't force her. Was it really because he was thinking of her, or was it because he didn't find her attractive enough to bed? And if he didn't bed her, would he find his satisfaction elsewhere on the island? The humiliation of that would be agonizing.

Meanwhile, Ian had already settled himself into his new life. Oh, he hadn't asked to live at the castle, but when he returned the day before yesterday after visiting the estate with Duncan, he couldn't stop talking about it.

"Mam!" he'd shouted as he ran into the house. "They have horses and dogs and sheep. And do you know what? Mister Duncan has a bow and arrows he brought with him from Texas and he said he would teach me how to use them. Wouldn't that be great? And remember, you said you didn't like the thought of me using a gun, so I wouldn't be. And you'd be happy about that, right?" He had gone on and on about everything he saw, everyone he met, and was absolutely in awe of his two cousins, Rory and Rabbie, who apparently had treated him like the long lost cousin he was.

Isobel sank into the chair by the fireplace, noting that the fire was almost out. Henry was getting more and more useless as time went on.

A knock on the door roused her from her daydreaming. She answered it and found Duchess Rosalyn standing on the stoop.

"Your Grace. Please come in." Isobel curtsied and opened the door wide. The beautiful, elegant woman stepped inside. She and the duke did make a stunning couple, Isobel thought.

"Isobel, since you and Duncan will marry and you will become part of the family, I'm not going to go through the formality of calling you Miss Crawford or Dunbar, or whatever it is. I intend to call you Isobel. It's such a lovely name, rather a quaint name for Elizabeth, if I remember right. And you must stop referring to me as Your Grace. I'm Rosalyn." Her smile was warm.

"I do appreciate that…Rosalyn, and I must say that I'm—should I say—apprehensive about this arrangement."

"I know the feeling. I had been rather badgered into marrying the duke—"

"You were?"

"Yes. My brother knew something about the lands and the fortune even Fletcher didn't know until after he arrived. It appears that if Fletcher didn't marry and have an heir before his first year was up, everything would go to a distant relative."

"And he asked you?"

Rosalyn laughed, a quiet, soft chuckle. "When Geddes first suggested it I nearly threw something at him I was so angry. I'd lost a child before that and for some reason Geddes thought if I had another bairn, it would make up for that loss." She looked pensive and inhaled deeply.

Isobel wouldn't reveal what she already knew, but said, "I don't know why men think one child will replace another."

"Aye, aye, sometimes they are so thick skulled. And it was rather accidental that we married anyway, but, you know," she said, giving Isobel a sweet, almost knowing smile, "things always work out one way or another."

Did she mean to say that perhaps Isobel and Duncan's unusual marriage might work out as well? Isobel couldn't imagine being comfortable with His Lordship ever.

"And of course," Rosalyn went on, "I now know why you never took me up on my offers to help. What an awful burden for you to carry all these years, Isobel. And to think it's all because we were away and Barnaby forgot you were there the moment he closed the door." She shook her head. "Things could have been so different."

"Could they have been?" Isobel tried to not sound harsh.

Puzzled, Rosalyn said, "What do you mean?"

Isobel rubbed her arms and walked the short distance to the kitchen door. "Can I make us some tea? Or would you prefer coffee?"

"Oh," Rosalyn said, "I'd love some tea."

"Do you mind stepping into the kitchen?"

"Of course not. Lead the way."

Isobel had never been embarrassed about her kitchen, and she told herself not to be now. It was a large, airy room, so clean one could eat off the floor. Except, she realized, glancing under the table, where Yellow slept, taking her usual afternoon nap. And today, Fifi was curled up beside the feline.

Rosalyn automatically took a seat on one of the long benches that bracketed the table.

While Isobel puttered about, Rosalyn repeated her question.

Isobel answered, "I was an orphan raised by an aunt who was the madam of a brothel."

"Ah, yes, that. Well, do you know where Geddes found Fletcher when he went to Texas?"

When Isobel shook her head, Rosalyn said, "He found him in an Army stockade, having been arrested for murder and waiting to be hanged."

Isobel nearly dropped the teapot. She turned slowly to catch Rosalyn's expression to see if she was simply fooling her. Rosalyn was serious as sauce. "He murdered someone?"

"No, but he was with the woman when she died, and he's always felt responsible. And I guess if you're a half-breed Indian in Texas, you're guilty no matter what."

"Who killed her?" She was being too nosy.

"She was the wife of an Army officer, who had actually pulled the trigger, and it was Fletcher's word against his."

Isobel finished going through the motions of making tea. She went to the pantry and pulled out some oat cakes that Delilah had made that morning, put them on a plate, and set them on the table. "I had no idea."

"And, before you even ask, Duncan, Kerry, and Gavin were living with their grandfather, a full-blooded Comanche, all this time because Fletcher was in the Army. Kerry, who was just a child, cooked for them and kept the place clean, but it was just barely a cottage by any standards, I'm told."

The family history was intriguing. "Their parents?"

"Fletcher, Duncan, and Kerry had the same father, the Scot, but when his wife died, he married his wife's sister, so Duncan and Kerry are really Fletcher's half siblings. Earlier on Fletcher's da found Gavin hiding in a root cellar after a raid. His parents, farmers, were killed. When both the Scot and his second wife died, I guess the grandfather was the only one there to care for them. You see, Fletcher hasn't always been the rock of the community," she finished with a wry smile. "He was once a bad boy, as was Duncan, as I'm sure you can verify."

Isobel felt heat go straight to the roots of her hair. There were many things she wanted to ask Rosalyn about, but instead she poured them each a cup of tea, relieved that her tea set was not chipped or stained, and joined Rosalyn at the table.

They spoke of the school, and Isobel briefly mentioned Lily, but Rosalyn didn't appear to be curious about the girl.

"Have you and Duncan made plans for the wedding?"

Isobel released a long sigh and nervously picked at an oat cake. "No. Actually, I've seen little of His Lordship since Ian was told he was the boy's father. At least that went over well; I truly didn't know how Ian would take being lied to all these years."

"He is a darling boy. The moment he met the twins, it was as if they'd known one another forever."

Isobel felt Rosalyn watching her.

"It bothers you that he felt comfortable with all of this so quickly, doesn't it."

"Truth be told," Isobel answered, "I continue to worry about how he feels every time he must return to this place after being on the estate."

"But this won't be your place much longer. The three of you will be a family and have a place of your own." She paused briefly. "I wanted to approach another subject. About Ian's schooling."

Isobel bristled. They were taking over her entire life! "What about his schooling?"

Rosalyn smoothed her hands over her skirt. "I presume you sent him to the mainland because you were afraid he might be recognized, and I understand that. But now, is it really necessary?" She paused briefly, took a sip of tea, and continued. "Once we have another schoolmaster and they have finished the renovation of the schoolroom next to the kirk, the twins will be enrolled there. I see no need to keep them tutored; they should get out and about more. And I would hope you would enroll Ian in the new school as well. I just hope we find a good teacher."

Isobel had thought of that as well. She knew Lily didn't qualify for the job but she had some hope; after all, the duke had suggested they might find something for her to do. "I guess it's worth thinking about," Isobel said. "It's getting harder and harder to scrape together the money for his tuition and room and board."

"Isobel, once you marry Duncan you won't have to worry about money anymore."

Suddenly the reality of her future dawned on her; she felt sick. "Oh, my. I hadn't really thought about that." She had never lived without worrying about money. "How will I ever get used to such an idea?"

"Knowing you now as I do, I don't imagine you'll change very much even after your wedding. I think you'll still squirrel money away for a rainy day, simply because you always have." Rosalyn paused briefly, then added, "Isobel, please don't take this the wrong way, but I'd love to help you prepare for the wedding. Have you decided what you will wear?"

At that, Isobel almost laughed. "To be perfectly honest, I have wondered what I will wear. I don't really have much of a wardrobe."

Rosalyn waved away the comment. "Not to worry. If you don't mind my interference, I think I can find something quite suitable for you." She stood up, stepped away, and studied Isobel from a short distance, her forefinger tapping her chin. "With your wonderful hair and your lovely skin, you will be a beautiful bride in a fawn or mushroom color. I know just the place to buy—"

"Nae," Isobel interrupted. "I canna afford to buy anything and I refuse to let you do it for me. Please, can we just use something that's already available?"

Rosalyn pursed her lips and sighed. "Oh, my dear, are you so set in your ways?"

"Aye, I'm afraid I am. Getting married is going to be hard enough—"

"You're treating this like some kind of punishment, Isobel." Rosalyn reached over and stroked her arm. "I don't know how to convince you that all will be well."

Isobel looked down at Rosalyn's dainty white fingers, noting that even she worked with her hands, because although they were not calloused or chapped like Isobel's, her nails were short and serviceable. Isobel tucked both of her hands into fists to hide them. "Nae, I don't think you can, but I do so appreciate your help and your concern. Now," Isobel finished, "I am happy for your help preparing for my marriage, but we must do it on my terms."

Rosalyn pondered a moment, and then said, "What if I can find something for you that I already have? Would you agree to wear it?"

"Look at us. We couldn't be more different."

Rosalyn squeezed Isobel's arm lightly and walked to the door. "I'll find something. It will give me an excuse to go through my wardrobes."

After Rosalyn left, Isobel sat, feeling a bit stunned. Rosalyn had more than one wardrobe. Of course she did. Even though Rosalyn's efforts had been meant to ease Isobel's discomfort, they did little in that regard.

For years, Isobel had done everything but sell her soul to pay for Ian's schooling, just to keep him safe. For years, she had scrimped and saved every penny, not allowing herself a shred of luxury. For years, she had prayed that each day would pass without another catastrophe that needed fixing with money she didn't have.

She felt something tug at her skirt. Fifi looked up at her and whined. "Oh, I know, lassie, your mam is gone and you're lonesome." She picked the pup up and walked through the house, remembering that she'd told Delilah that she would sort out some linen upstairs. But when she got to the second floor, her bedroom door was open and her bed looked so inviting. She looked down at the dog, who returned her gaze.

"I never nap during the day, Fifi. Never." But suddenly she was exhausted, probably from all the work she had ahead of her. The sale, the wedding, the marriage itself—was she really to be with Duncan MacNeil for the rest of her life? God help them both. She yawned and stretched out on the bed; Fifi snuggled right in. "Only for a few minutes, all right?"

• • •

Duncan had passed Rosalyn on the road. She had told him about Isobel's fears and her stubborn pride, and suddenly Duncan realized they had all been coming at her from every direction.

The house was quiet when he entered. He was on his way to the third floor when he noticed the door to Isobel's room was open. He looked in and found her asleep, curled up around that silly dog of Lily's.

How vulnerable she looked when she slept. And sweet. Her long lashes fanned her rosy cheeks and her lips were full and natural looking. No rouge for his Isobel. He nearly laughed. His Isobel? He gazed at the rest of her, vividly remembering what was beneath her drab clothing. She was full, succulent, luscious, and she would be his.

Or would she? Ah, yes, there was the rub. The promise he'd made in haste because he wanted to be part of a family—one of his own. He would not coax her. Somehow she had to come to him of her own free will, but in order for that to happen, he would have to be especially accommodating, and he could do that. There was movement on the bed.

"Is something wrong?" Isobel sat up so quickly the dog yelped and nearly fell to the floor.

Duncan straightened, hoping she hadn't been awake and merely watching him slaver over her. "No. Nothing is wrong. I was on my way upstairs and just happened to see your door open. Are you all right?"

She rose from the bed, smoothing her skirt as she stood. "Of course. How silly of me to have fallen asleep. It isn't as if I do this every day, for I do not."

"Of course you don't. Heaven forbid that you should have any moment of rest during a busy day."

She placed her fists on her hips. "Are you making fun of me?"

"Maybe a little," he answered. He reached for her hand and noticed that she flinched when he took it. Could she not even stand his touch? "I'm sorry all of this is such a burden for you. I don't want you to feel that way, Isobel."

"That's what everyone says, but it's not as easy as all that. I'm nearly twenty six years old and I've been living a certain way for all of it and I can't just change my ways because everyone says I should."

Duncan didn't know what else to say to her. He knew that everyone tried to make this stress-free, but apparently, according to Isobel, it wasn't that simple. And yet he still was anxious to make them a family, and he didn't want her to back down on their deal. And, like it or not, it was a deal. An arrangement.

He watched as she fussed with the bedding and suddenly felt deep warmth for her. Not pity, as she seemed to think he felt, but something stronger. Something he had begun to feel when she had hoped the damaged ceiling would fall on him while he slept. It puzzled him.

He shook his head. What a dolt he was. All he'd have to do to scare her away permanently was to tell her he was beginning to have strong feelings for her. Those feelings grew stronger as he watched her, and he forced himself to step away.

"Isobel, we are getting married. I understand your reluctance, but I insist that you pick a time when banns can be read at the church. It's foolish for us to continue to tip toe around one another. We're wasting time." With that he left.

She sank back onto the bed and closed her eyes. Oh, by the saints, why did this have to happen? Aye, she could be married to the man, but what kind of marriage would it be? Something unexpected had occurred to Isobel: each time he came into view her heart did a little jig against her ribs, and she felt a little breathless. One time she had even touched that soft part at her throat and found her heart pounding there, hard.

The arrangement they had made weeks ago had emerged as something of a life sentence for her. But there was no use putting it off any longer. She would set a date, and if he wasn't happy with her choice he could go to the devil.

Chapter Twelve

The day Lily returned from Ayr, Isobel sent a message to the castle, alerting the duke of her arrival. What he decided to do with this information, she didn't know. Even she had a case of nerves when she thought of the outcome.

She did find out first that the elderly couple had left Lily everything, which apparently was a tidy sum.

"I want you to have it," Lily had said.

"Nonsense! You keep it; you don't know when you might want to use it yourself," Isobel answered.

"But maybe we can use it to fix up the house so we don't have to move."

"That's sweet of you dear, but the deal is done and we won't be staying here any longer than we have to. There are going to be uncomfortable changes for all of us, so don't be so quick to give your money away."

"Where will you go?"

"I don't know, but I guess I'll have a husband who will figure that out."

Lily's expression was close to fear. "Where will I go?"

Isobel took Lily in her arms and hugged her. If Lily was indeed Rosalyn's daughter, she could live with her at the palatial castle. But, not knowing this for certain, Isobel said, "I would never allow you to be homeless, I promise."

The day had begun sunnily, but the breeze that accompanied the warmth promised rain and wind. Ian was at home, having spent much of the past week at the castle with his cousins. He did appear a bit down in the mouth about having to stay close to home, but to Isobel his discontent was normal. It didn't make her happy, but she understood.

Meanwhile, she had a meeting with Mr. Geddes and Duncan at the law office. She'd coaxed Delilah into coming with her for moral support. After telling Lily that Ian was outside somewhere, Isobel and Delilah set off to complete the sale of her precious home. As they walked, Isobel noticed the darkening of the sky. It sent shivers through her. She hated storms; she always had.

• • •

"Why are we stopping here?" Rosalyn asked, surprised that he'd halted the carriage in front of the old brothel. "It's raining and blowing, Fletcher, and I'm not entirely excited about stepping out into it. Can't I just wait here for you?"

"Just for a moment, Rosalyn. If you're quick, you won't get wet," he promised as he took her hand and hurried to the door. She sidestepped puddles and dashed with him.

Once inside, Fletcher found no one about. He called for Isobel and got no answer.

Rosalyn shook out her gown, sprinkling the floor with droplets of water. "Really, darling, what are we doing here?"

"Go over by the fire and wait for me. I'll be right back."

He found no one, not even in the schoolroom. But he heard the teacher's dog yapping wildly outside. He opened the door to the back, spying the dog on the water's edge, still barking feverishly. The rain came down in sheets, almost sideways, and he had to cup his hands around his eyes to see over the water.

"My God!" He tore off his boots, stripped off his jacket, and raced into the churning river, taking huge strokes to get to the little boat. When he reached it, he found Ian clinging to the side. He went to grab the lad, but with halting breath, Ian stuttered, "L-L-Lily! S-s-she just disappeared under the w-w-water." His teeth were chattering.

"Keep hanging on, Ian. Good lad!" Fletcher dove beneath the

surface and tried to see what was beneath. But with so little light and so much turmoil on the surface of the water, it was difficult to see anything at all.

He suddenly saw a wide wisp of cloth and swam to it; Lily appeared lifeless. Grabbing the girl around her waist, he swam to the surface quickly. He was grateful to see Duncan on the shore.

Duncan raced into the water, swam to the boat, and pulled Ian into his arms. They made it to the shore easily, just as Fletcher was running into the house with Lily. She was limp. Rosalyn appeared at the door.

Fletcher laid Lily on the box bed in the corner of the kitchen and bent to see if she was breathing. Her chest rose and fell slightly, and he let out a huge sigh of relief. At that moment, Isobel rushed in, Henry and Delilah loping along behind her.

"What's happened?"

"A little accident. Can someone get that fire going?" Fletcher asked.

"Henry, use the coal."

Henry hesitated. "But Miss Isobel—"

"Hang the cost, Henry, we need a good fire. Now go."

"I'll get blankets and some dry clothing." Delilah quickly left the room.

Rosalyn, always good in a crisis, went to Lily's side and, when she started coughing, helped her sit up and gently rubbed her back. "You poor dear," she cooed. Turning toward Fletcher, she asked, "Is this the teacher?"

Fletcher nodded, not trusting his voice as Isobel put a kettle on and Delilah rushed into the room with a pile of clothing and some blankets. They all exchanged worried glances.

Duncan came in with a sodden Ian, bringing Isobel to a swift stop. "What happened?"

"I'm not sure, but perhaps our son here can enlighten us?" He put the boy down by the fireplace and wrapped him in a blanket. With the addition of a fair amount of coal, the fire blazed hot.

While the women tended to Lily, both Fletcher and Duncan

waited for Ian's explanation. He had warmed up enough that his teeth were no longer chattering. "I was bored," he began, a spark of defiance in his tone. "I thought I could catch something for dinner, so I took my pole and the boat and pushed out into the water." He gave Duncan a look of pleading. "It hadn't been blowing or raining when I started, honest."

"And you lost the oars in the wind?" Duncan asked.

"Aye. And then the wind started blowing me about and I didn't know what to do. Then Lily appeared on the shore and jumped right in; she didn't even take off her shoes! She would've been all right if a wave hadn't pushed her against the boat and made her hit her head."

Fletcher and Duncan looked at one another. There would be time enough for punishment, if it was needed. Duncan took the boy by the hand. "Let's get you into some dry clothes." They disappeared up the stairs.

Fletcher turned away as Isobel and Rosalyn got the patient into dry bedclothes. Isobel was speaking to Lily in a low, calm voice, but she hadn't yet opened her eyes. Rosalyn had been curiously silent. The dog was curled up at the end of the bed, clearly guarding her mistress. Delilah and Isobel went to the stove to prepare tea.

Fletcher stepped to the bed. "Rosalyn?" She looked up at him, a peculiar expression on her face. When Isobel returned to the bedside, Rosalyn stepped away and she and Fletcher went into the next room.

Fletcher hardly dared breathe. "What's the matter?"

Rosalyn pressed her hands to her chest, her fingers nervously rubbing the locket Fletcher had given her years before. "I don't know. I just have the strangest feeling when I look at the girl, Fletcher." She raised her gaze to his. "A feeling like I have never had before."

He wondered if he should tell her what he, Fen, and Geddes suspected. He decided to wait. "Explain it to me."

She paced in front of him. "It's like I've been hit in the stomach, yet I feel no pain, only anguish. It's like looking at someone for the first time and thinking you've seen them before and you know them as well as you know yourself," she finished with an uncertain laugh.

Isobel called to her from the kitchen and Rosalyn hurried away. Fletcher followed her.

"She's coming around, Rosalyn. I have to run up and check on Ian, would you mind sitting with her so she isn't frightened when she wakes?"

Again, Isobel and Fletcher exchanged glances, and then she was gone. Delilah, who had been advised of the circumstances by Isobel, hovered nearby.

Rosalyn took a seat by the bed; Fletcher stood beside her. She was quiet, but she stroked the girl's brow gently, singing a song Fletcher had heard her sing to the twins when they were babes.

The girl made a noise in her throat and opened her eyes, blinking into the light. She smiled at Rosalyn. "I know that song," she whispered. When the dog saw she was awake, she nosed Lily's hand. "Good girl, Fifi," Lily said. "Good girl."

Momentarily startled at the name of the dog, Rosalyn asked, "Your pup is named Fifi?"

Lily nodded. "It's a name I remember from before."

"From before?" Rosalyn asked.

"It must be from before I was found by the river. I don't remember much else…"

Rosalyn looked up and found Fletcher's gaze. Her own was incredulous. She took Lily's hand and asked, "Do you know who I am?"

Lily studied her and smiled, closing her eyes briefly. "I dream of you every night. You used to sing that song to me. You are my mother."

Rosalyn collapsed on the bed, her body covering that of her long lost daughter, and she wept while her daughter stroked her hair.

• • •

Isobel stepped into Ian's room. Ian was in his nightclothes and Duncan sat with him on the bed.

"I'm sorry, Mam, I didn't mean to get into so much trouble."

And I hope Lily is all right, because it's my fault if she isn't." His expression was enough to melt her heart.

"Lily is going to be fine, thank God." She sat down across from Duncan on the bed and traced her son's chin with her finger. "I should be very angry with you, my wee lad. But right now I'm so relieved that everyone is all right, I just want to hug you and never let you go."

Ian moved his head away. "Aw, Mam. I'm getting too old for that."

Isobel clasped his hands in hers and felt the tears roll down her cheeks. "Never. Never will you be too old for my squeezes, laddie." She gave Duncan a quick look, trying to blink away her tears. "And you. I can't thank you enough for being in the right place at the right time."

They studied one another. Duncan held her gaze. "My life is just beginning with the two of you." He turned to Ian. "I won't lose you now that I've found you."

• • •

With the cannery deal concluded and signed, Duncan was anxious to start working on demolishing the building. That meant relocating everyone. It should have been a reasonably easy task, but for Isobel it was not. She feared she knew where they would go, and she was very uncomfortable with it. Castle Sheiling.

"Izzy," Duncan had said to her, "it's the only solution that makes sense. And it won't be for that long. Where else would there be room enough for all of us?"

"But the castle? I couldn't put all of this on Rosalyn. It's just not fair."

"She has plenty of help. She has a housekeeper who lives there, a number of girls from the village who come in daily, and with you and Delilah, she'll have that much more." He gave her a warm smile, that blasted dimple winking at her. "Don't let your pride get in the way, Izzy. And a wedding at the castle solves a multitude of problems."

A rush of heat spread through her. Lord, for her it was just one big drama after another.

"Nae, not the castle."

He gave her a quick glance. "Why not?"

"Because the little kirk that I've attended my whole life is where I want to be wed, whether the roof is done or not."

"Then I'll tell Reverend Fleming of the change. We'll do it right after sheep shearing."

Isobel looked at him, noting his warm brown eyes, his carved cheekbones, and his inky hair, which he still wore a bit long. She was head over heels. "You've taken this all upon yourself."

He gave her a mock scolding look. "If I didn't, I'm wondering if we'd ever get the deed done."

She had the decency to blush and look away. She'd fallen in love with her son's father. Shouldn't that make things perfect? Not for Isobel. She still had questions, but she was reluctant to speak of them. 'Twas easier just to let them fester inside her. Perhaps because she didn't wish to hear the answers.

Chapter Thirteen

Sheep shearing day dawned warm and dry. Duncan and Ian had gotten up early and met Fletcher, the twins and the crofters at the meadow where the fank, or stone pen, was standing, waiting for the commotion.

Rosalyn came by in her gig and picked up Isobel; they rode out to the meadow together, baskets of food and jugs of tea stacked in the back. They both knew that ale would flow, but hopefully it would be consumed after the work was done.

"I asked Fletcher how long he'd kept his suspicions about Fiona from me." Reins in hand, Rosalyn studied the rutted road ahead.

"It wasn't long. Then Lil—she had to leave for Ayr, so it was better to wait until she returned."

"I know. And that's another thing. She's been Lily for most of her life; I don't know if I can get used to that."

"Seems a small matter, wouldn't you say? Ye can always call her your wee lassie, little dumpling, darlin' girl, or some such thing," Isobel suggested, albeit not seriously.

"She's all of those things to me." Rosalyn teared up.

"It is such a miracle." Isobel brushed a wild curl from her face and tucked it under her bonnet. In the bright sky a hawk circled lazily above them.

"Aye, it is that. But all those years…" She inhaled sharply. "I can't dwell on that, can I? It's in the past; we have the future together, and I'm so joyful I may shed tears of happiness every day for the rest of my life."

After her rescue, Lily had caught a terrible chill and fever. Isobel wanted to keep the girl at the house, but she knew better than to argue with Rosalyn, who insisted she be transported to Castle Sheiling so Mrs. Gordon and Dr. Mac could tend to her there. Isobel understood; now that Rosalyn was reunited with her daughter, she would do anything to keep her close. She was still recovering, and although she wanted to join the festivities, both Mrs. Gordon and Rosalyn flatly refused to let her.

The shearing had already started when they arrived at the site. The sheep had been brought to the fank by the collies, which placed themselves at the entrance so none of the imprisoned sheep could escape.

Isobel and Rosalyn joined Fergie the Burn's wife, Birgit, and Donnie the Digger's wife, Elizabeth, on a small hillock overlooking the activity. Both Birgit and Elizabeth had young daughters who played together near their mothers. Other children ran about noisily. A long-beaked curlew screeched in the distance, perhaps having found lunch in the marshes below.

"We hear there be a weddin' soon," Birgit spoke, all smiles.

Isobel drew in a deep sigh. "Aye, there will be, but don't ask me when."

Elizabeth gave her a sly grin. "With a buck like that, and ye haven't tied him down, yet? Ye best watch out or some lassie will ferry him away to her own bed, believe it."

Isobel blushed but didn't respond. She looked for Duncan. He and Fletcher were working side by side, each handling a sheep, deftly working the large, metal shaped shears through the fleece. They were shirtless, and among the healthy-looking yet pale Scotsmen, they looked dangerous and almost feral, their black hair blowing in the breeze, their skin brown and their muscles chiseled in stone.

Isobel's mouth went dry. She had never imagined Duncan could look so untamed. It thrilled her. She'd seen a few half-dressed men in her day—Hamish for one, who was big, bulky, and so white he was almost blue.

But by the holy, Duncan MacNeil was splendid. Magnificent. Now and then someone said something that made him laugh, and he threw his head back, allowing Isobel a look at his chest and his throat. There was nothing more beautiful to her than his body. Ten years ago she had thought she could look at him every day for the rest of her life and not get tired of it. She still remembered that very moment. And now he was going to marry her. And he promised to leave her alone. She wanted that, didn't she? Looking at the miracle of his body, she seriously began to wonder.

Rosalyn stepped up beside her. "I know."

Isobel swallowed, her throat dry, and turned abruptly. "What?"

"I know how it feels to see him this way for the first time. It was the same for me."

Isobel couldn't even respond. She just nodded, not taking her eyes off the father of her son. When she finally spoke, her voice was raw. "I had no idea."

"Aye," Rosalyn said, putting her arm around Isobel's shoulders. "And trust me, you'll never take it for granted, I promise you that."

She wanted to confide in someone; she needed to. How would she feel when she learned he'd slept elsewhere, and not in her bed? How would she feel when gossiping fishwives snickered and sneaked behind her, telling the stories of where he *had* spent the night?

"Isobel, if you ever need to talk, I'm always ready to listen. I may not be in your exact situation, but I also had many, many issues marrying a man I barely knew."

Oh, Isobel thought, *it would be so good to just let it all out!* But something still held her back. The only confidants she had ever had were her aunt and Delilah. Even Hamish didn't know her deepest, darkest secrets and desires, and now he never would.

"When can we expect you to come stay with us?" Rosalyn's question broke into Isobel's thoughts, but she was grateful for the disruption.

"Oh, Rosalyn, that's such a wonderful invitation, but how can we possibly impose on you? We have no idea how long this entire situation will go on. It could be months, maybe even a year."

Rosalyn squeezed Isobel's shoulders. "Then we'll really get to know one another, won't we?"

A shout alerted them to company. "Ah, Duncan," Fletcher said, wiping his face with his forearm, "there are our maidens now, ready to give us food and drink and whatever else we deserve for all our hard work."

"Ocht, you rascal," Rosalyn said with a wide smile. "You'll get your food and drink and nothing more." She tossed him a large bath sheet so he could wipe himself down.

Duncan's gaze fell on Isobel, and she managed a smile, although inside she was all aflutter. She handed him a bath sheet as well, and he began to dry himself. Sweat ran in rivulets down his hard, wide, brown chest, saturating the already-wet work pants he wore. His skin was smooth, his nipples dark brown. A puckered scar up toward his left shoulder was the only thing that marred the beauty of his skin. There was a small strip of black hair that ran from his navel and disappeared beneath his clothes. There were times, like now, when the evening she spent with him all those years ago came back crystal clear. She remembered the hard length of him as he'd held her close; she remembered vividly cupping it through his clothing. She still remembered the brief bite of pain when he entered her and the pleasure he brought her…

She shook herself and went to help Rosalyn with the food.

The brothers settled beneath a tree, allowing the women to wait on them. Fergie and Donnie climbed to the rise, their wives having settled by a nearby oak.

Suddenly the twins and Ian came rushing toward them, dirty and greasy from handling the fleece, demanding nourishment, and quickly Isobel was once again in her comfort zone.

The conversation turned to poaching, for unlike the land, Fletcher still owned all of the wildlife. "Is there much problem with poachers on the island?" Duncan asked.

Fletcher took long, deep gulps from the jug of tea. He wiped his mouth and handed the jug to Duncan. "Now and then, but I usually turn a blind eye to it."

"Why would you do that?" Duncan took a meat pie from Isobel, giving her a quick smile as he did so.

So this is what it would be like, she thought. Companionable. Comfortable with one another.

"It's a give and take thing," Fletcher explained. "For instance, last winter I learned that Red Forest, the crofter who works the land nearest the woods, had felled a deer, so his family was well fed through the winter."

"Why let it go?"

"Because, Red is an excellent blacksmith, better than the one in the village, and when I need a little work done, all I have to do is ask and he's on the job immediately."

"So, he knows you know about the poaching."

"Yes, and if any of them were to take terrible advantage of it, I'd do something about it, but so far, we're all quid pro quo." He polished off a meat pie and then took another from the basket nearby. "Isobel," he said. "When are you and Duncan going to decide what kind of cottage to build?"

Duncan answered, "A cottage? No sir, brother. We're going to have a house with a second story, a garden, and a beautiful view of the ocean. Maybe it will be a mansion."

Isobel gave him a sharp look. "You don't mean that."

Duncan gave her a puzzled look. "You don't want a mansion, my Izzy? With servants and gardeners and a butler, maybe a maid or two to help you dress in the morning?"

She reached over and gave him a gentle punch on the arm. "You are a big tease."

"I'm sure you'll probably need more than two bedrooms," his brother suggested.

Once again Duncan's gaze landed on Isobel. "Indeed we might."

Isobel could barely breathe. Her insides shook like leaves in the wind. It was one thing to speak of the house, quite another for them to banter back and forth about such an intimate thing.

"And, because I want you to be happy," he said to Isobel, "I want it to be a home where you will be comfortable. That's most important."

Isobel looked off into the distance, still anxious about her future. "It all sounds lovely."

Duncan came and stood in front of her. Once again, she noticed the rucked-up scar on his shoulder and suddenly felt a pang of anxiety for what may have happened to him. "It will be everything you want it to be."

Chapter Fourteen

BAYOUS OF LOUISIANA—SEPTEMBER 1864

His eyelids fluttered. He winced as he tried to rise, and fell back against the cot. Something wet poked at his face. Forcing his eyes open he found a big, mangy mutt eyeing him.

"Titan, down."

Duncan blinked repeatedly, searching for the sound of the voice. A young woman appeared next to him, her hair a shimmering mass of gold curls that created a halo around her head. "Are you an angel?" His voice was raspy; his throat hurt.

She giggled. "No, silly, I'm Kitten."

"I'd have sworn you were an angel," he answered, his mouth dry.

She turned and shouted, "Daddy Beau, he's awake." Her voice was smooth as maple syrup over a thick stack of cakes. He'd missed the sweet sound of a southern woman's voice.

"Daddy Beau" entered and the mutt ambled to him, tail wagging, head down submissively. Duncan's gaze wandered up the length of the man, for he was big and tall and imposing. He had long, stringy white hair and a healthy, if filthy, beard. His ragged eyebrows hung over his eyes like two pale caterpillars on the move. A tight shirt, that once had probably been white, was stretched over his portly gut. In spite of that, an apron of fat hung over his pants. He grinned at Duncan; he was missing a front tooth. "Well, good to see you're awake, boy."

Boy. Duncan didn't like the sound of that. He tried to clear his throat.

"The damned Yankees got ya. My dog was barkin' something fierce, and Kitten here and I found ya lyin' 'neath a cypress after the fight." He swore. "Them damned Yankees thought you was dead." He leered again, revealing a mouth full of empty spaces where teeth used to be. "Thought so myself at first."

"Water." Duncan tried to swallow.

"Kitten! Get the jug."

The girl scurried away, returning with something for him to drink.

"Water's precious, boy; you'll have to make do with what we got."

Kitten bent over him, taking care not to spill as she helped him. Duncan struggled to his elbows, wincing at the pain in his shoulder, and allowed her to put the tumbler to his lips. He drank greedily, noting it was bitter and warm, but he didn't care. When he'd finished, he asked, "Where was I shot?"

"They got ya in the shoulder, but when ya fell, ya broke yer ankle. Kitten here patched you up real good." He gave the girl a lewd smile. "She's a crackerjack, she is."

Kitten offered the old man a smile, but Duncan saw something else in her eyes. Was it fear?

"Oh, Daddy Beau you make me blush." To Duncan, her words sounded forced.

Daddy Beau laughed, a lascivious sound that rumbled up from his belly. "Blushin' is one of the things you do best, Kitten."

Duncan closed his eyes against the uncomfortable feeling in his gut. "Where are we?"

"I got me a little place deep in the bayou, boy. 'Fraid there's no way to get you back to your outfit, the condition you're in. You'll have to stay here 'til you're able to travel, and the good Lord only knows how long that'll be."

Duncan mouthed a curse, but he knew the old man was right. Once again he tried to sit up, but dizziness overcame him and he flopped back on the cot. His left shoulder and his right ankle throbbed like hell. And oddly, he couldn't move his left ankle either.

"Now, now," the girl—Kitten—soothed, "I'm going nurse you back to health, soldier, just wait and see. We got very little medicine, but we have plenty of Daddy Beau's hooch." She smiled, wrinkling her little nose. "That ought to take the edge off."

Duncan studied the girl. She was older than he'd originally thought, though probably not yet out of her teens. She was pretty and petite, and he wondered how in the hell Daddy Beau could keep her cooped up in the backwaters of Louisiana.

"So," he began, trying to make conversation, "why do they call you Kitten?"

She giggled sweetly again. "My papa and my mama, bless their souls," she added, crossing herself, "named me Kitten." She busied herself by fluffing up the gray and smelly pillow and straightening the bedding on the cot, which was in the corner of a large room that held a fireplace and a makeshift kitchen. "They told me when I was born I sounded just like a new kitty when I cried.

"You rest now," Kitten ordered. "When you wake up, I'll bring you some squirrel broth. You'll have to start eating or you won't heal. My mama always told me that."

Later—he wasn't sure how long he'd slept—he lay still and listened to the sounds around him. Insects hummed steadily; birdsong and bird calls drifted in through the windows. With nothing to keep the bugs out, they flittered and flew about, landing wherever they pleased. Duncan stopped a shiver. Good thing he didn't hate bugs; Texas was rife with them, as was this place deep in the swamp.

It was light; he thought maybe late morning. But of what day? He heard Daddy Beau outside, talking to someone and cursing a blue streak. When he stepped inside, he saw that Duncan was awake.

He, with Titan following behind, lumbered over and pulled up a chair next to the cot and hefted his bulk into it. The hound curled up at his feet. Duncan smelled the man's sweat; liquor and body odor wafted over Duncan and he swallowed hard.

"Them damned Yankees," Daddy Beau muttered. "They went into Ponchatoula and sacked the town. Looted homes, took what they wanted and left a goddam mess. Dammit." He shook his head, the jowls beneath his beard moving rhythmically. "They even sacked the post office, letters and torn newspapers scattered everywhere. Hell, they even got hold of Lenny's fine stash of liquor, toting it away like they owned it." He turned and spat. Duncan watched the ugly brown wad fly through the air into the spittoon, where it pinged against the side.

"They got soldiers stationed there, guardin' the town. That's another reason you can't leave, boy. It ain't safe." He studied Duncan. "Where you from?"

Duncan didn't feel much like talking. "Texas."

"You're an injun, ain't ya?"

Duncan nodded. "Half."

"So they let redskins fight for the Confederacy? I'da thought you'll be more likely to be on the other side."

"I fight for Texas," Duncan answered.

Kitten moved toward them and Daddy Beau threw her a rough gaze. "Got that squirrel cookin'?"

"Yes, Daddy Beau." Duncan wondered if both she and the dog had reason to fear this behemoth of a man.

"What do you do in Texas?" Kitten and her sweet voice were the only things palatable in this hellhole.

How much to tell them? "I work on a ranch," was all he said. For some reason he was reluctant to tell them more.

"It is a big ranch?" As she attempted to move away from Daddy Beau, the corpulent man put his arm around her in a way that sent a jolt of revulsion through Duncan. Kitten stood stiffly in his grip as the fat man fondled her breast.

Duncan wanted to look away from the scene, instead he focused on the big man's forehead. "I guess it's big." He noticed the fat man's caterpillar eyebrows move up with interest. Duncan would say no more.

"I've always wanted to go to Texas," Kitten said, her voice wistful.

"Like hell you'll ever get out of the swamps, girl." Daddy Beau sounded threatening, and Kitten maneuvered her way out of his grasp and started fussing with the bedding over Duncan's legs.

"Lotsa open spaces, 'that right, boy?"

Kitten gave Duncan one of her sweet smiles. "He has a name, Daddy Beau. Don't you?"

For some reason he didn't want to divulge that information to this filthy man. "Daniel. Call me Daniel." It was the first name that popped into his head. Feeling a trifle stronger, he tried once again to change the position of his left ankle. It moved slightly but it was as if he were shackled. The thought was ludicrous and he snuffled a quiet laugh.

"No sense tryin' to pull free, boy," Daddy Beau said, noting his confusion.

Something cold and alarming washed over Duncan. "What?"

"Now, me and Kitten had to make sure you wouldn't hurt your injuries, ya know?"

Duncan shook his head to clear the fog between his ears. "You've shackled me to the bedpost? But...but why?"

Daddy Beau rubbed a huge paw over his face and sighed. "I got me some items here that might strike you as strange, being a Rebel and all."

Duncan was still confused. "What do you mean?"

Daddy Beau snorted a derisive laugh. "You half-breeds a bit slow witted, are ya?"

Duncan closed his eyes. "Listen, old man, I don't care what you're hiding or for whom. I just want to get out of here."

"Yeah, well here's the thing, boy." Daddy Beau drummed his sausage fingers against his heavy thigh. "I got me some information that tells me you might be worth somethin' to the enemy, and I don't just mean 'cause you're a fightin' Reb."

Comprehension dawned. Of course. Before he was injured, he'd led a small band of men down to the Tickfaw where they had capsized a steamer, killing all men aboard. He must have stood out, and it was likely because of his coloring. "This is war, old man. Killing your enemy isn't a crime."

Daddy Beau's jowls shook with laughter under his beard. "Boy, it's a crime when they're transportin' secrets and you sent them down into the sluggish, muddy Tickfaw. And believe me, nothin' save a miracle can bring them back from that sludge. Might as well be quicksand."

So he was being held prisoner by a southerner who played both sides.

"But," Daddy Beau continued, "before I turn you over, I'm gonna get you healed up a bit. Don't want you dyin' on me, since there's a reward if yer turned in alive." He smirked down at Duncan. "And I gotta keep my Kitten happy. She's taken a likin' to ya, despite the fact that yer half savage. No accountin' for the taste of some young gals." His laugh was loose and phlegmy as he pulled out a cigar butt and stuck it into his mouth. He didn't light it; he just chewed on the end. It seemed to fit perfectly in the gap between his teeth.

At least a week had passed since Duncan had been "rescued" by the maniac Daddy Beau. In that time he had witnessed the ups and downs of the man's personality. One minute he could be calm, and the next he would fly into a rage. The mutt was in tune to his master's changes and sulked away with his tail between his legs when the fat man started to blow. And Duncan had witnessed the abuse he heaped on the dog when he was in a foul mood. It curdled Duncan's stomach the way Daddy Beau treated the dog, who still loved him unconditionally. And his abuse didn't stop with the dog; Kitten received her fair share, and Duncan prayed the old man would simply have a stroke and fall over dead.

The more he watched the chemistry between Daddy Beau and Kitten, the more Duncan realized she pacified him, if only to save herself from abuse. It didn't always work. She sported bruises on her thin arms, and he was sure he noticed a fading bruise on her neck.

He was also certain they were putting something in his food or water, because he slept much of the time. And his shoulder throbbed like hell.

Most nights, Daddy Beau left the cabin for a spell, not long enough for Duncan to form any sort of plan for his escape. He left Kitten alone with Duncan, which surprised him. She joined him, sitting on a chair by the bed. Sometimes she would read to him from a tattered old Bible. Despite the fact that she probably hadn't bathed in weeks, she looked winsome and sweet, and Duncan felt a brotherly protection toward her.

"Daddy Beau beats you and the dog."

She jerked her head up, her blue eyes huge in her delicate face. "Yes," she murmured.

"What's making me so sleepy, Kitten?"

A flash of alarm lit her eyes, then was gone. "I don't know what you mean."

"I'm sleeping all the time. What are you giving me?"

She threw a furtive glance at the doorway, then in a whisper, she said, "Daddy Beau thought it best for your healing if you slept, so he makes me put something in your food."

Duncan took her hand and looked at her. "Please. Don't do it anymore."

She looked down at his big, brown hand as it covered her small white one. She squeezed his fingers, turned to the door and back again. "What will I tell him?"

"Don't tell him anything. Just stop doing it, please?"

She chewed her lower lip. "But Daniel, why don't you want to sleep?"

"I need a clear head, Kitten. Somehow I've got to get out of here." They continued to hold hands; Kitten appeared reluctant to let him go.

"You think you can leave?" She appeared incredulous.

"I've got to. If I don't, you know as well as I do that I'm a dead man."

She threw him a guilty glance. "Your ankle isn't broken."

"What?"

"Daddy Beau said it was a sprain, but that it didn't seem broken."

"Then why tell me it was?" he demanded.

She studied the dirt floor. "He thought you wouldn't try to move it too much if you thought it was broke."

Duncan knew a sprain was sometimes worse than a break, but he could deal with the pain. "Do you know your way out of here?"

"Sort of. My papa always told me I had 'dead reckoning,' which I guess means I know my directions."

He wondered how long she'd been imprisoned in this hellhole with that bullying masochist. "Will you help me?"

Her sparkly blue eyes were wide. Myriad emotions played over her face and she knelt by the cot and grabbed his hand again. "If I promise to help you, you have to take me with you."

He would need her to get clear of the bayou. After that...hell, he couldn't just leave her to the old man's rage.

He gave her a tender smile. "We'll figure something out, Kitten."

"Oh, Daniel, we'll make it, I just know we will!"

Her enthusiasm was so great he almost felt like they had a chance.

Chapter Fifteen

ISLAND OF HEDABARR—1872

Isobel was in the kitchen nursing a cup of tea. She was thinking about her decision not to sew Duncan a wedding sark for fear he would automatically assume she was thinking of their marriage bed, because after all, even though the sark could be worn anywhere, under anything, a marriage sark was for, well, the marriage bed. And for all she knew, he wore nothing to bed. She honestly couldn't envision him in a nightshirt. Heat rushed to her cheeks and her ears at that thought.

Delilah strode in, her hands on her hips. "Tomorrow be your wedding day and here ye are, sitting around as if ye've not a care in the world."

Isobel inhaled deeply and looked up at her. "Looks can be deceiving, Delilah. My insides are whirling around in such a flurry I don't even dare drink this tea for fear I'll toss up everything I've eaten today."

Delilah made a clucking sound and left for the root cellar, returning with a basket of vegetables. "It's high time you quit frettin' and start believin' that it'll be all right."

Isobel pushed the teacup aside; tea sloshed over the lip, onto the saucer. "That what will be all right? That we are all expected to descend on the Castle Sheiling and put down roots there for God knows how long?" She stood and began to pace. "Just what exactly do you believe will be all right?"

Delilah screwed up her face. "I was thinkin' about the fact that you'll be married and all that. I do believe you should be preparing for it, rather than worryin' about things you can't control."

"And you think I can control my marriage?"

Delilah stopped washing the vegetables, wiped her meaty hands on her apron and took Isobel by the arm. She sat her down at the table and scooted in next to her. "If ye won't control it, who will? Do ye want a real marriage or one that just looks good from the outside?"

Isobel's starchy demeanor deflated, and she rested her elbows on the table and put her hands over her face. "I think of little else, truth be told, but he's already told me he wouldn't force me into anything…"

"Do ye suppose that was just to get ye to agree?"

She looked up and caught Delilah's gaze. "But what if it isn't? What if he's not interested in me that way?"

Delilah snorted. "He was once; he will be again, if he isn't already."

Isobel stood and marched to the sink to take over the job Delilah had left, more to keep busy than anything else. She took a small brush and scrubbed a potato, digging at the eyes to get them clean of dirt. A hysterical giggle escaped. She was beginning to attack the vegetables just like Lily had when she'd first arrived. "And what if he isn't? Then what? What if I'm too fat or too short or not submissive enough? These are traits I can't change."

Delilah slapped her palm against the table, causing Isobel to jump. She nearly dropped the potato on the floor. "Lord a'mighty, can't ye just take things as they come and not worry yerself into an early grave?"

Isobel rested her forearms against the sink. Her wedding dress, one that Rosalyn had provided for her, was hanging upstairs in her nearly empty wardrobe. It was a lovely mushroom silk, with embroidered forest green flowers stitched over the skirt and green ribbing at the neck and sleeves. It was the most beautiful gown Isobel had ever seen. It was certainly more beautiful than anything she had ever believed she would wear.

Lily had promised to do something with her raucous, unruly hair, which Isobel seriously doubted was possible, and Rosalyn was providing a bouquet of flowers from her own garden for Isobel to carry, complete with a sprig of white heather for good luck. She'd likely need a bushel of that.

The entire reception was to be handled and paid for by the duke, and she and Duncan were to wed in the wee kirk Isobel had attended most of her life, the service conducted by the Reverend Fleming; it would be one of the last official duties he would perform before he retired. Ian would walk with her down the aisle. Isobel wanted everyone to attend, if not the ceremony, then at least the party afterward. An open invitation to the villagers and the crofters. Duncan thought that was a fine idea.

Everything seemed perfect. What could possibly go wrong?

There was some commotion in the outer room, and Lily, who had been cleaning up the schoolroom, stepped in carrying a small package.

"What do ye have there?" Delilah asked.

Lily sauntered up to Isobel and handed her the small parcel, appearing to bite back an enormous grin.

Isobel frowned. "For me? Who came to the door with it?"

"Some laddie from the castle," she answered. "And before you ask, he said it was specifically for you."

Isobel wiped her hands on her apron and carefully took the small box from Lily. Her heart was pounding and her mouth was dry. She could not imagine why anyone would send her a gift, unless it was Rosalyn's wedding gift to her. That had to be it. She stared down at.

"Well, open it—or have ye lost the ability to move?" Delilah's voice was impatient.

Isobel slowly unwrapped the package and discovered that under the paper, there was a small, velvet-covered box. Slowly she opened the box, and when she saw what was inside, she brought a hand to her mouth and let out a small scream.

"Land sakes," Delilah sputtered, "is it a snake?" When Isobel didn't answer, Delilah added, "With that screechin' it better be a snake."

Isobel made her way to the table and all but collapsed onto the bench. Shaking her head, she answered, her voice wobbly, "Not a snake, Delilah."

Delilah peered over Isobel's shoulder and took the box. "Lord Almighty. It's a luckenbooth." Her voice was reverent.

Lily stepped close, anxious to see the gift. "What is a luckenbooth?"

Delilah waited for Isobel to speak, but when she couldn't, Delilah explained. "'Tis a brooch. A love token. A gift from the groom to the bride to be, and by the holy, it's real silver."

Lily gently touched the brooch. "There are two hearts entwined." She gasped. "Oh, that's so romantic!"

Isobel started to hyperventilate. She rose from the bench. "I need to be alone for a bit, please…" She was so addled she couldn't finish the sentence. She left the box on the table and raced up the stairs to her room.

She flopped onto her back on the bed and stared at the cracks and stains on the ceiling. What could he be thinking? What…what did he want of her? Was it simply an innocent gift, or did he actually know the myth behind such a gift? A luckenbooth wasn't something given lightly. No, indeed not. But of course, he could be ignorant of the meaning behind it.

Delilah appeared in her doorway. "Ye forgot something." She tossed the box on Isobel's bed and left.

Isobel reached for the box and slowly opened it again, studying the magnificent piece. She began to make little sobbing sounds in her throat, and she started to cry. She was so bewildered she didn't know if they were tears of happiness or of panic.

The last thing she wondered before she dozed off was whether or not she had time to sew Duncan a wedding sark after all.

• • •

As per most traditions, Duncan could not spend the night before his wedding in the same house as his bride to be. Although it was close to nine at night according to the tall, stately clock in the entry hall, Duncan was restless. He went outside and walked toward the stables. A number of hounds ran up to him, sniffing at his pant legs. "Sorry, fellas, it's just me." They followed him into the barn anyway.

A light flickered at the other end, drawing him to it. There, on a stool, sat Kerry, nursing a pup with a makeshift bottle. She looked up briefly and smiled. "The runt of the litter," she explained. "I'm supposed to let the weakest take his chances with the rest of the bigger pups." She looked up at Duncan and then glanced at the huge Scottish wolf hound bitch that was curled around her bevy of whelps. "That hound had thirteen pups! What chance does the smallest have? We'll be lucky if half survive as it is."

Duncan squatted down beside Kerry and studied the hound. There was something so massively beautiful about these dogs. Yes, there were a number of collies on the premises for herding, but these hounds owned their space; they didn't have to have a purpose to survive, although he presumed they were used for hunting. "I hear that's nature's way; survival of those who can endure without human intervention, or something."

"Oh, I know," she answered, her voice soft. "But I can't just ignore her and let her die. Could you?"

Duncan settled down beside his sister, resting his back against a board that reinforced the roof. "Back in Texas at the ranch, we had a mare that foaled twins. One, a filly, was born healthy and strong. The other, a handsome colt, was weaker and unable to stand as quickly as his sibling." He stopped, remembering the incident. "He had what we called base-narrow stance in his hind legs, which kind of kept him off kilter."

"I've heard of that. If I've learned anything at all from our brother, it's what constitutes a healthy horse." She stroked the pup in her lap, who had fallen asleep. "What happened to the colt?"

"The mare seemed to sense the colt was weak, because she would side step when he tried to nurse. One of the stable boys, who himself had a bum leg, pleaded with me to let him bottle feed. There's an old saying, you know, 'no legs, no horse.' Even though I was pretty sure the colt wasn't going to make it, I let the kid nurse it. Somehow it survived, but it had a strange gait and it never would have survived without intervention. And it wasn't of any use to us—as a horse, anyway."

"But I sense it brought the young lad profound joy, am I right?"

He nodded, recalling the bond between the damaged horse and the crippled boy. "It gave me a feeling of peace. I realized a person doesn't always have to follow the rules." He almost laughed. "That probably sounds crazy coming from someone who broke as many as he could find to break ten years ago."

Kerry studied him. "You're a good man, Duncan MacNeil, no matter what you did back then."

"From your lips to Isobel's ears."

Kerry put the sleeping runt down on the blanket with the furry little pups that were already asleep. It nuzzled its way into the pile. "I don't know her well at all. From time to time I would see her in the village, and she always answered my greeting, but I gathered she wasn't interested in getting further acquainted." She glanced at Duncan. "I guess we all know why, don't we?"

"I hate to be reminded of what I did back then, especially now when I have a son of my own. I do know she was afraid of the lot of you."

"Rosalyn says Isobel has a lot of fears. All of us have done everything possible to bring her into the family with ease. From what I understand, she is a proud, stubborn woman, and strong in her own right, but certain she won't live up to our expectations." She put the empty milk container in a wicker basket beside her. "Despite the fact that she knows all of the MacNeils' sordid history, she still isn't convinced we're just regular folks."

Duncan stood and brushed hay off his buckskins. "I sent her a brooch today."

Kerry struggled to stand, and Duncan took her hand and pulled her up. "A luckenbooth? You did? Oh, she must have been delighted."

"I haven't heard one way or another, but knowing Isobel as I do now, she will read some meaning into it that will either scare her or anger her."

They reached the stable door and stepped out into the cool night air. The sky was awash with billions of twinkling stars; it seemed a good omen for tomorrow. Duncan said, "It's like my whole youth has come back to haunt me. I never had a problem getting any woman I wanted. That sounds arrogant, but I was always so sure of myself, I couldn't see how any girl could refuse." He laughed at his naivety. "Even with Isobel—" He shook his head, not willing to go into that night ten years before.

"And now?"

"And now, I'm nervous as a jungle cat, wondering how I should approach her. Will she tell me to go sleep with the devil? Will she make it clear that our 'arrangement' was to be all business?"

Kerry gave him a sisterly punch on the arm. "I can't give you answers, brother dear. I have no experience at all in the ways of love. But I do believe that both of you are worrying yourselves over nothing."

They returned to the castle in silence, Duncan's only thought being it was likely he'd spend a long, restless night awake.

• • •

Isobel's little escape nap ended when Delilah thumped on her door. Isobel sat up, searched for her gift, and stuck it into her pocket. "What is it?"

"'Tis Henry," Delilah said, her voice solemn.

Isobel was up like a shot. "Is he all right?"

Delilah snorted. "More'n all right, I'd say." She handed Isobel a letter. "From his sister in Ayr."

Isobel looked at the letter. "I didn't know he had a sister."

"Well, if ye aren't goin' to read it, I'll just tell ye. His sister wants him to come and spend his days with her, as she's recently widowed. Guess she wants the company." Delilah snorted again. "Henry is about as much company as Yellow the Cat. At least the cat is useful around here."

Isobel gave Delilah a look of warning. "Since he's leaving, you could be nice to him for a change."

"Hard for me to change, Izzy."

Isobel opened the letter and scanned it. "When does he plan to leave?"

"He says right after the nuptials. He's itchin' to see ye finally wed, as we all are."

"Well, at least I won't have to worry about him after tomorrow." She gave Delilah a forlorn look. "How can we possibly descend on Rosalyn, the two of us?"

Delilah shrugged. "Ye'll be busy with His Lordship, and I'll make sure things are running as they should be."

"That's what I'm afraid of. Just remember that it isn't your place to order anyone around."

Delilah planted her meaty fists on her hips. "Huh. Then what in the devil will I do with meself all day?"

Chapter Sixteen

The morning dawned bright and beautiful. Isobel had been up before dawn, however, trying to prepare herself for a demanding day. After a nice warm bath and clean hair, she had sat by the fire and toweled her hair dry. Now she perched on a stool before the mirror, while Lily worked on the mess.

"So many curls, Isobel," Lily said, her voice filled with awe.

The feeling of Lily's hands in her hair was comforting; it relaxed her. "Aye. I've never been able to do anything with it but pull it back away from my face and stick it into a roll at the back of my neck. Even then it springs loose like it wants to get away."

"The Travelers had beautiful hair," Lily recalled. "I could sit for hours and play with my mum's—" She paused midsentence. "Oh, I don't even know what to call them anymore."

"Don't fret about it with me. They rescued you, raised you, and kept you from harm. We shall all be grateful to them for that." Isobel wondered how Lily's idiosyncrasies affected her new life at the castle.

Lily made a noncommittal sound, one that made Isobel catch her gaze in the mirror. "What's wrong?"

As Lily pulled Isobel's hair into a series of corkscrew curls, she said, "I've asked my…Rosalyn, to explain how I came to be in the river. So far I've not gotten a very good explanation."

"It's not my business, but if you were very young and asked that question, I too would wonder how to answer. But, and again this isn't my worry, you're a lass full grown. I'm sure they will tell you, but you must be prepared for something possibly unpleasant."

"I've gathered there wasn't a good reason for me being there.

Rosalyn appears heartbroken every time I bring it up. She does promise to tell me one day, but I'm wondering when that day will come, if ever."

"Then be patient, lassie. Be patient." Isobel almost laughed at her advice. At this moment she was about as impatient as any person on the planet. But impatient for what?

Moments later, Lily announced, "There. A masterpiece."

Isobel glanced at her reflection in the mirror. "Oh my." Lily had brought all of her hair to the top of her head and fashioned the curls securely with pins and a circle of pearls. Tiny, wispy curls framed her face. "How did you do it? I can't believe how neat and tidy it looks." She touched the curls gently. "Unfortunately, by morning it will look like I've been struck by lightning."

"You're too hard on yourself, Isobel." Lily stood back, her hands clasped together under her chin. "It's the least I can do for you. Without you, I may never have known who I really was. Now," she added, "let's get you into that dress."

A short time later, a stunned Isobel stood in front of the mirror and studied her reflection once again. Why, she was almost beautiful. The mushroom silk with its green embroidery complemented her fair skin. The bodice dipped low, revealing more than she'd ever revealed before, and immediately her neckline flushed with heat. Her luckenbooth was pinned on the left side of her gown, and the gown hugged her small waist and womanly hips and then draped itself beautifully to the floor. She wore mushroom-colored silk and low-heeled shoes decorated with a green bow. She had the urge to reach out and touch the mirror to make sure it was really her.

"Ye right look like a lady," Delilah announced behind her. "Ye'll dazzle your lord, ye will."

Isobel pulled in a sigh. "Oh, Delilah, can you believe I'll actually have a title?" She glanced at the big woman and they both began to giggle again.

"Ye think I should probably practice me curtsy?"

"If it's anything like the last one, I'd say aye, practice, practice, practice!"

They were still laughing when Ian skidded into the room, all combed and polished and dressed in an adorable MacNeil plaid kilt made just for him. His mouth fell open when he saw his mother. "Is it really you, Mam?"

"'Tis." She enjoyed his expression. "And you look very handsome." She studied her son. When had he become all arms, legs, and knobby knees? Oh, he was growing up so fast. Too fast. She supposed all mothers felt that way.

"It's not a skirt, it's called a kilt; Mister Duncan is wearing one, too." He frowned.

"What's wrong, laddie?"

"Oh, I'm just sorry Hamish can't be here," Ian murmured.

"Aye, I wish he were here too, but when the sea calls him, he must go, whether there are important nuptials taking place or not." She reached out and straightened Ian's collar. "You know," she began, "Mister Duncan or even his proper title, His Lordship, probably won't do. You're going to have to decide what to call him."

Ian checked his reflection in the mirror, strutting around like a lad in a costume. "We've talked about that."

"You have?"

"Aye. He says to call him whatever is comfortable for me. He hopes that someday I'll call him da."

"And what do you think? Will you?" A twinge pricked Isobel's heart, nudging open the hard shell she'd wrapped around it for so many years.

Ian stood before the mirror, thoughtful. "I've given it some thought."

Isobel bit back a smile. How grown up he sounded! "And what have you decided?"

"Well, I've only known him a little while, but he is my real da, and he treats me like a grown up, just like Hamish does. I told you that he promised to teach me how to use his bow and arrow, and he says that's not a plaything for a little lad, but a grown up weapon." He turned from the mirror and looked at her. "I'll guess he'll be my da soon enough."

Isobel released a sigh of relief.

Delilah stormed back into the room. "Lands' sakes, 'tis time. Come on, come on, or ye'll be late for your own wedding!"

• • •

He had kissed her. At the conclusion of the brief ceremony, her new husband had taken her into his arms and kissed her as though he meant it. When he raised his head, he had looked into her eyes and whispered, "You look beautiful."

And now, after the Wedding Scramble, where both Duncan and His Lordship had tossed coins into the air for the children, everyone walked toward the pier where the lavish reception was to take place. Isobel and Duncan, seated at a small table near the groaning benches that held the food, greeted everyone. Ian and the twins were somewhere, undoubtedly trying not to get into too much trouble.

Duncan leaned toward her. "The whole town must be here."

Isobel soaked in his nearness, as happy as she'd ever been. "Aye." A roar went up, and the duke made his way through the crowd and presented Isobel with the Loving Cup. She took it from him, lifted it to her lips, and took a small drink of the whisky. She tried not to cough as the fiery liquid slid down her throat. She then passed it to her husband. Their fingers touched, and she felt a tingle race up her arm. Their glances held as he took a drink, and then he passed it on to his brother. When all in the wedding party had partaken, the duke raised a glass to the couple.

"I'll repeat the toast that was given to us at our wedding," he replied, smiling warmly down at Rosalyn, who was at his side. "'Lang may your lum reek.' Or, may there always be a fire in your fireplace. I should mention that by the time that toast was given to us, most of the men were in their cups. I was never sure which fireplace they were talking about, for there was nudging and guffawing all around."

Isobel blushed at the innuendo, which, she was certain, everyone thought was very bride-like, indeed.

Duncan reached under the table and took her hand; she was so shocked she almost pulled away. His thumb circled her palm. Her breathing was ragged. His thigh touched hers, and even through the fabric of their clothing, she felt the heat of him.

"I'm going to have you tonight, Lady Isobel," he whispered, close to her ear.

She still felt silly having a title but refrained from giggling. "Are you, indeed?" she answered, hoping her voice didn't shake.

"Are you going to stop me?"

She swallowed. "Big, strong man that you are, how could I?"

"You could tell me to go sleep with the devil." His breath caused the curls by her ear to flutter, tickling her skin.

"I'm thinking you've already slept with the devil many times, my husband."

His chuckle was warm, making her skin tingle. "How well you think you know me."

"And I don't?" she asked, anxious to keep the game going. "Did I marry a stranger?"

"About as likely as I married a virgin," he volleyed, his face dangerously close to hers.

Without thinking, she answered, "I might as well be."

He gave her a questioning look. "What?"

A drop of whisky had made her brazen. "Does having relations only once in my lifetime make me something less than virginal? I think not."

He took her chin in his fingers and turned her face toward his. "Once?"

"Aye," she answered, her heart banging her rib cage. "With you."

She watched his Adam's apple bob up and down in his throat. She had shocked him. "I suppose it would be better for a bride in my position to have some experience, but I don't, and I have you to thank for that."

He released her and sat back against his chair and gazed off into the distance. Suddenly it was as if he didn't even realize she was there.

Isobel was baffled. What had changed his demeanor? He couldn't possibly be upset that she had never slept with another man. She knew men held virgins in high esteem; why wouldn't he? Of course she hadn't meant to blurt that out; it had just happened. But he should know that she had no experience at all. None.

• • •

Duncan had procured rooms for them at an inn on the other side of the island. There was a bottle of champagne chilling in a bucket, plus fine cheeses and sweet and nutty breads.

Duncan watched as Isobel stepped further into the room. She still looked stunning, although she had changed into one of her own gowns, which complemented her hair and coloring. He was pleased that she still wore her brooch. He had said as much when they started their journey.

"I may even pin it to my nightgown. I thank you, it's so beautiful." There were actually tears in her eyes.

"Isobel, I—"

"Nae," she interrupted. "Let me speak first." She took a deep breath and said, "I don't know what would make a husband more pleased, that his wife had been with only him and only once in ten long years, or that she had many partners, which meant she probably knew what to do in the bedroom. I guarantee you, I do not. So—"

He pulled her to him and put a finger to her lips. "You are amazing." He wanted to ask her how she could possibly have gone so long, but decided he didn't need an answer.

"Nae," she answered, "not really." When he released her she crossed to the window, pulled the heavy drapes aside, and looked out into the night. "You see, after Ian was born, I decided I wanted nothing more than to raise him up to be a healthy, honest, and caring man. So I created a dead husband for me and da for him so he wouldn't ask pesky questions about everything, and I proceeded to become the proper widow, raising my son the way I promised myself I would, sometimes even believing the lie myself."

"And how did that work out for you?" he teased.

She bit back a smile. "Fine, until you came back into our lives."

"Do you wish I hadn't?"

"Of course I did, at first. But," she added, "now that you're here I truly hope we can have the home that Ian deserves."

"You mean with two loving parents?"

She hung her head. "I know, I know—'twill not be an easy task to convince people we are close."

"Why do you think they'll need convincing, Izzy?"

Her head jerked up at the familiar sound of her name. Confusion and worry creased her features. "Because…because…"

He took her hand and pulled her toward the loveseat opposite the bed. "Do you dislike me, Isobel?"

Her eyebrows shot up. "What? No! Of course I don't dislike you."

"And I don't dislike you, either. Maybe we can start from there, all right?" It really wasn't all right with him, but he wasn't about to scare her off by telling her how much he wanted to undress her, drink in the luscious beauty of her body, take her to his bed, and make love to her until dawn.

Something flashed in her eyes, then was gone. "Aye," she said with a smile, "I guess that's a place to start."

• • •

That night, as a storm raged on the coast, she lay in bed, lightning and thunder crashing nearby. When she was a girl, she thought the lightning would pierce the window and hit her. She would curl herself into a ball and put her hands over her ears.

Duncan had been such a gentleman that he'd taken the extra bedding and made himself a bed on the floor. Isobel grew cold under the luxurious covers, her fear of storms heightened and she shivered. "Duncan?"

She heard the bedding rustle. Actually, he seemed to move

around a lot, looking for a comfortable position on the hard floor, no doubt. "Yes?"

"'Tisn't fair for you to sleep on the floor. The bed is big enough for both of us, and I'm cold. The bed is unfamiliar and I can't relax. And truth be told, I hate storms."

"You want me to join you in the bed?"

She rolled her eyes in the dark. "Isn't that what I just said?" He seemed always to repeat her sentences back to her.

"I just wanted to make sure."

He crawled in beside her and stretched out on his back. She felt his arm and the cloth. "You're wearing the sark?"

"That's what it's for, isn't it?"

"I have a feeling you're not accustomed to such foolery as bedclothes."

"Well," he said, turning away from her, "there's always a first time. Now, go to sleep Isobel."

She continued to smile in the darkness. And suddenly she was sleepy and comfortable despite the storm outside. She turned the other way to face the door and soon fell asleep.

• • •

Duncan woke early; the sun was barely peeking through the drapes. He shook his head and sighed. This was a first. He'd spent the entire night in bed with a woman and had only slept. He eased his bag of tricks into a more comfortable position; they weren't used to it.

Isobel slept on her side, away from him. What folly it would be to spoon her while she slept! Could he catch her off guard? She could push him out of bed, he supposed, but he had to take the chance.

Slowly he moved toward her until she rested in the hammock of his body, her nightgown soft against him. He placed his hand on her hip, and when she didn't wake, he moved it around, over her stomach and up to her breasts, which were resting on her arm.

He felt her stir, and then stiffen. He waited to be elbowed in the gut. Surprisingly, she relaxed a little against him. "Izzy?" he whispered against her ear.

"Tell me what to do." Her voice shook.

"Relax and try to enjoy it." He stroked her stomach and her breasts through the fabric of her nightgown, enjoying the tensing of her nipples as he did so. "I have thought of these many times, Izzy." He gently squeezed her breast, rubbing his thumb over the taut nipple.

"Ye have?"

"Yes."

She moved, allowing him more access. "What else have you thought about?" Her voice was timid.

"You're sure you want to know?"

"Aye."

"Ever since the first time I've wondered about the color of this," he said, moving his hand to just above her thighs.

"The color?"

"Is it as red as this?" He ran his hand over her head, nudging a curl around his finger.

"'Tis not red, remember?" She sounded more amused than upset.

"Ah, yes. Nutmeg."

She chuckled. "Nae, not nutmeg, you fool."

"Cinnamon?"

She shook her head, continuing to laugh. "Nae."

"I just may have to take a look and find out for myself," he threatened.

"Aye, and if you can remember the color, I'll not call you a fool ever again."

With that he threw the covers back and lifted her gown, slowly exposing creamy calves and smooth, white thighs. A burst of color appeared, rich and thick and… "Ginger."

"Aye, ginger."

He was hard and ready and knew he had to hold back. He laid his head on her stomach and breathed, trying to get control of himself, wanting desperately to put his mouth on her fiery mound and breathe in her scent.

She timidly touched his hair, stroking his head with her fingers. "Duncan?"

He lifted his head and looked at her; her eyes were heavy with arousal. "Yes?"

"What do we do next?"

He was holding himself together by sheer force. "What do you want to do next?"

She squirmed. "My nightgown is riding up; 'tis uncomfortable."

"Then we must remove it."

She was quick to do so, and when he saw the glory of her breasts he bent over her and took a nipple in his mouth, listening to her harsh intake of breath. "I remember the beauty of these," he said, nuzzling her breast with his lips.

"Oh, I feel that all the way down here." She touched her mound briefly with her fingers.

He cupped her and dipped a finger inside; she was wet. "Here?"

She spread her legs a bit and lifted herself off the bed. "Aye."

Suddenly she pushed his hand away and sat up.

Afraid he'd gone too far, he asked, "Izzy? What did I do?"

There was still arousal in her gaze. "The sark."

He glanced down at the nightshirt she had made him. "What about it?"

"Will you take the blasted thing off, please?"

He grinned at her, and pulled the shirt over his head and tossed it on the floor. "Better?"

She reached out and touched him, her fingers moving over his skin, stopping briefly at the scar near his shoulder. Suddenly she bent and kissed it. "I'm sorry you were wounded."

"I have a bigger wound that needs tending." He pressed himself against her, letting her feel his hard length.

She sighed. "I remember that."

He returned to the lushness of her sweet body, moving his

finger around and around her nether lips. She raised her bottom off the bed, her thighs quivering. "Please…"

He moved between her thighs and poised himself at her opening. She spread her legs wider, inviting him in. He eased in, finding her tight, then went in deep and stopped, trying to gather patience.

She wrapped her legs around his waist and her arms around his neck and began to rock against him. The rhythm was all he needed. They rocked together, the cadence of their movements driving them both higher and higher toward ecstasy.

When she cried out, he kissed her, muffling the sound. She continued to weep and laugh, tears running down into her ears. Finally able to speak, she said, "Oh, my God."

Duncan let himself go, felt the release and rolled her over on top of him. They both breathed heavily; Isobel's eyes were closed. Her cheeks were flushed, as was her neck and chest. She opened her eyes. "Oh, my." She put her cheek against his chest and relaxed against him.

Oh my indeed, he thought as he stroked her buttocks and hips. He certainly was no novice to lovemaking, but it was hard for him to compare this morning to anything else he had ever experienced. The thought scared the hell out of him.

And, as so often happened when his blood ran hot, the scar at his shoulder began to throb.

Chapter Seventeen

BAYOUS OF LOUISIANA—DECEMBER 1864

Another two weeks had passed, and Duncan was certain he had Kitten on his side. She was an excellent actress, giving Daddy Beau no reason to think she would betray him, even going so far as to take his abuse as if she deserved it. So far, Duncan had kept his mouth shut, but after seeing Kitten limp around the cabin one morning, he couldn't stand it any longer.

Daddy Beau lumbered into the cabin from outside, sweat already staining his shirt. When Duncan noticed him toss the limping Kitten a glance, he said, "Does it make you feel like a big man?"

"What's that, boy?"

"Do you feel like a big man when you hit a little girl?"

Daddy Beau reached the cot and raised one white caterpillar eyebrow. "You better watch your mouth, son. How I treat my woman is my business."

"Is she really your woman, old man? She's young enough to be your granddaughter."

Daddy Beau chuckled. "Jealous?"

Duncan looked away. It killed him to be so damned helpless. "I don't have to beat on my women to keep them interested," he murmured.

Daddy Beau took a step closer to the cot. "No, I bet you don't, boy. Do the ladies swoon over your brown pecker?" He leaned in closer still and Duncan smelled the man's filth. He said in a raspy voice, "I heard tell that Injuns got teenie weenies, boy."

Duncan knew he was being pushed. "Haven't you heard, old man? It's not the size that counts; it's what you do with it."

Daddy Beau actually threw back his head and laughed. "Boy, I'm gonna miss you when yer gone."

"The feeling isn't mutual," Duncan answered.

The old man studied his prisoner, his eyes slits in his head. "No, I don't imagine it is."

Most evenings, when Daddy Beau was sleeping off his liquor on the rickety front porch, Kitten helped Duncan strengthen his weaker ankle. After a while, he knew he could at least put weight on it when he had to. And, because Kitten had quit putting a sleeping potion in his food, Duncan had to feign sleep so the big man wouldn't get suspicious. But one morning, something changed.

Daddy Beau strutted to the bed, his thumbs in his empty belt loops, his belly hanging over his pants, and leered down at him. "Time's near ready, boy." He whipped the covers off Duncan's body and studied his shackled legs. "Swelling's down. Good sign." Duncan reached for the blanket and covered himself. "We got a meetin' place, boy."

Duncan tried to steady his beating heart. "When is my doomsday?"

The fat man laughed, big and hearty. "Now, you expect me to tell you that? I thought it'd be a nice surprise for ya. I don't want you worrying over when your last day on earth is. Although you already know they'll prob'ly blast a hole through your heart."

Or hang him, like they nearly hanged Fletcher. "All right, let's just get it over with." He pretended to struggle as he sat, appearing weaker than he was.

"Easy, boy, not today." Daddy Beau belched loudly and left Duncan in a very tentative state of relief.

That night Kitten moved quietly around the cabin cleaning up after the fat man, her usual task. When she finished, she sat on the side of the cot so she faced the door and could watch for any movement. She leaned in close. "It's going to be the day after tomorrow," she whispered. "We don't have much time."

Duncan couldn't rise to any level of excitement. "How in the hell are we going to do this?"

She scooted closer. "I've been putting some things aside that we'll need once we're in the bayous." She cast a quick glance at the door, then continued, "Dried meat, water, and alligator oil. If we don't grease up, we'll be eaten alive by mosquitoes."

"Do you have any sort of weapon?"

She wrinkled her nose. "Daddy Beau has a rifle, but I noticed the other day that it wasn't where he usually keeps it. Might be that he doesn't trust me anymore." She winced and stretched her back. "I do have this." She bent down *and pulled up her shift, revealing a homemade sheath and a knife attached by a leather thong around her thigh. "I'll have to leave it with you; there's no place I can hide it." She unfastened it and shoved it between the pillow and the dirty muslin case that covered it. Her eyes were huge. "All right, this is the plan."*

She proceeded to tell him the details of their escape—how she would drug Daddy Beau's hooch, and, "I'll even have to give some to Titan. You've probably noticed that he barks at shadows."

Duncan asked her how they would maneuver once they left the cabin.

"I have a friend," she said, her voice low. "He's an Atakapa, full blood, not half like you. He has a dugout we can use to maneuver the rivers, and he'll take us as far as he can. After that we'll be on our own." She glanced at the doorway again. "We'll have to leave as soon as Daddy Beau falls asleep and get as far away as we can in the dark. My friend was born in the bayous and knows the streams we need to take to get to Bayou St. John."

Duncan began to believe it was really going to happen. He felt a flutter of excitement. He took Kitten's hand and squeezed it. "I don't know how I'll ever repay you," he said, tossing a quick look at the door, "provided we get out of here alive."

"You must take me with you, all the way, Daniel. You must." There was panic in her eyes as she nervously pressed her fingers over a recent bruise. The fat man was sneaky; he never hit her in front of Duncan. "You know that when Daddy Beau discovers us gone, he'll be madder and meaner than a cottonmouth. If he catches up to us, we're both dead. If I go back, he'll beat me so bad I'll want to die."

Duncan realized Kitten was risking her life to save his. If they got out of here, he vowed to make sure she was safe, and as far away from Daddy Beau as humanly possible.

• • •

ISLAND OF HEDABARR—1872

Isobel woke slowly and stretched. Her first notion of reality was that she wasn't wearing her nightgown. She blushed and bit her lip to hide a smile.

"Good morning."

She gasped and pulled the covers up to her neck. He stood at the foot of the bed holding a tray covered with a cloth. He wore his sark. She groped under the covers for her nightgown and couldn't find it.

He put the tray down on a table beside the bed and reached for something, bringing up her wayward bedclothes. "Looking for this?"

She felt shy and reached out to take it from him. "Aye, please."

"To make things even, I can take off my own."

"I don't want to encourage you," she managed. "I'm not sure it's legal to eat breakfast without clothes on."

He picked up the tray and placed it in the middle of the bed. "Oh, I'm sure there's a law about it. Someone somewhere has always got a law against anything, especially if it feels good."

She cleared her throat and wiggled her fingers at him. "My nightgown, please?"

He frowned, appearing to think about it. "Well, ya see, lassie, me bride sewed me this here nightshirt and—"

Isobel started to giggle and put her hand over her mouth.

"What's so funny, lassie?" He feigned indignation.

She shook her head and tried to stop laughing. "Your burr is the worst I've ever heard."

"In that case…" In an instant, the sark was on the floor, and he stood before her naked and very proud.

She couldn't look away. A strip of hair grew from his navel down into a thatch of the blackest hair she'd ever imagined. And springing from that was what had given her so much pleasure earlier. She looked up into his eyes. "I've never seen one before." She could swear the thing moved as she spoke.

"You keep looking at it and breakfast will have to wait," he threatened, his eyes dark with desire.

Even under his weightless threat, she couldn't tear her gaze away.

"Izzy." His voice was low and menacing.

It seemed to get even bigger before her eyes. She glanced up briefly. "Why is it growing?"

"Obviously because you're looking at it like you want to, I don't know, maybe eat it?"

She couldn't tear her gaze away. "Oh, be serious."

"You can touch it if you want to, only I can't prevent it from getting even bigger if you do."

Her whole body shook with need. She had no idea a person could feel such hunger for someone and something. She could barely breathe as she watched him remove the breakfast tray and then join her on the bed, facing her.

"Sit on it, Izzy."

Without a second thought, she moved to straddle him, closing her eyes and holding her breath as she eased herself down onto his shaft. She put her legs around his waist and felt him go even deeper. She put her arms around his neck and he held her shoulders to steady her. As she moved against him, she felt that tingling part of her come even more alive and she continued to move, pressing and rubbing herself against him as he thrust into her. Once again, the beautiful wildfire spread through her, sending her into spasms of joy. She pressed her lips against his shoulder to keep from crying out. She felt him come as well, and when her breathing finally steadied a bit, her ears were ringing.

She stayed where she was, pulled tightly against him, feeling languid and lazy. She lifted her head and looked at him. He was smiling at her.

She struggled to get off him and punched him on the arm. "Am I so very humorous this morning?"

He continued to smile. "It's not humor that makes me smile at you, Izzy. Look at my shoulder."

She glanced at it and gasped, pressing her fingers to her mouth. "I did that?"

"Yes, ma'am. It's my badge of honor."

She quickly tucked herself under the covers. "I'm sorry I bit you."

"I don't think I've ever known anyone who seemed to enjoy a good roll in the hay as much as you do."

She snuggled against the pillow, turning away from him. "My goodness, aren't you the sweet talker?"

He was quiet behind her. "What did you want me to say, Isobel?"

What had she wanted him to say? That she was the best he'd ever had? That he had fallen in love with her? She didn't know. All she knew for sure at this moment was that she didn't want to break the mood. "Are you going to spoon me or not?"

He chuckled and accommodated her. "I guess breakfast will just have to wait."

"My, yes. After all that spent energy, I need a nap."

He hugged her close. "That's my girl."

Yes, Isobel thought, *be his girl.* It was better than nothing.

Chapter Eighteen

Rosalyn joined her daughter on the wide brick patio next to her garden and watched as Fifi played havoc with the big hounds and the collies.

"She isn't afraid, is she?" Rosalyn put the tea tray down on the table and took a seat beside Lily.

"She's fearless," Lily answered.

"Of course you realize that the men in this household have a bet going to see how quickly one of the big hounds has her for lunch."

Lily continued to watch her pup. "I think I overheard that. They'd just as well try to eat a rabid ferret."

Rosalyn watched the animals cavort on the lawn. "She does appear to have the upper hand for some reason. Someone new for the dogs to play with besides the sickie sheep." She put her hand on the girl's arm. "Something troubling you?"

Lily turned to her and looked straight into her eyes; there was a coolness there that concerned Rosalyn. "I think you know."

Some of the spirit went out of Rosalyn. "Why do you have to learn about this?"

"Because it involves *me*. Whatever it is, it's part of who I am."

"It's not pleasant."

"I guessed that, otherwise it wouldn't be so hard to tell me about it."

It was time, Rosalyn knew, especially as long as Lily wouldn't let it go. "It has to do with your father."

"I rather guessed that, too. There is never a mention of him."

"Before I say any more, I will tell you that he charmed me.

He had a way of making me believe everything he said. He was a manipulator."

"And," Rosalyn added, "he did things to children that hopefully sent him straight to hell." She nearly choked on the words.

Lily's hand flew to her mouth and her eyes were wide. "You mean, he—"

"I discovered this after I became pregnant with you. He'd been touching the young girls whose mothers worked for us; one of them was brave enough to tell me."

Lily sat quietly, one hand in her lap, the other still over her mouth, as she gazed into the distance.

"Naturally I divorced him," Rosalyn went on. "I took you and came here, to Hedabarr, where my friend Fenella was practicing nursing. I felt safe here; your father didn't have any knowledge of my friendship with Fenella, so I wasn't concerned that he would show up here. We stayed with Fenella for over two years before he found us."

Lily turned to her, her eyes still wide, her voice a whisper. "He found us here, on Hedabarr?"

Rosalyn nodded. "Somehow he tracked me down. He was relentless. A normal man would have gotten the hint that what we had was over, but not him. He didn't like to lose. He had seen so little of you because I left him as soon as both of us were strong enough. He was a very possessive man as well. What was his was his for all eternity." She shuddered and rubbed her arms with her hands. "So even though he had rarely seen you, you were his. And so was I."

"What happened when he found us?"

Rosalyn rolled her head around to loosen her stiff neck. "He must have been watching the place for a while, because he waited until Fenella and Reggie, her handyman, left in the buggy to get supplies in Sheiling.

"There was a short knock on the door, and at first I thought Fen must have forgotten something, so I opened it, expecting to see her standing there. Much to my surprise and dismay, it was your

177

father." Rosalyn swallowed hard, remembering how she'd felt the moment she saw him.

"Where was I?" Lily asked.

"You were napping. You'd had a bit of a cold and Fen had given you some syrup so you wouldn't cough; it made you sleepy." She took Lily's hand in hers and squeezed it.

"He walked right in as if he belonged there. He even brought a bottle of champagne and some chocolates, believing that if he gave me gifts I'd soften and forgive him." She shuddered again. "He really didn't know me very well." Rosalyn stood and paced in front of Lily.

"He got down on his knees and begged for my forgiveness." A grim smile appeared on her lips. "He even cried. I wondered how long he'd been practicing that. But I'd lived two happy years without him and I wasn't taken in by his drama. He pleaded with me, saying he couldn't live without his little family."

Rosalyn paused in front of a trellis, where a climbing rose bush blossomed. "I didn't fall for any of it. He was so full of himself I doubt he thought I'd refuse. When I told him to get out and leave us alone, he appeared contrite, although I knew it was just another act.

"He slumped into a chair, pretending to give in. I remember him looking up at me with his soulful eyes, asking if we couldn't at least drink a glass of champagne together before he left. I thought only to get rid of him, so I agreed." She sat again, her eyes filling with unshed tears. "But he didn't just give me champagne; he put something else in it and I fell asleep. When I awoke, you were gone. He had kidnapped you." Rosalyn wiped away her tears with the back of her hand.

"And then what happened?" Lily's voice was almost a whisper.

Rosalyn sniffled. "There was a search, and on the other side of the water, near Ayr, they found a small capsized boat with your father's body floating nearby. But you were nowhere to be found. They combed the river and the area around it, but nothing. You were gone." Her voice squeaked as she finished the sentence.

Rosalyn sat, feeling spent and anxious.

Lily rose from her chair, knelt on the bricks, and put her head in her mother's lap. "And you were unhappy."

Rosalyn stroked her daughter's hair. It was so very much like hers, thick and easy to care for. Even the color was similar. Rosalyn often wondered if she would ever have recognized her darling girl under any other circumstances. "Unhappy hardly describes the pain and heartache that stayed with me until the day I found you again."

Lily hugged her mother's knees, and neither spoke or moved until the dogs alerted them of the arrival of company.

Lily's gaze went to the road. A man on horseback trotted toward the castle. On a swift intake of breath, she stood up. "Stefan?"

Rosalyn stood as well. "You know him?"

Lily nodded. "It's Stefan. He a friend of my brother's. How in the world did he find me here?"

Rosalyn noticed the pulse at her daughter's throat throbbing hard beneath the fragile skin. Lily walked swiftly toward him when he dismounted. He smiled and held out his arms, an invitation for an embrace.

"Stefan." Her voice was filled with disbelief. "What…how…"

Stefan swept Lily into his arms and hugged her. She couldn't believe it. She thought she might never see him again.

They both laughed, the sound joyful, excited. He put her on the ground but kept his arm around her.

"I have disturbing news," he began, his voice suddenly somber. "It's Mum. She's very ill and she wants to see you before she… gets worse."

Surprised, Lily asked, "She wants to see me? Why?"

Stefan ran his fingers along Lily's cheek and she put her hand over his. "Ever since you left she has felt guilty about how little she showed her affection for you."

Comfortable warmth cloaked Lily as she heard the words. "Oh, I never wanted her to feel any guilt."

"I know, I know," Stefan answered. "But I've come to take you to her, just for a while, perhaps until…she passes on. It would mean a lot to her, Lily."

The two spoke softly to one another, the young man obviously carrying some sort of message to Rosalyn's daughter. Rosalyn felt a bite of jealousy toward the intrusion into her now nearly perfect life.

Rosalyn, who had been watching them with apprehension, pasted a smile on her face when Lily brought him over and introduced him; Rosalyn was grateful she was introduced as Lily's mother. God, would she ever get used to calling her a name that another woman gave her, clever as it was?

"I'll take you and your mount to the stable so he can be fed and watered," Lily offered. "We can talk there." She gave her mother's arm a squeeze and left with a very tall, dark, and handsome gypsy. Rosalyn raised her eyebrows and glanced toward the path she often took to see Fen and was grateful to find her friend hiking over the grass toward her.

Fen frowned. "What's wrong?"

Rosalyn felt rattled and nervous. "Would you believe my daughter, Lily, Fiona, whatever you wish to call her, is in the stable with a very handsome young gypsy?"

Fen raised her eyebrows. "Ooo la la. But how do you know he's a gypsy?"

Rosalyn frowned at her. "He came looking for her, found her, embraced her, laughed with her, and now he's in my stable with her, talking about God knows what."

"Well, at least they're just talking…"

"Fenella! This is serious. I never envisioned her old life would come back to haunt me, but it has." She rubbed her hands nervously over her arms and stared at the stable.

"You kind of wished there was simply a big gap there, between her kidnapping and her latest rescue?"

"I don't know. It's foolish, I realize that, but I knew all I had to know, to be honest. I knew she was saved, she was cared for, she was fed, and she wasn't abused. I just didn't think about the entire life she led when she was taken from me."

"And here it is, in the guise of a handsome young gypsy." Fen tucked her arm through Rosalyn's. "Any inkling at all why he's here?"

Rosalyn didn't take her eyes off the stable entry. "I imagine we'll find out soon enough." She felt Fen studying her.

"You want an excuse to go to the stable, don't you?"

"Of course I want to go to the stable. And the nosy woman inside me wants to listen to their conversation without being seen."

Neither noticed Delilah until they heard her wheezing behind them. She stopped, and when she'd gotten her breath, said, "Anyone going to stop me from washing all them windows? I can hardly see outside, they're so dirty."

Rosalyn gave her a look of gratitude. "If you want to wash windows, Delilah, who am I to stop you? But ask Mattie and one of the girls to help. It's a big job for just one person."

They both watched as she trudged off toward the castle.

"Does she seem all right to you?" Rosalyn had noted how breathless the woman was when she reached them.

"Something's going on. I wish she'd come to see me; I don't know how I'd approach her otherwise. Do you think Isobel has noticed the change?"

"I don't know. But that's the last thing she needs when she gets back from her little wedding trip. She's always waiting for the other shoe to drop."

"Meaning?"

"Meaning, Isobel can't believe she could finally be happy. So, if Delilah is ill, it would prove that Isobel is right. Again."

Shoes crunching on gravel alerted them to Lily and her guest's approach.

Rosalyn's gaze immediately went to her daughter's face, and she knew something was wrong.

"Stefan is staying the night, Mother."

Rosalyn simply nodded. "He can use the room to the left of the stairs. Ask one of the girls to get it ready."

Lily took Stefan's arm and they walked toward the house.

Fen let out a whoosh of air. "Now, that's some handsome gypsy. Did you see those eyes? A girl could fall into them and never be the same ever again."

"You're not helping, Fen." Rosalyn continued to watch the couple as they walked toward the castle. One was slender and fair and pretty, the other tall, dark, and unabashedly handsome.

"Oh, come now," Fen cooed. "She's a grown woman, remember?"

"Am I going to lose her now, just when I've found her?"

"You're overreacting, Roz. Don't create trouble where there isn't any."

"I know, I know." She shoved her fists into the pockets of her apron. "I wish I could simply take things as they come; but with her, I want to cushion every possible thing that could hurt her."

"You just have to remember that she lived an entire life without you, and she survived very well. Don't smother her, Roz."

· · ·

Over dinner, Stefan appeared completely at ease with the family. He told stories about Lily when she was growing, telling his table mates that her nickname had been "Worm" because she always had her nose in a book. Lily blushed prettily, and swatted his arm when he exposed some of her secrets.

All of which made Rosalyn hope her dinner stayed down. They obviously cared for one another. Had this been something brewing before she left the family? Had they been in touch over the few years she'd been alone?

Later, while Evan was showing Stefan around the grounds, Lily took Rosalyn's hand and led her into the library. Rosalyn was nervous as a cat with its tail on fire.

"I won't beat around the bush," Lily began. "Stefan brought me news of my…the woman who raised me."

Suddenly Rosalyn's selfishness made her feel a terrible guilt. She clasped Lily's hands in hers. "Dearest, did you call her 'Mother'?"

"She was 'Mum.'"

"Then call her what makes you feel comfortable. It won't

bother me. I'm your mother. She was your mum for all the years I mourned you. Nothing can erase any of it."

Lily drew in a breath, releasing it slowly. "Dika—that's her name—has fallen very ill." Lily chewed on her lower lip. "She has asked for me."

A cold wash of dread spread through Rosalyn. She held her tongue.

Lily pressed nervous fingers to her cheeks. "It seems she feels she must atone for how she treated me, not giving me the love and gentleness she gave my sister Kizzy and my brother, Pali."

Rosalyn spoke. "Why didn't one of your siblings come instead? Why send someone outside the family?"

"Pali is in Germany and Kizzy is married and expecting another baby. That will be her third, Stefan tells me. So that just leaves Papa to care for Mum and he's not good with sick ones, even when they are his own." She gave Rosalyn a weak smile. "Stefan is, well, sort of like me in a way, but he wasn't wanted by his mother. She was raped by some titled nobleman when she tried to sell him vegetables. So, Stefan lived with us."

"Did your Stefan need atonement from Dika, too?"

Lily shook her head. "Mum adored Stefan. She preferred Pali to Kizzy too." With a shrug she added, "She liked boys better than girls. It wasn't a secret; we just accepted it."

"And now she wants to make up for all of those years she treated you badly?"

"I wasn't treated badly, I just wasn't loved," Lily corrected her gently.

Rosalyn wanted desperately to urge her not to go, to stay here with her and all of those who had come to love her. She never wanted to be separated from her daughter ever again, and though she knew she was being foolish, her heart had been battered for too many years to listen to her head. She put her face in her hands and shook her head.

"You don't know how badly I want to tell you not to go," she finally said as she looked at her beautiful daughter and smoothed back a curl from her forehead. "But I can't do that, can I? As much as I still think of you as my baby, you're a grown woman. These people were your family for most of your life, and of course I'm grateful, but I have to admit I'm a little jealous too. After all, they had all those years with you and I…well, I won't say I had nothing, but the void in my life was deep."

"So, you think I should go?" Lily's expression was cautious.

"I would have to be very, very selfish to stop you. And then I'd feel guilty. No, my darling, you must go." She swallowed a sob. "Just please know that we all want you back as swiftly as you feel you can return. Tell your mum, Dika, that I didn't accept your decision easily." There was so much more she wanted to say, to remind her daughter that she was loved and would be missed, even if she was to be gone only for a short while.

They sat quietly, shoulder to shoulder, heads touching, hands clasped together. Rosalyn broke the silence. "When will you go?"

"Stefan believes it should be as soon as tomorrow; he only hopes Mum hangs on long enough for me to see her. And we have to take the boat to Ayr, then down the coast a bit. It will take us two or three days, at least. I promise to let you know when I'll be back."

"Remember when you wanted to give Isobel your inheritance? Maybe there's something you can do for your family, for Dika's care, something."

Lily broke into a wide smile. "I can tell you're my mother; we think alike." They embraced. "I will miss you and I promise to come back." Lily pulled away and looked into Rosalyn's eyes. "Remember, I never forgot you, either."

Chapter Nineteen

The carriage stopped in front of the castle and Isobel was relieved to see Rosalyn hurrying toward them from her garden, waving and smiling. Duncan helped Isobel down. She had not tired of his touch. Would she ever? Nae, she didn't think so. He winked at her and she blushed, still feeling like a new bride.

Rosalyn ran to them and embraced Duncan first, and then Isobel. "Oh, you both look wonderful! Was it restful? I hear there's a superb walking path in the hills there above the ocean. Did you happen to take advantage of it?"

Isobel hid a grin. They had gone out for a walk along the cliffs, but it was only because both she and Duncan decided they needed some fresh air. They had rarely left the cottage. That, too, made Isobel blush.

Duncan said, "We did a little walking but we kind of just stayed close to the cottage. The weather, you know…" He clucked his tongue. That coastline could be rough and often whitecaps were as high as a house—but the days they were there, things were calm.

He touched Isobel's sleeve. "I'll put the rig away and get the horses settled. Evan can bring in the luggage." He looked down at her, his eyes smoldering. "I'll see you inside."

Rushing warmth spread through her. Had she been worrying for nothing? So far, things were marvelous. Better than marvelous.

As they walked toward the castle, Rosalyn prattled on. "I have rooms ready for you; I hope they will be all right."

Isobel gave Rosalyn a strange look. "And why wouldn't they be? I wish you wouldn't treat us as guests, Rosalyn. I am ready to do my share of work, and if you refuse, I'll be very angry with you.

You know I am unable to sit around and do nothing." She suddenly remembered Delilah, and she was almost afraid to mention her.

"Did Delilah behave herself?"

Rosalyn rolled her eyes. "It's a good thing our housekeeper is a mild-mannered woman, else I think they might have come to blows."

"Oh, dear, I told her she was not to interfere."

"Not to worry," Rosalyn assured her. "I found just the thing for her to do."

"What, pray tell?"

"I have so many exotic plants in the solarium and find I have so little time to tend them. Some need repotting badly; they've outgrown their pots. Delilah's eyes lit up when I asked her if she had a green thumb."

Isobel raised her eyebrows. "I suppose hers is as green as anyone's. She does plant a grand garden, and raises the roof when the deer and the rabbits come in to dine on her handiwork."

"We also got the windows washed; she was adamant about doing them, and I thought it would be all right as long as she had enough help."

Before they entered the foyer, Isobel took one last look at Rosalyn's rose garden. It was breathtaking. Everything Rosalyn touched seemed to flourish and thrive. She wondered if there was anything at all Rosalyn couldn't do well.

Isobel entered the splendid foyer and followed Rosalyn up the wide winding staircase. Portraits of MacNeils going back for generations lined the wall. There were a few pieces of art on stone pedestals in the hallway, but otherwise, it was quite unadorned. Plain, yet elegant.

She stepped into the rooms Rosalyn had prepared for them. "Rosalyn, this is more beautiful than the finest hotel in Edinburgh."

Rosalyn fluffed the pillows on the enormous bed. "When have you been to Edinburgh, My Lady Isobel?"

The title still made Isobel want to laugh. "Nae, I haven't, but it's what I imagine when I think of where the rich and famous stay when they come to town." The bed was big and wide and canopied.

There were at least a dozen pillows artfully strewn across the top, near the headboard. The bedding looked like lush velvet.

"The dressing room is through here." Rosalyn opened a door and allowed Isobel to walk through first.

The room was as big as her entire bedroom and bathing area at the brothel. Isobel was very grateful, but also felt they were imposing. She reached up and pulled the long hat pin from her hat and took the feathery bonnet off. She tossed it on a shelf, wondering what had possessed her to think she would look like gentry just because she bought a new, garish hat. And she certainly felt out of place here in this splendid castle.

"Do get comfortable, Isobel." Rosalyn showed her where everything was and before she left, she announced, "There will be tea in the morning room when you're ready to come down."

The morning room. What luxury to have so many rooms that they must be named! Isobel shook her head and checked herself in the bevel-edged mirror. She thought she would look different now after all of the lovemaking, but she was her old self, hair like a bird's nest, oversized bosom, pink cheeks and, she thought, looking down at her hands, the hands of a woman who worked for a living.

She understood that lust was a passing thing. At the moment, both she and her new husband were wallowing in it. She was almost ashamed to admit that every time she saw him, she wanted him. But how long would it last? What would they have when he tired of her? He surely would eventually tire of her. The joy would seep out of her existence like water from a sieve. But not yet.

Isobel strolled around the bedroom, her thoughts on the big old brothel house that would soon be rubble. There were many things she wanted to save, and the furniture could be stored until they were ready to use it again. Duncan had told her there must be some family on the island that needed her old furniture more than she did. It gave her pause.

There was a knock at the door, and Evan poked his head around it. "I have your luggage, Isobel."

"Yes, bring it in, Evan and thank you so much. I hope we aren't going to be any trouble." She watched him deposit the trunk in the corner. He was such a handsome young man.

He tossed her a warm glance. "Rosalyn told me you worried too much."

"'Tis a hard thing to do, changing habits that one has had for a lifetime." He brought in more luggage pieces and set them near the trunk. He left her and she wondered how he fit into the family picture. Later, when she and Rosalyn were having tea, Isobel broached the subject.

Rosalyn leaned back in her chair. "When I first arrived, I was told his parents had drowned. I guess no one knew the real story." She lifted the fine china teacup to her lips and took a sip.

"As it turned out, we all learned that his mother was seduced by one of the MacNeil lords, and Evan is the result of that union."

Isobel raised her eyebrows, surprised. "And no one knew this until you came here?"

"Actually, it was after Kerry and the boys arrived. Evan and Kerry became close friends, and he had confided in her that his mother was ill and living in a small cabin in the foothills. He swore her to secrecy. He would leave every day at a certain time to care for her."

"But why would he keep his mother a secret from your family?" Isobel asked.

"It was her wish. She had begged the old laird to take Evan on as a stable boy so he would have a place to live. When all of them died, the secret went with them to the grave."

"Until Kerry came along," Isobel finished.

"Exactly." Rosalyn rose and poured Isobel more tea and passed her the plate of scones. She studied her. "All is well with you and Duncan?"

The blush began at her cleavage and raced upwards. She merely nodded. By the holy, she could run on and on about other people and their problems and offer advice and solutions by the bushel, but ask her about her own affairs and she became a mute. Just as well; what she and Duncan had wasn't exactly dinner conversation.

Duncan poked his head into the room; he appeared very serious. "Ah, there you are. Izzy, I need you to come upstairs with me for a minute."

"Yes, yes of course," she answered, placing her teacup on the tray and getting to her feet. She thanked Rosalyn for the tea and followed Duncan up the winding staircase to their suite of rooms.

When they got inside and he shut the door, she asked, "What is it?"

"I can't go another minute without having you."

Her immediate reaction was the hunger she'd had so frequently these past days. Then, realizing where they were, she said, "We can't do that here."

He looked at her, surprised. "Why not?"

She glanced around nervously. "Because someone might hear us."

He stood in front of her, legs spread apart and arms crossed over his chest. "Do you mean to tell me that while we're living here, we won't…how can I say this nicely…do the marriage dance?"

She clasped her hands together and brought them to her chin. "That would be an awfully long time, wouldn't it?"

His expression became pained. "We could do it quietly," he suggested, taking a step toward her.

She tossed him an amused look. "Have I yet to be quiet?"

"I'd allow you to bite me over and over again," he teased, moving closer still. When he reached her he bent and planted a kiss on her exposed cleavage, sending shards of fire through her blood. She pressed his head into her bosom and ran her fingers through his silky hair.

Her heart racing, she pulled away and ordered, "Lock the door."

He was already disrobing. "No one will come in without knocking first, Izzy."

"Lock the door or…or—"

He was naked. "Or, what?"

"Just please lock it, Duncan." She flashed him a winning smile. That did the trick; he strode from her, his beautiful brown buttocks flexing with each step, and turned the latch on the door. "There." He turned to face her, his erection already full and heavy. "Satisfied?"

Timidly, she answered, biting down on her lower lip, "Not yet."

"Oh, woman, you are such fun." He helped her pull off her clothes, leaving them in a pile on the floor, and they fell onto the bed together.

Chapter Twenty

An hour later Isobel slipped from the bed, careful not to wake Duncan. As she dressed, she marveled at how much she enjoyed what they did together. Again, however, she knew it wouldn't last forever. Should she stop being and doing everything he wished, she would lose him.

She sat down at the dressing table and tried to make herself presentable. Her cheeks had high color and her eyes were wide and actually sparkled. Her hair, of course, looked like someone had taken an egg beater to it, but she didn't really care too much. That was a part of her she couldn't change.

Trying to manage the mane with a brush, she thought about their venture outdoors at the inn. She had secured her hair with pins and even a bonnet, but the bonnet was the first thing to blow off, out over the water.

She had cried, "Oh, no!" It was a fine new bonnet, the first time she'd ever worn it.

Duncan had put his arm around her waist, reached up and caressed her breast. "Ah, Izzy, don't worry. I like you better without it anyway, just as I like you better without clothes."

It had been a good day, wind and all. The proprietors of the inn had made Duncan and Isobel a lunch and they had looked for spots to spread out on the sand for the picnic. Isobel was excited; she hadn't been on a picnic in years. But instead of finding a place to spread the blanket, they found a cove, hidden from the sun and the wind and the world, and lunch was the last thing on their minds. When they had finished their lovemaking, they looked over and found the tide had come in and their lunch was under water.

But oh, what a splendid time they had, examining one another. She tentatively stroked him and watched ecstasy play over his features. On an impulse she squeezed his length and he had told her to squeeze it harder, harder still. "Trust me, Izzy," he had said, "a man loves a good hard squeeze."

And he had scrutinized her bushy mound and had even bent to kiss it, which nearly made her fly apart. "One day I am going to put my tongue in there."

Shakily she had said, "Is that a threat?"

"No. A promise, sweet Izzy."

They never did have a picnic. She glanced in the mirror and saw him awake, watching her.

"You know what I haven't done in a very long time?" she asked.

"Masturbated?"

The idea of it made her blush. "I will have you know I have never done that."

"Never? Ever?"

"Never. Ever."

He rested on his elbow and studied her. "Haven't you ever wondered what it would feel like?"

She put down her brush and looked at him in the mirror. "Until you came along, again, I wasn't even interested. Especially in doing…that."

"I could watch you and be your coach."

Aye, and he'd probably be a very good one. "No, you awful man. I want to go on a picnic and actually eat the food that's prepared."

He sat up and flung his brown, muscular legs off the bed. "Were you disappointed in our last attempt at a picnic?"

Their eyes met and she shook her head. "Not even a little bit."

He stood and walked toward her, his manhood at half-mast. "To be honest, I can't imagine going on a picnic with you and not wanting to ravish you."

"Get dressed. You are incorrigible."

"So I've been told." He sauntered away toward where his clothes were strewn on a loveseat.

Aye, she'd guess there were dozens of women who had experienced with him that which made her want him for herself. She sometimes wondered if she would be the last. It was something she could only hope for, but she wouldn't hold her breath.

Out in the hallway, she met Delilah. They embraced. Her friend felt different as she hugged her. "How are you?" Isobel was concerned.

Delilah huffed as they separated. "How do you think I am? I've nearly been booted from the kitchen, where I can make a finer clootie dumpling than anyone on the island. The cook they have makes scones that are as solid as rock and impossible to eat unless dunked in tea, her ginger cakes are nowhere near as good as mine, and the list goes on."

"I hardly think Rosalyn would keep someone as bad as that in her employ," Isobel reminded her. She looked into Delilah's dark eyes. Were the whites of her eyes yellower than usual? She hoped she was just imagining it.

"I've been relegated to that room with all the windows and ordered to repot plants. 'Tisn't all that bad, I guess." She studied Isobel for a long minute, and then announced, "I think you're already carrying a bairn."

Isobel stifled a cry. Aye, she had gotten pregnant very easily the first time, actually with no intention of doing so at all. "Don't repeat that to anyone, please." But the thought of carrying another of Duncan's children made her want it to be real, if for no other reason than she loved him. Yes, she had fallen in love with her husband. And, if she was with child, she would not tell him until she absolutely had to. She didn't want to spoil what they had.

"By the by," Delilah said, interrupting her thoughts, "have ye seen that Barnacle fellow?"

Isobel frowned. "Who?"

"Oh, that ancient old sod who shuffles about the castle, passing wind like it's the only thing propelling him from room to room."

Isobel remembered that the valet or butler or whatever he was, had been ancient when she'd first seen him all those years ago. "Be generous, Delilah. I think you mean Barnaby, and I'm sure he can't help it. Whatever do you want him for?"

Delilah adjusted her scarf, tucking in stray strands of kinky black hair. "Nothing, really, I just want to avoid him if I can." She shook her head, her dark neck wattle moving from side to side. "Being downwind of him is sorta like being in the stables."

She ambled away, leaving Isobel to wonder how they all would tolerate each other for another two or three months. And she did worry about her friend. Had she lost weight? With Delilah it was hard to tell. Isobel descended the staircase and went in search of Rosalyn, but was told the mistress had gone to visit her friend, Mrs. Gordon.

Before Isobel stepped outside, Duncan came down the stairs and gave her a quick peck on the cheek. "Fletcher and I are going over to talk with Archie, Fergie the Burn's son. Hopefully he has some good news about possible workers for the cannery." And he was gone.

Isobel watched him lope to the stables and disappear inside. Moments later, he and his brother left on their mounts. Isobel returned to the foyer, picked up the green cashmere shawl she'd gotten from Hamish all those years ago. She had truly missed him at the wedding; he was still one of her very best friends.

Isobel stepped outside again and began to stroll the grounds. Fifi and a collie dog ran up to her and the collie nuzzled her apron. She stroked the dog's head. "Am I going to have to start carrying around treats?" She bent and picked up Fifi, who licked her face. "So you are without your mistress, are you?" She had wondered how little Fifi would get along with all the big dogs at the estate, but she need not have worried. The little dog looked right at home.

The collie scampered beside her, often running around her in circles. She found a rocky ledge partway between the castle and the cliffs and sat so she could watch the ocean. Fifi stayed on her lap and the collie settled beside her and curled up at her feet.

In the distance, she saw Duncan and his brother on horseback, riding out toward the beach. Her husband was a very open man;

he seemed to have few secrets. However, when she had asked him about his time in the war in America, he became quiet and pensive. He had been wounded, she knew that. And he wasn't reticent when he talked about how he got his wounds. Perhaps he was quiet because his side lost the war. Of course, she really didn't understand any of it.

Isobel heard children laughing and whooping it up. Ian and the twins came running from the back of the castle and nearly bowled her over.

"Mam!" His face was flushed and his cheeks rosy. "You're home!" He glanced around. "Where's Mister Duncan?"

"We just returned a few hours ago, and he and the duke went over to see Archie." She pointed at the two disappearing figures. "I hope you lads haven't been getting into too much trouble." She tried to keep her voice stern, but she was just happy they were getting on so well together.

The three of them echoed one another, promising they hadn't gotten into any trouble. "At least," one of the twins said, "not when anyone could see us." All three boys laughed heartily.

"Mam, are we really gonna live here for a while?" At her nod, the three boys whooped and hollered again, and tore off for another adventure, the collie deserting her for a more exciting escapade. Fifi stayed with her the rest of the day.

• • •

BAYOUS OF LOUISIANA—JANUARY 1865

It was almost dawn. Traveling the braid of rivers at night was nerve wracking for Duncan; he'd peered into the darkness, wondering how Kye, the Indian friend of Kitten's, could tell where he was going. Kitten spoke to him in a mixture of English, French, and some other language, and the swamp native seemed to understand her.

Their escape was anticlimactic. Daddy Beau and Titan each had fallen into a deep and drugged sleep. Kitten took the keys for the shackles from his unconscious body and freed Duncan. Everything went as planned.

Kye had a paddle and a long stick, both of which he used to maneuver through the sluggish waters. He was lean and brown and although he appeared to be a slight individual, Duncan had no doubt he fought with stealth and skill. He had a knife at his waist, sheathed in a leather pouch. Duncan touched the knife Kitten had given him, tucked into the waistband of his trousers.

The next day they hid, waiting again for evening before going on. Kye left them for a few hours, telling Kitten he would return at nightfall. Kitten removed her disguise, an old hat and a pair of overalls, and stretched her legs. Her hair tumbled down around her shoulders. She looked at him, a question in her gaze as she shrugged her shirt off over her head, revealing her small breasts.

He had not thought of her that way, maybe because she reminded him of his sister, Kerry. But suddenly his arousal came hard and strong. Hopefully Daddy Beau was far behind them. Kitten stood before him naked.

As aroused as he was, he couldn't quite make the move. "Kitten, I don't think—"

She pressed her fingers to his lips. "Don't think, Daniel."

Never before had he felt he was taking advantage of a woman. But she was so willing...

When Kye returned, they continued their journey. He often noticed that Kye and Kitten spoke quietly with one another; they seemed genuinely fond of each other. Duncan's ankle was weak, but he ignored it, knowing that he would suffer for it later on. His shoulder was healing nicely, and he could move his arm without pain.

As dawn broke, steam rose up from the water as it met the cool morning air. Cypress trees leaned over the river; their mossy branches dangling close enough to touch. Mangrove trees spread their roots out into the water, down deep where there was murky soil. Birds awakened; birdsong filling the air. Night critters scuttled into hidey-holes to wait for the next evening. Katydids and crickets continued their tunes; they never seemed to sleep.

Kitten leaned close. She had put on her disguise again. At a distance she could pass for a boy. "We should be at the mouth of Bayou St. John soon. New Orleans isn't far. We can go on foot from there."

Duncan still wondered how he was going to get Kitten away safely, but at this point she was in better shape than he was and looked inconspicuous in her attempt to appear a boy. He had no reason to believe they would not succeed. They had already decided that he would take her to the ranch, where she would stay until he returned from the fighting.

The mouth of the bayou opened up and they found the best spot to get out of the dugout. Duncan jumped out onto the marshy grass, turned to help Kitten only to hear Kye speak. Whatever he said surprised Kitten, and she turned to him. "Why?"

Kye placed his hand on her shoulder and spoke to her softly. There was affection in his eyes.

She put her hands to her face, and then turned back to Duncan. "He wants me to stay, to go back with him," she said with surprise.

"No," Duncan replied. "Come with me, Kitten. You've got to get out of the bayou. Think about Daddy Beau!"

Kye said something again, and Kitten translated. "He said Daddy Beau has been…taken care of."

Frustrated, Duncan asked, "What in the hell does that mean?"

"Daniel, it's all right. Kye and I have been friends for so long. I'd hate to leave him."

"Then tell him to come with us," Duncan answered. He spoke without thinking, but he didn't want to leave Kitten behind.

She gave him a wan smile, although he saw the shine in her eyes. "Go, Daniel. Go. Please, take care."

Tempted to go after Kye with the knife Kitten had given him, he thought better of it. "I'll come back after the war," he promised. "I'll find you."

She waved at him.

That was the last time he saw her.

Chapter Twenty-One

ISLAND OF HEDABARR—1872

Isobel stood in front of her new house. The front faced the ocean. In fact, one could see the ocean from every window. It was a solid structure, no frilly grill work, no fancy columns. The front windows were bowed, and Isobel already imagined setting plants on the ledges inside. And it was quite near the castle, Fletcher having given them land that was lush and green, but unused. The nearness to the castle didn't bother Isobel; she enjoyed being close, for she and Rosalyn visited often.

Imagine. It truly was hers and Duncan's, although it wasn't nearly ready to move into yet. It had been two months since their wedding, and Duncan had hired carpenters from the mainland to build the house of Isobel's dreams. That was really a contradiction, if she thought about it. In all of her life, she had never had a dream house. All she'd wanted was a house without a leaky roof, or slanted floors, or warped wall boards.

She still couldn't believe it was all true. She felt shame that she expected something catastrophic to happen any minute, because everything was just so absolutely perfect. How could it last?

She and Duncan still had a wonderful time together, in bed and out. They had picnicked and had placed the basket somewhere safe from wind and water, and he had ravished her first. They took long walks on the cliffs over the ocean, speaking of dreams and ambitions. Duncan was eager to get involved in the cannery. He had admitted to her that fishing was one of his favorite sports, and now he was able to offer the young men of Hedabarr work. He worked with Archie, getting the men together for the work on the building; he was gone most mornings until early afternoon. Isobel's only dream was that things continue as they did now.

She hadn't wanted to watch them demolish her home; she had made wonderful memories there. But as Delilah had once said, the building was only a place to hang one's clothes. And always, she and Duncan made love with abandon. How had she lived so long without knowing such bliss? Such pure, untainted joy? Any reservations she had she tried to keep locked up in the attic of her mind.

She had taken a trip to the kirk and saw the work they were doing on the schoolroom. She felt a stab of envy that she would no longer be involved in the schooling of children. Aye, she had known it was temporary from the onset, but she had refused to think about what she would feel when she was no longer needed. But life went on; she had a new one and was determined to make her home a happy one.

A shay rumbled to a stop beside her and Rosalyn waved to her before getting out. She made her way to Isobel and glanced at the house. "'Tis going to be a beauty, Isobel."

"Aye. I still can't believe it will be mine."

Rosalyn tucked her arm under Isobel's. "But it is."

"Has Lily heard anything about the teaching position?"

Rosalyn shook her head. "I'm afraid the big issue will be that she has no proper training as a teacher."

"How has she been since she returned from the mainland?"

Rosalyn looked pensive. "Rather quiet, although she did tell me that her mum had always had a weak heart, so it wasn't a surprise when she took a turn for the worse."

"But she was able to stay for the funeral."

"And spent a little time with her siblings and her papa. And," she added, "she paid for her mother's burial and gave a big chunk of her inheritance to her papa. It's no secret that Travelers often live from hand to mouth."

Isobel shook her head and toyed with the ribbon on her bonnet. "She's a darling, that's for sure."

They were quiet a moment, and then Rosalyn said, "Stefan came back with her."

Isobel turned swiftly to look at her sister-in-law. "To make sure she got home safely?"

On a sigh, Rosalyn answered, "Perhaps, but since they've been back, he's spent a lot of time with Evan in the stables. Apparently he's an excellent horseman and quite knowledgeable."

Isobel tilted her head to one side. "My, my. Two exceptionally handsome young men, both clearly available. I'm surprised you haven't had to build a moat around the castle to keep away the lassies."

"And they are handsome, both of them. Piercing blue eyes, black hair—the only big difference is that Stefan is rather swarthy and Evan is very light skinned."

They quietly studied the house for a while, then Isobel asked, "Has Lily been keeping busy?"

"So far. She's taken the three boys and given them projects to work on so they aren't simply running around the grounds with no purpose other than making noise."

"I'm so grateful Ian has fit into your family so easily," Isobel mused.

"It's your family too, Isobel."

"Aye, so it is. Eventually I may get used to all the changes." She turned and looked at Rosalyn. "About the teaching position…His Lordship doesn't have influence in that regard?"

Rosalyn gave Isobel's arm a gentle squeeze. "I'm afraid you give him more credit that he deserves."

"What will she do if she can't teach there?"

Rosalyn was quiet a moment. "We haven't really talked about that. I want her to stay with us, forever. There will never be enough time for us, at least not for me."

The women walked toward the unfinished house and stepped onto the path that had been made by the tradesmen with their wagons of lumber and tools. "I don't want her to get bored. And I really don't know what other skills she has. It's something she and I will have to talk about. I want her to feel useful, not at loose ends."

Isobel thought about that. "Aye, there's precious little to do here on the island, especially for a bright young lass like her."

"Kerry is different. She's comfortable working with the horses and the sheep, she loves all the dogs, and she's never been interested in girly things. Like Gavin, I think she's read every book in the library."

"Aye," Isobel agreed. "It will be a strong, no nonsense man who will finally make her tumble."

"I rather doubt there's a man like that here on Hedabarr."

"I guess we've got the only two," Isobel quipped with a smile.

"Indeed we do."

They strolled around the grounds that would, Isobel hoped, grow fine vegetables and perhaps even some flowers. "I worry about Delilah."

"Yes, as do I. I hadn't realized how ill she really was. She's a very private person, isn't she?"

Isobel recalled the conversation she'd had with Mrs. Gordon after they returned from their honeymoon. Mrs. Gordon had found Isobel outside, weeding Rosalyn's roses.

"I'd like to speak to you about Delilah," Mrs. Gordon had said.

Isobel got to her feet, removed her gloves and brushed off her skirt. "Yes?"

"I don't know if you're aware that she came to me while you and Duncan were away and complained about severe stomach pains."

Alarmed, Isobel had said, "She did? I had no idea."

"She also admitted she hadn't been eating, that her appetite seems to have, as she put it, 'flown the coop.' She also told me not to tell you."

Isobel's alarm grew. "I had noticed she'd lost some weight, but with her girth, it's not always easy to tell."

Mrs. Gordon had given her a long, serious look. "The whites of her eyes are also turning yellow."

"Yes, I had noticed that," Isobel remembered.

"I think she has a wasting disease that is eating away at her liver and her pancreas."

Wasting disease. "Cancer?"

When Mrs. Gordon had nodded, Isobel had struggled to a bench in the garden and sat down. "Is there anything to be done?"

Mrs. Gordon had said no.

And Isobel knew at that moment that she would do whatever was possible to make Delilah's last weeks or months as comfortable for her as possible.

"She's very private. Before I was informed, I may have been suspicious a time or two, but she never let on there was anything wrong. Thank heavens Mrs. Gordon noticed the change in her."

Rosalyn nudged her. "You can call her Fen."

"I will not," Isobel said fervently. "She's a formidable woman, she is."

"Look who's calling the kettle black."

Isobel drew back. "I am not formidable."

"My dear, you are the only person who thinks that way. You are, in a very good way, as daunting as Fen Gordon."

Isobel huffed a little, unsure if that was a compliment or not.

"Will you be able to keep Delilah here until the end?"

Sadness swamped Isobel. "She will live with us here. She still has a lot of strength and I don't intend to see her simply waste away, doing nothing. I'll let her do whatever she's able to do." Isobel fought tears. "She raised me, you know. She's as close to me as my aunt was, and after Paula died, Delilah was all I had." She absently put her hand on her stomach, praying that Delilah would be around when the bairn was born.

"I'm sure Duncan is fine with it," Rosalyn murmured.

"Aye, he has fond memories of her when he was a lad here before. And Duncan has such a positive view on everything. He's cheerful and optimistic and I must admit some of that has rubbed off on me."

"You've changed, Isobel, and it's a very good change."

Isobel released a deep sigh. "Aye. I'm happier than I've ever been in my life."

"Have the two of you come to some kind of truce regarding the furnishings of your new home?"

"He has convinced me that my old furniture will be someone else's treasure, so indeed, I'll have to adjust to new things."

"Gone is the Isobel who vowed she'd never fit in."

"Aye. But I'm still not comfortable being called Lady Isobel and I don't think I ever will be. Actually, it makes me want to collapse into fits of laughter. Delilah and I sometimes do, you know."

"Collapse into fits of laughter?"

"Aye; the first time she curtsied and called me 'My Lady' we laughed so hard it was difficult to catch our breath." She still stifled a giggle when she thought about it.

"I never really found it all that humorous," Rosalyn mused.

"Of course not; you weren't born and raised in a brothel, where anyone who watched over you was a prostitute, a madam, or a big, black woman from Africa."

"But you don't sound bitter," Rosalyn noticed.

"Nae," Isobel answered, remembering her childhood. "I was loved and cared for, fed and given a proper education. I didn't have what many young girls had; I never had a gown that wasn't sewn by either Paula or Delilah. The nicest pair of shoes I ever had was an old pair that one of the girls in the house didn't want anymore. I was taught to be frugal, and it simply stuck."

And she continued to be thrifty and she still had a pall lingering over her heart, for she now knew she was pregnant, as Delilah had suggested. Not that she wouldn't love having another of Duncan's children, she just couldn't be sure the life she currently lived was the one that she would be living a few years from now. Would she ever be certain of her future? Nae, she thought not.

Chapter Twenty-Two

Duncan met with Archie and learned he had found three carpenters, a mason, and a roofer, plus a couple of men who could do a number of jobs. Duncan was anxious to get the project underway. There were also some younger fellows who would help with the demolition, hauling the rubble away.

The two of them sat at Danny's by the Glass, each nursing a pint.

"So, have ye a plan for the building?" Archie asked.

Duncan pulled out the floor plan that had been drawn for him by an architect in Edinburgh and spread it out on the table between them.

Archie nodded as he studied it. "Looks mighty fine."

Duncan rolled it up and placed it back in his leather satchel. "Archie, you've been a great help to me through all of this. I went out and saw your shed; it's finely constructed. I've talked with the men you recommended; they all speak highly of you. Most consider you a leader in the community. I'd like to offer you the position of supervisor over the workmen."

Pleased, Archie reached out to shake Duncan's hand. They had a deal.

• • •

A few days after that meeting, Fletcher had just come out of the livery when he noticed Duncan returning from delivering the wreckage from the brothel, his wagon now empty. There were more young lads who were interested in being hired on. Fletcher hated to turn any of them away, so tried to see that each had a job they could do.

He strode toward Duncan and paused when he saw someone walking toward the cannery site. It was Hamish, and he was leading a young woman and a girl of perhaps six or seven, both of whom had to hurry to keep up with the big man's strides.

Duncan sprang from the wagon seat. "Hamish?"

"Aye, mate." Fletcher noticed the fisherman didn't smile. He gave Duncan a withering glance, left the woman and girl, and strode back to the pier.

Fletcher moved into the shadows as Duncan gazed at the woman, whose smile was wide and shiny and whose hair under her bonnet was a glorious shade of gold. "Kitten?"

Fletcher frowned and looked at the woman. *Kitten?*

The woman ran to Duncan and flung her arms around him. "Daniel!"

Fletcher blinked. *Daniel?*

The two embraced like long lost lovers. Duncan swung her around and then embraced her again. "I can't believe it's you." His voice was filled with tears. "I thought when Kye took you away, you wouldn't be safe, that you even might die. I worried so…"

Who were these two, and what had they to do with Duncan? Fletcher had a sick feeling he might know. Knowing he should find out just what their relationship was, he also knew he was too angry to approach the three of them.

He watched as Duncan held the young woman from him and studied her. There was such a look of adoration on his face, Fletcher had to look away. And he'd seen enough. Turning back toward the livery, he retrieved Ahote and rode swiftly to the castle with this unsettling news.

•••

Rosalyn paced the library, wringing her hands. "Are you sure about this? I mean, maybe she's just an acquaintance from Texas or somewhere."

Fletcher's hands were balled into fists at his sides. "I'd like to believe that, but you didn't see his reaction when he saw her. Or hers, either. They embraced like long lost lovers. There wasn't a hint of guilt or remorse in Duncan's manner or what he said. Whoever she is, he thought she was dead."

Rosalyn whipped around, her skirt whirling in a circle. "Oh, God, you don't think…"

"That because Duncan thought this lovely, golden-haired creature was dead, he'd willingly decided to propose to Isobel?"

Rosalyn's shoulders sagged, and she stumbled to a wing chair by the fireplace and sat. "What this will do to Isobel, I just can't imagine," her voice quivered.

"And here I thought everything was going along so well," Fletcher said, rubbing the back of his neck. "Then there's the little girl she has with her."

Rosalyn sat up. "A daughter? Could…" She clamped her lips shut and finished the question with her eyes.

He gave her a quick, sympathetic nod. "The coloring and the time is right; she appears to be about seven, which means she was conceived when he was fighting in the war. I guess Duncan hasn't changed as much as I'd hope he had." He swore and pounded the top of the desk with his fist.

"What will we do?"

Fletcher swore again. "What will *he* do?"

They were both quiet, each thinking things they didn't want to say out loud. "Poor Isobel. She was uncertain about this marriage from the very beginning. She was sure he didn't truly care for her; he just wanted to be a father to Ian. Think how this will affect her."

"Well, we'd probably better not jump to any conclusions until we've talked to Duncan, but on the surface, it doesn't look good."

There was a noise behind them, and both Rosalyn and Fletcher turned to find Isobel standing in the doorway.

Rosalyn shot to her feet and ran to her sister-in-law, grabbing her hands and giving them a loving squeeze. "Oh, my dear, what did you hear?"

Isobel was nauseous. There was a lump of dread in her stomach so debilitating she nearly stumbled. She let Rosalyn help her to a chair. "I heard enough," she managed.

Rosalyn patted her hand and motioned for Fletcher to get her some port. "We don't know the whole story yet, dear. We were just—"

"You were just assuming what's probably the truth." Isobel's voice reached barely above a whisper. This was her worst nightmare. She knew things had been too good to last, but she hadn't wanted to think about this…

Fletcher offered her the wine. With shaky fingers, Isobel took it and had a small sip. What would she do now? She was pregnant with Duncan's child, and an old love, who probably also had a child by him, had returned to stake her claim on him. With difficulty, she asked, "Is she pretty?" She knew why that mattered; she'd never felt pretty in her life and to be pretty usually meant you got whatever you wanted.

Rosalyn shot Fletcher a warning look but Fletcher ignored it. "You'll see for yourself sooner or later, so I won't lie to you. She's quite lovely."

"Fletcher!" Rosalyn scolded.

He grimaced at his mistake. "She would have seen for herself. Maybe now the worst is over."

"Of course the worst isn't over. This is just the beginning of what could become the most horrible thing to happen to this family. Ever! And that includes you being in the stockade for murder." She bent down beside Isobel and glared up at her husband. "Now go. Go and find your brother; you have to learn the truth."

Fletcher went to the door. "What if this is the truth?"

Rosalyn gave her husband a fierce look. "Then I may have to do away with Duncan myself." She gathered Isobel in her arms and they sat there, quietly pondering the dreadful future.

Chapter Twenty-Three

Fletcher rode Ahote hard into Sheiling and went to the cannery property. No one was about. He was so angry with his brother he wanted to ball up his fist and smash him in the face. Never had he been this outraged before.

He rode to the docks and found Hamish working on his boat. He dismounted and strode to the big fellow.

Hamish raised his head in greeting. "Looking for Duncan? He—"

"I want to talk with you first," Fletcher interrupted. "How did you come to meet this young woman?"

Hamish drew out his pipe and stuck it between his teeth. "I was returning from sea and when I got off me boat, she and the lassie were standing there." He pointed to the decking that was built over the water. "I asked her if I could help, and she told me who she was lookin' for, y'see. I was confused at first, her callin' him Daniel and all, but then she described him, y'see."

"And you don't know anything else about her?"

"Nae. But from what I did see, my poor Izzy is going to be heartbroken." His eyes clouded over and his expression became cruel. "I'd like to take that brother of yours and toss him into the ocean as shark bait."

"Get in line," Fletcher growled. He glanced over and saw his brother leave the tea room and walk toward them.

He waved and smiled. As he approached them, he said, "I just got Kitten and Dannie—"

Fletcher planted his fist in his brother's face, the shock of the impact racing up his arm and into his shoulder. He hoped he broke Duncan's damned nose.

Duncan simply lay there and stared at his brother as blood ran into his mouth. He spat it out and wiped his nose with his sleeve, wincing at the pain. He didn't get up right away. "Fletcher, what in the hell is wrong with you?"

Fletcher swung around, unable to control himself. "What's wrong with me? What's wrong with *you*, you big jackass!"

Duncan slowly got to his feet, glancing at Hamish, who glared at him, his meaty arms crossed over his massive chest. "What do you mean?"

"What do you mean?" Fletcher mimicked, itching to toss another punch.

Duncan pulled out a handkerchief and blotted his nose. "Hell, I think you broke it."

Fletcher got into his face. "I hope to hell I broke it, you bastard."

Duncan frowned and continued to baby his nose. "What's this all about?"

"It's about a pretty little 'Kitten' and a kid who has Indian blood. Do you think I can't add?"

Duncan's eyebrows shot up as he understood his brother's insinuation. He glanced away as if unwilling to meet Fletcher's angry glare. When he returned his gaze, he said, "So, you think Dannie is mine?"

Now both Hamish and Fletcher stood before him, feet wide apart and arms crossed over their chests, eyebrows slammed down over their eyes.

"Convince me differently," Fletcher ordered.

Duncan sucked in a deep breath through his mouth. He nodded slowly, a sardonic half smile on his face. "You know what? I don't have to explain a damned thing to you."

Fletcher was ready to punch him again. "How do you think Isobel feels?"

Alarmed, Duncan asked, "What has Isobel got to do with this?"

"She already knows about Kitten."

"What?"

"What happened," Fletcher asked. "Did you promise to marry

this Kitten, thought she was dead, so came home to court Isobel? Or had you already married her and then thought she was lost, so then came back to Isobel? Don't even think you can lie to me; I saw how the two of you embraced, like long lost lovers."

Duncan's face was unreadable. "How does Isobel know Kitten is here?"

Fletcher still had his hands balled into fists. "Trust me, she knows." Before he could take another breath, his brother took a swing and hit him in the face. Defending himself, he lunged at Duncan and the two brawled on the pier. Suddenly he was in the water, as was Duncan, both flailing and treading water. Fletcher looked up to see Hamish on the dock, dusting off his hands.

"Christ almighty," the fisherman growled, "do ye know how ye look? Two grown men, one the laird and 'tother his brother, wrestling on the pier like a couple of ruffians. Now get up here and straighten this out, Duncan, or I'll have me a piece of ye meself."

• • •

Rosalyn returned to the library with a tray, a teapot, and two cups. She put it down on the desk and looked over at Isobel. Her heart sank. Isobel sat there like she was in a trance. Rosalyn didn't think she'd moved since she'd sat down after hearing the news.

Suddenly Isobel spoke. "I've lost him."

"We don't know that, dear." Rosalyn poured Isobel a cup of tea, added just a few drops of whisky, and handed it to her.

Isobel's hand shook, but she took the cup, lifted it to her lips, and took a sip. "I can't bear the thought of losing Duncan now, after all we've…" She shook her head and gave Rosalyn a sad smile. "What does it matter?" She returned the cup to the saucer and pressed her hand over her stomach. "The only thing I will regret is that…" She glanced at her stomach and rubbed it, her expression both joyful and sad.

Startled, Rosalyn asked, "You're pregnant? Why didn't you tell me?"

"I would have, sooner or later, but with Delilah's condition and everything in such an upheaval, I didn't think to do so. And I'm not so far along that I'm showing anyway."

"So Duncan doesn't know."

Isobel shook her head, fresh tears streamed down her cheeks. "And now I can't tell him." She looked up at Rosalyn. "What if he married her and then he thought she was dead? Our marriage wouldn't even be legal, would it? And I'd have another bastard."

"Oh, Isobel," Rosalyn said, "let's not go there. We don't know anything for sure, yet."

"But I've always been prepared for the worst. In everything. It's how I coped with life. I was always grateful when the worst didn't happen, even if what did occur wasn't particularly pleasant, because at least it wasn't what I had dreaded.

"And I shouldn't be surprised at this turn of events." Isobel shook her head. "No, I expected something to happen. I knew I couldn't be happy forever; it just isn't the way life is for me. I just didn't think…" She sniffed again. "I just didn't think it would be this." She put her face in her hands and wept.

Suddenly there was a racket in the foyer. "Isobel! Izzy?"

Both she and Rosalyn turned toward the door as Duncan, Fletcher, and Hamish came crashing through.

Fletcher's eye was beginning to blacken and Duncan's nose was swollen and his face was bloody. Their clothing was wet and clinging to them.

Rosalyn stood. "What happened to you two?"

"Later," Fletcher replied.

Duncan stood in front of everyone, flashing Isobel a tender look. "I have a story to tell, and I don't want any interruptions until I'm done."

Both women sat, eagerly awaiting his explanation.

"When I got shot in the war, Kitten and another man saved my hide. At first I was grateful, then I realized that the big, old, fat slob of a man had shackled me to the bed where I was to recuperate. He discovered I had done some irreversible damage to one of the Yankee boats and there was a bounty out on me if I was delivered alive.

"He smacked Kitten around, left bruises on her and, well, I shouldn't have to mention what else went on in that little cabin in the swamp." His anger spread. "His name was Daddy Beau and he played both sides of the war."

"Was this Daddy Beau her father?" Rosalyn asked.

Duncan snorted. "Hell, no. Yankees had burned her home, killing her parents, and somehow Daddy Beau found her. She was every bit a prisoner as I was. She tended to my wounded shoulder and made sure I had nourishment, all the while trying to stay out of Daddy Beau's way."

He glanced at Isobel, noting the fear and confusion registered on her face.

"As it turned out, Kitten was as anxious to get away as I was, so together we planned our escape. Since she had no family, I thought I'd take her to the ranch, leave her with people I trusted, then decide what to do after the war was over." Once again he looked at Isobel. "She saved my life, Izzy. But," he added, remembering it all, "even though I had promised to take her with me, the Indian guide who led us out of the swamps pleaded with her to stay with him. She stayed. I didn't know what would become of her. I couldn't save her."

He paused and dabbed gently at his nose. "I felt like a coward for not going after her; maybe we both would have been dead, I don't know. After the war I did return to the bayou, but it's impossible to find anyone if you're not acquainted with the swamps. So I gave up trying, all the while wondering if she was dead and knowing that, if she was, it was my fault. I've never felt such guilt in my life."

Duncan sat down beside Isobel. He wanted to take her hand but she had both of them balled into fists in her lap. No one spoke for a long time. Finally, Rosalyn asked, "So, after she and her Indian friend got you to safety, he kidnapped her?"

"Well, I suppose, but she did go willingly. As I watched them slink back into the bayous, all I could think of was the look on her face, like she knew her fate. Yet she urged me to leave her; I shouldn't have, but I did. Now, as we spoke on the docks, she assured me Kye had planned to take her away from Daddy Beau himself. We had given him the perfect opportunity. Kitten was grateful and grew to care for him. Eventually, she had his baby. A little girl, Dannie. Or Danielle." He let out a short laugh. "She named her after me, or the name I'd given her in the beginning."

"Why did you do that?" Fletcher asked.

"At first I didn't trust either of them to know who I really was, and that I was going to inherit a ranch in Texas. Daniel was the first name that popped into my head."

"And she named her child after you, and not this other fellow?" Rosalyn's voice was quiet and sympathetic.

"That's right."

Isobel studied him and slowly reached up, gently touching his nose. He tried not to wince. "What happened? And why are you so wet?"

Duncan and Fletcher exchanged guilty glances. It was Hamish who spoke.

He pushed his bulk away from the mantle and crossed his arms over his chest. "One punched the other because he thought his brother was going to be unfaithful to his wife, and the other punched his brother because he learned his wife had overheard the other brother's assumption about the entire situation, y'see."

It was a roundabout answer, but they understood. Rosalyn asked, "And they're wet because…?"

Hamish shrugged his huge shoulders. "I tossed 'em both in the drink."

Fletcher pulled at his wet shirt. "I apologize for assuming the worst of you, Duncan. But, with only the past to go on…" He left the insinuation hanging.

Duncan glanced away. "I will admit there were a few moments of temptation—after all, it's what I would have done in a heartbeat any other time." He gave Isobel a shameful look. "But, beauty that she was, she felt more like a sister to me. And I thought of Kerry, and what I would do if someone abused her like Kitten had been abused by Daddy Beau, and I just couldn't." He closed his eyes and shook his head. "I just couldn't."

Isobel was quiet, still trying to piece everything together.

"Then," Rosalyn asked, "how did she end up here, on Hedabarr?"

Gathering his composure, Duncan answered, "She married one of the young missionaries who freed her from the tribe. The reason she and Dannie are alone at the moment is because her husband is meeting with Church officials and Reverend Fleming. Apparently he's to be our new minister here on Hedabarr."

"Well," said Rosalyn. "Isn't that a coincidence?"

"At least I know she's safe," Duncan said. "And she seems very happy."

There was total silence in the room. Hamish, who had returned to the mantle, chewed on his pipe. Rosalyn sat beside Fletcher on the settee. Duncan wondered how Isobel would take the story, hoping she hadn't actually thought the worst of him.

"I think it's time for us to leave the two of them alone, don't you? And you, dear husband," she said, tugging on Fletcher's arm, "need to get into some dry clothes." She motioned to Hamish and Fletcher, and the three of them left the library, closing the door softly behind them.

Isobel waited for Duncan to speak. He turned her face toward him. His nose was a mess and had begun to swell.

He wiped away tears from her cheeks and ran his hand over her chin and down her neck. "We look a lot alike right now, all puffy and red."

Isobel tried to smile, but her lips trembled instead.

Duncan stroked her cheek. "What you must have thought of me."

"I expected something to happen, you know."

"What? Why?"

"Because I was so happy, and I just knew it wouldn't last. I didn't know what it would be, but I didn't think I was lucky enough to live happily ever after."

Duncan frowned. "What makes you think you won't live happily ever after?"

Tears leaked again. "Because you love fun and you love sex and I can't always be there to enjoy it with you, especially when I'm big as a cow with another bairn. I—"

"You're having my baby?"

"Aye, and when I look like a cow, where will you go?"

Duncan hugged her and tried not to laugh, but failed. "Why would I go anywhere else?"

She tried to push him away, but he held her tightly. "Oh, Duncan, of course you'll want to find your pleasure elsewhere. Who'd want to have sex with a cow when there are fresh young lassies all about?"

Duncan's face fell. "You think so little of me?"

She gazed at him, knowing that everything she felt for him was in her eyes. "No, it's just that you married me to make Ian legal and I'll always be grateful for that. And I—" She clamped her lips together as if to prevent herself from saying more.

"You, what?"

She shook her head and looked away, unable to say the words out loud. "I can't tell you."

He turned her toward him. "Izzy? What is it?" His forehead was creased with concern. He gently shook her shoulders. "Tell me and maybe I can help. Maybe I can do something about it."

She actually laughed. "Aye, if you can do something about the fact that I'm in love with you, I'll be eternally grateful." She didn't want to look at him, but couldn't stop herself. She couldn't read the expression on his face, and her stomach twisted.

"Izzy, Izzy." He pulled her up and brought her close to his chest. She noted the dampness of his clothing and the faint fishy smell.

He cupped her face. "I think I fell in love with you when you wanted the roof to collapse on my bed with me in it."

"Not when you saw me naked in the tub?"

"I think I was already pretty far gone by then," he admitted.

She started to cry; she couldn't stop herself. "I canna believe that."

He hugged her close. "You canna?" he mimicked gently then held her away from him. "Well, believe it. We are going to be a loving family, the four of us," he said, rubbing his hand over her stomach.

"And ye won't mind if I get as big as a cow by the time the bairn is born?"

He waved the question away. "I've always been known to be a rutting bull."

"And ye don't mind if I'm not thin and willowy like Rosalyn and Kerry and Lily?"

He gave her a look of disbelief. "I love your curves, Izzy. I loved them ten years ago, I loved them when I found you in the tub the day I discovered I was a father, and I will love them always."

She stepped into his arm again, closing her eyes and inhaling all of the myriad smells he was today, finding, if she concentrated, that she could smell just him. "How can I be this lucky?"

He chuckled close to her ear. "You might change your mind, love. I'm not exactly easy to live with."

She pulled back, surprised. "And I am?"

He laughed again. "I will love you forever."

• • •

That evening, Kitten, Dannie, and Kitten's husband, the Reverend Lawrence Samson, dined with the MacNeils.

Isobel watched the pretty, animated woman, completely comfortable in the company of strangers, tell them her story. She described how her friend, Kye, had taken her back to his tribe, explained that he'd been preparing this for a while and helping Duncan escape fit right into his plans.

Fletcher said, "I heard you call him Daniel, and it added to the puzzle."

"That's what he said his name was." She gave Duncan a scolding look. "I guess he didn't trust us enough to tell us who he really was. Now that I understand things, it was probably because if Daddy

Beau had learned that Duncan would eventually inherit a large ranch in Texas, he would have found some way to get his hands on it."

"So," Isobel asked, "whatever happened to him?"

"Oh, I heard tell he was so angry that we both got away that he eventually had a stroke and keeled right over dead on top of his dog, Titan." She shook her head. "Poor Titan; we both suffered from Daddy Beau's abuse."

Ian leaned toward his father. "I like the way she talks. It's sort of like singing."

Duncan ruffled his son's hair.

"How did you finally get rescued?" Rosalyn asked.

Kitten shot her husband a shy, warm glance. "I guess it was a rescue, but I was treated well by the tribe. Shortly after Dannie was born, Kye got the blood fever and died." She lifted one slender shoulder. "I had no place to go, so I just stayed with them." She looked at her young husband again. "Until the missionaries came and with them the handsomest man I'd ever seen in my entire life. His eyes were warm and his face held no judgment when I introduced him to my daughter, Danielle. I was drawn to him immediately."

"And now you will make your home on Hedabarr." Fletcher raised his glass. "To the Reverend and Mrs. Samson and Danielle. Welcome."

Glasses were raised all around, and a kind of peace settled over the families at the table.

• • •

After they were alone and curled together under the covers in their big bed, Isobel said, "I'm glad she came, Duncan. I'm happy that circumstances brought her here."

"You don't feel insecure?"

Isobel smiled in the dark. "No. Aye, she's a beauty, she is, but when I saw the way she looked at her husband—the way I look at you—I was just grateful that she had been there to save you."

"As am I," he answered. "And I don't want to be anywhere else, with anyone else, ever again but you."

He pulled her against the hammock of his body, curled his arm around her, and they slept.

Epilogue

1873

Big as the cow she had promised to be, a very pregnant Isobel carefully made her way around the kitchen table, looking at the great mounds of food she and Delilah had prepared for the celebration to formally bring the new reverend and his family into the community.

Kerry and Evan were considering going to America to manage the family ranch. Isobel recalled the relief her husband had shown when they agreed to think about it. He was seriously concerned of late, because word of what was happening there had stopped arriving.

Lily didn't get the teaching job for the very reason Rosalyn was worried she wouldn't. The church hired a tall, thin young man with a spare beard and lank hair. In spite of his looks he was a good teacher, and even asked Lily for help from time to time.

Fletcher had asked Stefan to stay and learn to manage the grounds, since Evan would probably be leaving sometime soon. Stefan and Lily could often be seen off together, their heads close, talking and laughing. Isobel was sure that Rosalyn was happy Lily chose to stay, but wondered if they would, indeed, become a couple. Isobel reminded her that love wasn't always sensible. Time would tell.

Delilah was still as peppery as usual, but they all noticed that she napped more frequently than she used to. She did a lot of knitting, which she still did better and faster than anyone Isobel had ever known, and Isobel thought that maybe this time she was actually making something for the bairn. But she continued to lose weight, for she had no appetite. It broke Isobel's heart to see Delilah's health failing; she couldn't imagine life without her.

The cannery was open and fully staffed with island men, all

of whom were grateful they didn't have to leave the island to make a decent living. With that and the scotch distillery, Hedabarr's popularity was growing.

Isobel felt a kick and brought her hand to her stomach. "Aye, little one, I will have you to care for then, won't I?"

Duncan came into the kitchen and hugged her from behind. His hand, too, went to her stomach, and he was also blessed with a good, strong kick.

Isobel leaned into him.

"Are you tired, my sweet?" he whispered into her ear. His voice and his touch still sent chills down her arms.

She shook her head. "I'm fine, but I don't know how much longer I can carry this bairn around without the use of a wheelbarrow." She felt him shake with laughter.

"Do you know what I think?"

"Rarely do I know what you think, my husband."

"I think there's more than one in there."

The thought startled Isobel. "Nae, how could that be?"

"How, indeed," Duncan mused. "Look at Fletcher and Rosalyn. It could happen to us, you know."

Isobel turned in his arms and looked up into his handsome face. All those years ago, she thought she could look into his face and never tire of it. She was right. She was more in love with him now than she had been when they married. To think she could have two bairns...The thought made her almost giddy.

"And guess what?" he asked.

"What?"

"I overheard Ian talking to one of the twins. His exact words were, 'my da said when I'm older I can have his bow and arrow.'"

"He called you his da?"

"It's a start. Are we lucky, or what?"

"Aye," she answered, putting her arms around his neck. "We are lucky." And she finally believed it.

WINTER HEART

Desperate to escape a dark past, Dinah Odell will do anything, even risk her freedom by posing as a nurse and accepting a job to care for Tristan Fletcher's mentally fragile sister. She thinks she's prepared for anything, except the sensitive, generous, and mysterious man behind the facade that Tristan Fletcher presents to the world.

With a dark past of his own, Tristan survived the barbs of childhood by closing his heart off from the rest of the world. He sees something similar in Dinah, a desire to flee, and it sparks his desire to protect her. To marry her, even. But to love her? When Dinah's secret past is revealed, it threatens to ruin everything she and Tristan have worked so hard to create. Will it tear them apart, or strengthen their bond even more?

A TASTE OF HONEY

Seeking one last night of passion before entering into a loveless marriage, Honey DeHaviland finds that and more in the arms of Nick Stamos—the very man tasked with delivering Honey to her betrothed. Although it is in Nick's embrace that Honey finds the love she longs for, she knows that marrying a penniless man would mean her father's financial ruin.

But when Honey discovers that Nick is indeed wealthy beyond comprehension, she knows that she cannot give in to her yearning to stay with him without appearing shallow and mercenary.

When he learns the reason for Honey's arranged marriage, he vows to have her for himself. Will he convince her that he's all she needs before he loses her forever?

THE DRAGON TAMER

Widowed, alone, and penniless, Eleanor Rayburn is devastated when she learns that her late husband sold his shares of the ship before he died. Desperate to take back what she believes is rightfully hers, she sets out to fight back against the handsome but arrogant owner of the whaler.

Marine naturalist Dante Templeton survived a hard life, and has found success as an activist against the killing of whales or any marine animal for profit. But it's his own personal grudge against an enemy from his past that fuels his disdain for Eleanor, and his determination to keep her from reclaiming her share of stocks in the whaler.

As the feud heats up between Dante and Eleanor, so does the blaze of passion. But is Dante's love for Eleanor enough to smother his fiery hatred for her husband?

DANCING ON SNOWFLAKES

Susannah Walker has fled to Angel's Valley with her three-year-old son, seeking safety and a place to anonymously restart her life. What she didn't count on was bounty hunter Nathan Wolfe being hired to find her and take her home to stand trial for her crimes. Carrying his own wounded past in his heart, Nathan is committed to fulfilling the job, until he gets to know Susannah and begins to wonder if she's truly the criminal he's been told she is. But in order to get to the bottom of the mystery he'll have to gain her trust, and trust is one thing Susannah does not give easily.

FIRES OF INNOCENCE

An act of kindness may lead to her greatest loss, or the greatest love she's ever known.

The wilderness of Yosemite Valley is no place to be caught alone. When Scotty MacDowell rescues a wounded stranger from a fierce blizzard, she is thinking only of saving a lost traveler. She never expects to find a passionate lover in Alex Golovin through nursing him back to health.

Seven months later, Alex returns to Scotty's tiny cabin in the wilderness, but not to take her back into his arms. Instead of the man she loved, Alex returns as an angry lawyer, determined to run Scotty off of her beloved land. Caught between passion and responsibility, Scotty and Alex endure a daily struggle to stay true to their hearts, no matter the cost.